THE
SILENCE
OF MALKA

Editor Dean Mullaney • Art Director Lorraine Turner
Translated by Carlos Guzman-Verdugo

Additional translation by
Jeremy Melloul (Introduction and Epilogue) and Edward Gauvin (Afterword)

Lettering font based on hand-lettering by Frank Engli.

EuroComics.us

EuroComics is an imprint of
IDW Publishing
a Division of Idea and Design Works, LLC
2765 Truxtun Road, San Diego, CA 92106
www.idwpublishing.com

Distributed to the book trade by Penguin Random House
Distributed to the comic book trade by Diamond Book Distributors

ISBN: 978-1-68405-287-5
First Printing, June 2018

IDW Publishing
Greg Goldstein, President & Publisher
Robbie Robbins, EVP & Sr. Art Director
Matthew Ruzicka, CPA, Chief Financial Officer
David Hedgecock, Associate Publisher
Laurie Windrow, Senior Vice President of Sales & Marketing
Lorelei Bunjes, VP of Digital Services
Eric Moss, Sr. Director, Licensing & Business Development

Ted Adams, Founder & CEO of IDW Media Holdings

Thanks to Rubén Pellejero, Laureano Domínguez-Caamaño,
Nolwenn Lebret, Tina Tonero, Justin Eisinger, and Alonzo Simon.

THE SILENCE OF MALKA

Written by JORGE ZENTNER
Art and Colors by RUBÉN PELLEJERO

EURO COMICS
ENGLISH EDITION   GRAPHIC NOVELS

An imprint of IDW PUBLISHING

Thanks to the jury members of the Angoulême Festival and the Ecumenical Jury of Comics, which awarded their prize to this book in January 1997.

—Jorge Zentner

To Jorge Zentner, for having offered me, at the time, this story that would change my horizons as a draftsman.

—Rubén Pellejero

IN 1876, IN ARGENTINA, THE "AVELLANEDA" LAW WAS PASSED, intended to promote immigration. A short time later, the government opened an information bureau in Paris and tasked various European intermediaries with recruiting colonists and chartering vessels bound for the port in Buenos Aires. The reasons for such a policy seemed obvious: the entire territory of Argentina—a quarter of the size of the entire United States—was home to only three million inhabitants.

In 1881, a terrorist attack ended the life of Alexander II, the Russian Czar. His death bore severe consequences for millions of Jews who, until that point, lived under his protection in the region known as the Pale of Settlement, the only area in which Jews were allowed residency. Following that, a wave of pogroms—systematic or sporadic attacks against Jewish homes, businesses, and synagogues—spread throughout the Russian empire: Kiev (1881), Balta (1882), and Ekaterinoslav (1883) among the most notorious, but there were also attacks on many small villages in the province. In 1887, Jewish delegates from the most affected communities met in Katowice (Poland). They came primarily from Podolia and Bessarabia. They soon reached a conclusion: to live in peace, they would need to emigrate, flee, and leave their homes in search of new horizons. There were three possible places they could go: Palestine, Africa, and North America.

They chose Palestine and sent Mr. Eliezer Kauffman to Paris in search of the financial support needed to make the journey. His efforts in the French capital failed, but while there Kauffman met agents from the Argentinian government's information bureau. The two parties came to terms and signed contracts that would send one hundred thirty-five families (eight hundred twenty-seven people) to settle the land owned by Mr. Rafael Hernández (the brother of poet José Hernández, the author of *Martín Fierro*). The emigrants paid the agent four hundred francs per person to cover the trip to Argentina, food, farming tools, livestock, and more.

The emigrants boarded the steamboat *Wesser* at the German port of Bremen and, after a difficult journey, arrived in Buenos Aires on August 14, 1889, in the middle of the Argentine winter. There they discovered that the so-called agent had swindled them, acting without the authority of the landowner. The new arrivals were brought to the Immigrants' Hotel, a massive complex of buildings by the dock.

According to the statistics, there were 1,572 Jews living in Argentina at the time. Pedro Palacios, a doctor, lawyer, and landowner in the province of Santa Fe, was the legal representative for the Israeli Congregation of Argentina. Henry Joseph, a rabbi, told him of the immigrants' plight, and the doctor offered to sell a portion of his land and set out to furnish the settlers with animals and the necessary tools.

At the same time, the Argentinian government had sent Doctor Wilhelm Loewenthal, a Berlin-trained Rumanian bacteriology specialist, on an epidemiological study. One morning, during his visit to the province of Santa Fe, the dusty train that he rode on dropped him off at the tiny Palacios train station. "Here," wrote Loewenthal in the report he made to the Minister of Foreign Relations, "I found five hundred immigrants living in railway cars. Often, the only food they have to eat is a bit of stale wafer every forty-eight hours; many of them were sick, and more than seventy children had already died, while others remained on the brink of death." The passengers of the *Wesser* had been exploited again.

Back in Europe, Doctor Loewenthal met with Zadoc Kahn, the Chief Rabbi of Paris, and other members of the Jewish community. He proposed a detailed project to help the survivors of the *Wesser* and settle several thousand additional Jewish families in Argentina. Baron Maurice de Hirsch, a wealthy Jewish philanthropist, took up the cause. Born to a wealthy Munich family in 1831, at a very young age he married Clara Bischoffsheim, an heiress to an equally large family fortune. If the legend is to be believed, after the death of his son in 1887, Baron Hirsch said: "I have lost my son, but not my heir." Afterward, he gave a large part of his fortune to the Alliance Israélite Universelle, an organization founded in 1860 to safeguard the rights of Jews around the world.

Baron Maurice de Hirsch entrusted Doctor Loewenthal with investigating the opportunities Argentina might offer immigrants. The results of this study served to found the Jewish Colonization Association in 1891, whose board of directors included members of many prominent Jewish families in Europe: Avigdor, Klee, Leven, Phillipson, Errera, Dreyfus, Montefiore, and Reinach, among others. Baron de Hirsch contributed fifty million francs to buy arable land, choose candidates (families with children under eighteen years of age), organize the transportation of the settlers, and hire teachers—as well as to build schools, sanitation infrastructure, and synagogues. This new colonial enterprise purchased almost 700,000 hectares of land in the provinces of Santa Fe, Entre Ríos, Buenos Aires, La Pampa, Santiago del Estero, Rio Negro, and Chaco.

But the immigrants didn't have an easy time of it. They were expected to reimburse all that the Jewish Colonization Association had advanced to them with the fruit of many years of labor, and with that money enable the arrival and settlement of new colonists. Unfortunately, most of them were former craftsmen who knew little or nothing about working the land. With its flooding, droughts, and abundance of locusts, the

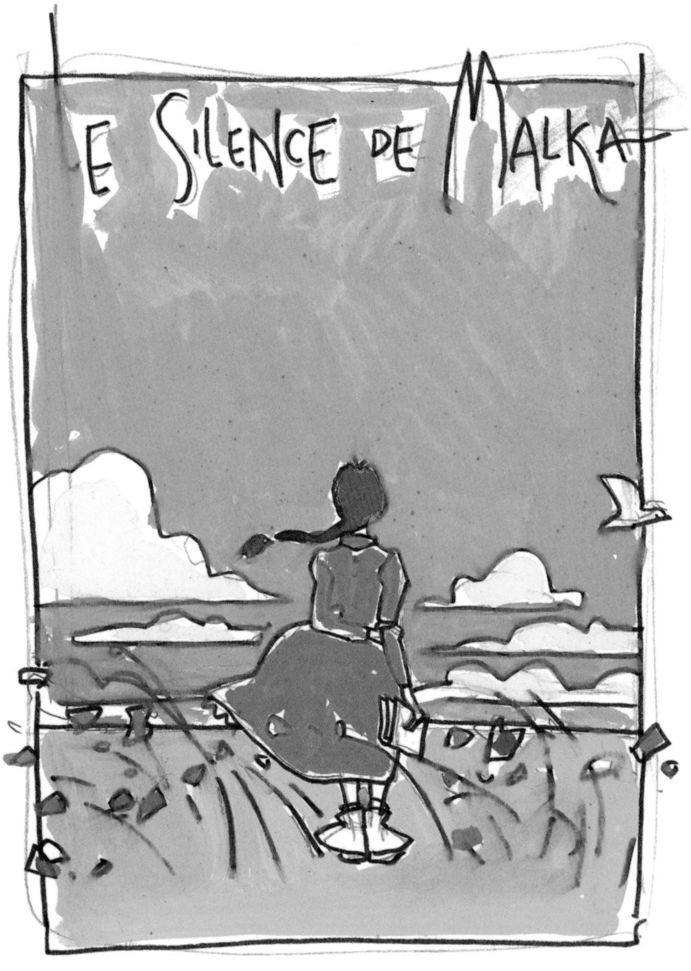
E SILENCE DE MALKA

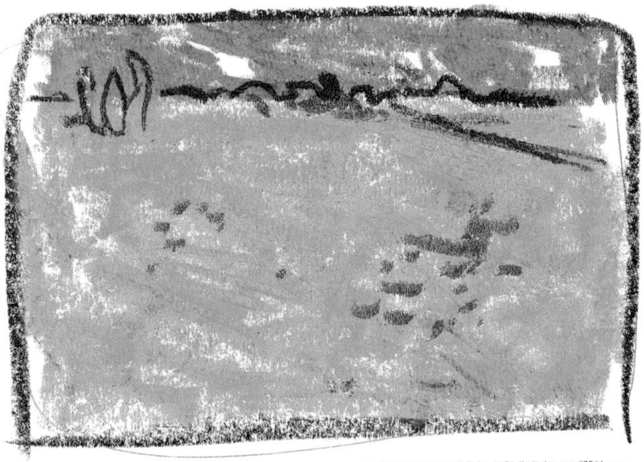

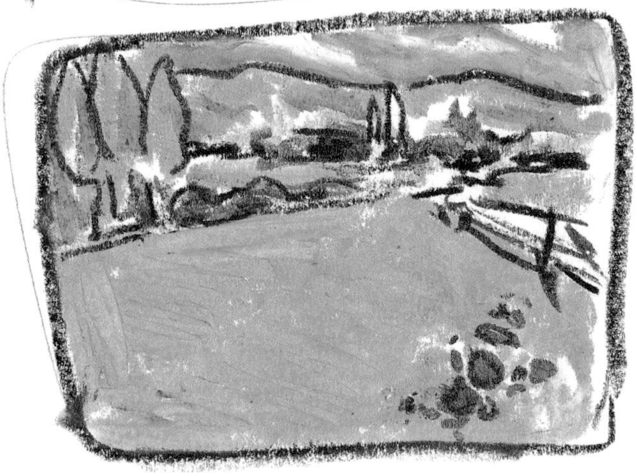

Argentinian pampas were far from the paradise of which they dreamed. Over the course of the first five years of the operation, however, the Jewish Colonization Association succeeded in settling around 10,000 European Jews in Argentina.

Baron Maurice de Hirsch died in 1896. Two years earlier, in the Argentinian province of Entre Ríos, the Jewish Colonization Association created a colony they called Lucienville, in homage to Lucien, the baron's son. It was on these lands that my family eventually washed ashore.

The story I'd like to recount for you took place more than forty years ago: at that time, my grandmother, Teresa (*Bobe Tuve*) had already spent more than seventy years in Argentina. Like others of her generation, despite having spent so many years in exclusively Jewish colonies, she had learned to speak Spanish very well, despite her accent and certain Bessarabic Yiddish expressions which still bled over from her mother tongue.

Over the course of those seven decades, I don't doubt that she had, on numerous occasions, read or heard the word "London." I saw her crying on many afternoons as she listened to the radio soap operas she so passionately followed; I must have seen her thousands of times slowly murmuring the words as she deciphered them (she never managed to read in silence) in popular novels filled with love and betrayal. But assuming she'd actually heard it, the word London didn't seem to mean anything to my grandmother; it was simply the name of a distant capital, practically a nonsense word. Until, one afternoon, on television, someone said the word "London."

"London!" exclaimed Bobe Tuve, upset, "I lived in London!"
"In London!?" I asked. "But Bobe, that's impossible. You were born in Bessarabia and you arrived in Argentina when you were just five or six years old. You couldn't

have lived in London. It's in England!" I told her.

What followed was a brief series of old and muddled childhood memories; obscure relics from her mind that told of Anti-Jewish pogroms in Russia, the Tsarist police raids, the difficulty of obtaining passports, her father's escape to London, his return, a new trip with the entire family to the British capital, and an eventual return to Bessarabia.

"We spent more than a year in London's port," she said. "My parents worked in a laundry. But because we couldn't find a boat to take us to America, we returned to Russia. Part of the family did find a boat to New York and we never saw them again. Then, from Odessa we went to Argentina. And as we were sailing off the coast of Brazil, there was a storm. The ship rolled a lot, and all of a sudden it listed so much I almost fell into the water, but luckily my cousin saved me; he was standing next to me and managed to catch me by my braids."

It was in this tale, in these red braids, that I found the seed of the story for *The Silence of Malka*.

—Jorge Zentner

CHAPTER ONE

FAR FROM THE SEA...

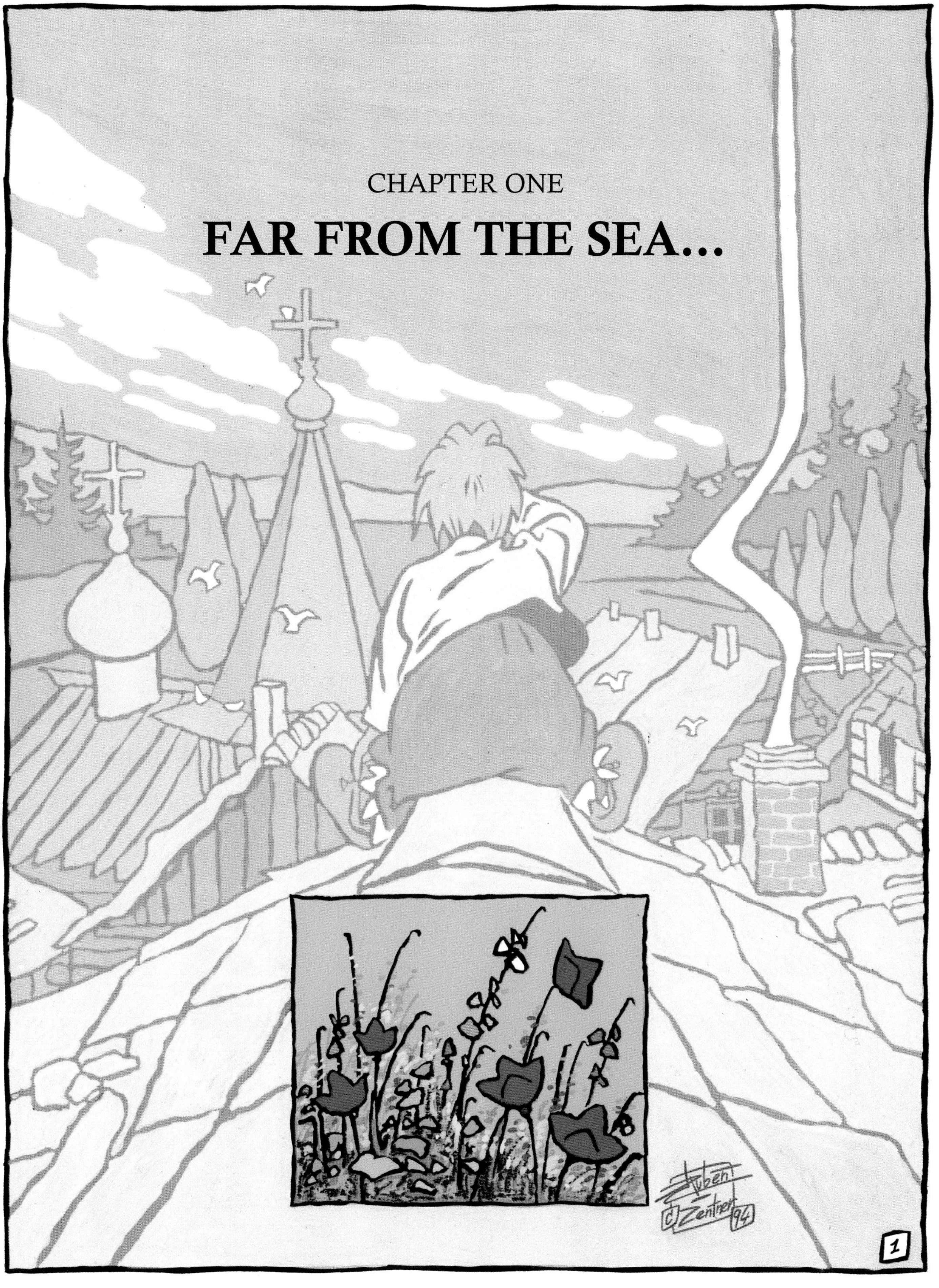
1

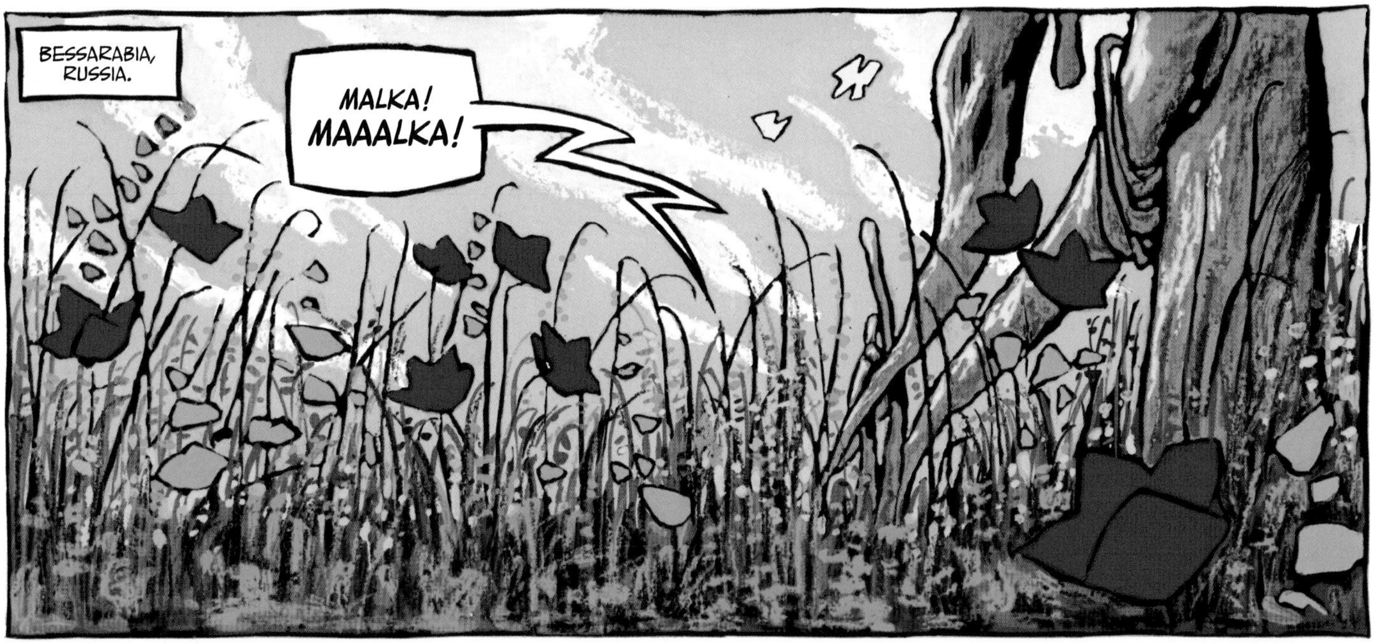
BESSARABIA, RUSSIA.
MALKA! MAAALKA!

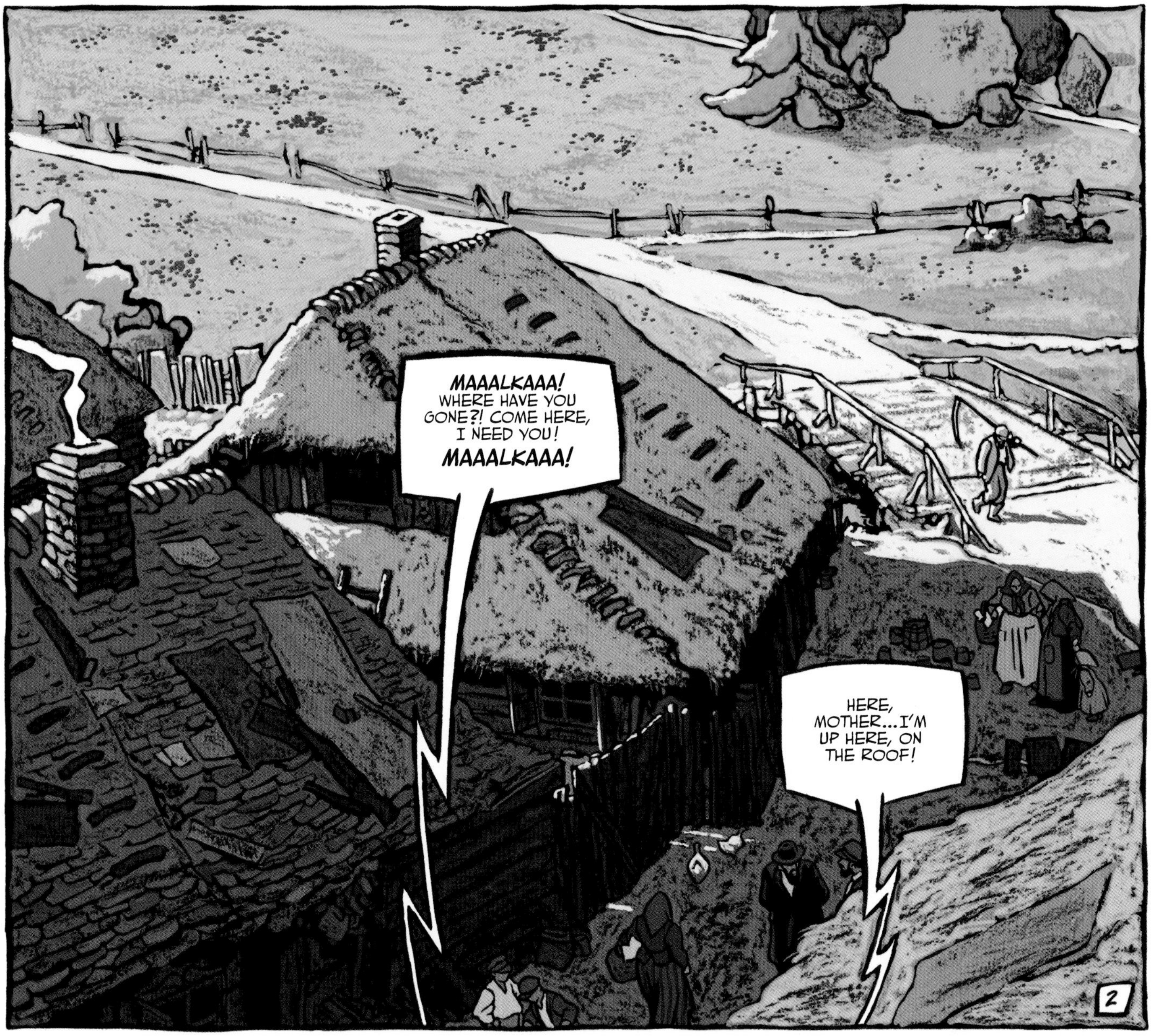
MAAALKAAA! WHERE HAVE YOU GONE?! COME HERE, I NEED YOU! MAAALKAAA!
HERE, MOTHER...I'M UP HERE, ON THE ROOF!
2

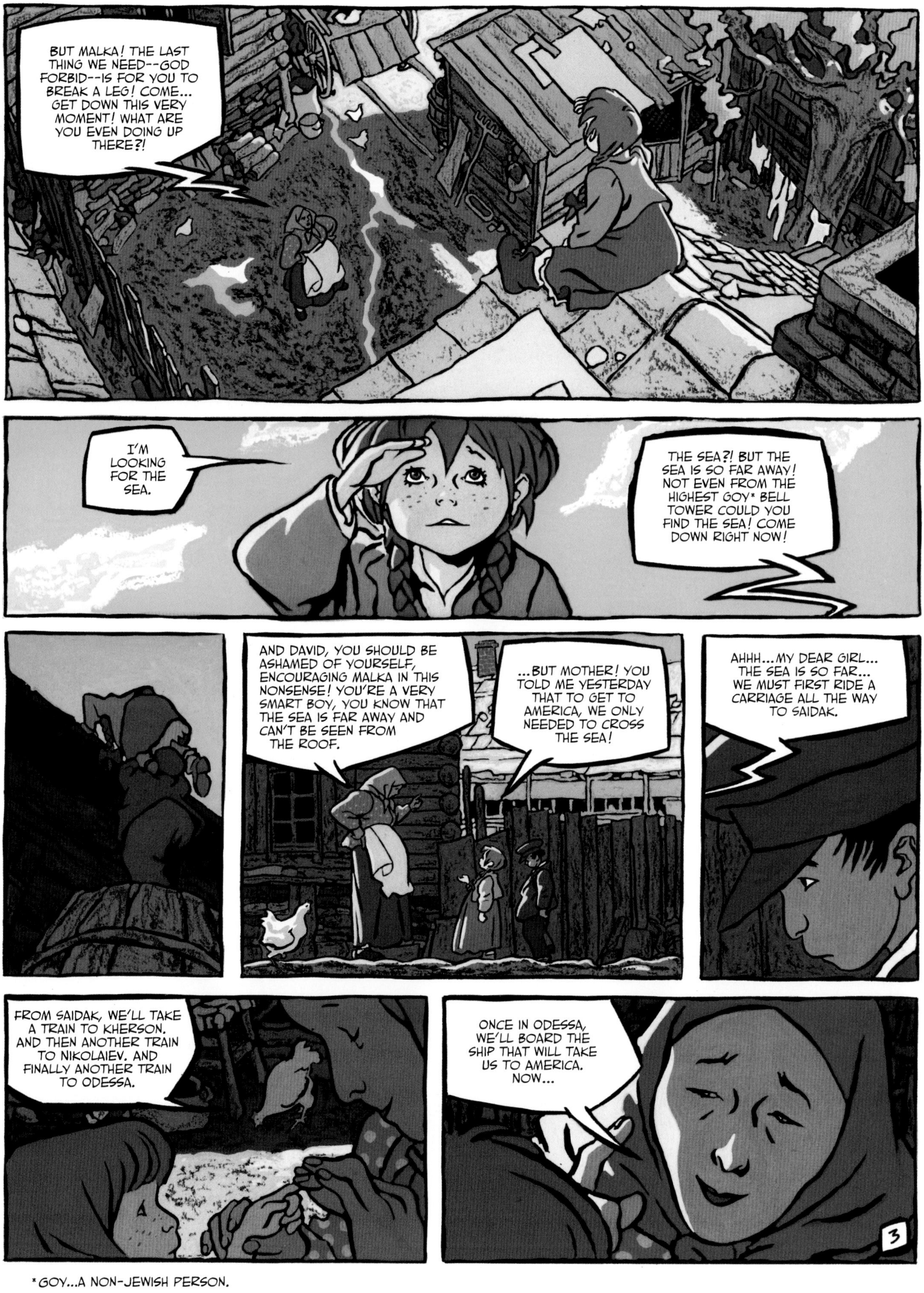
BUT MALKA! THE LAST THING WE NEED--GOD FORBID--IS FOR YOU TO BREAK A LEG! COME... GET DOWN THIS VERY MOMENT! WHAT ARE YOU EVEN DOING UP THERE?!
I'M LOOKING FOR THE SEA.
THE SEA?! BUT THE SEA IS SO FAR AWAY! NOT EVEN FROM THE HIGHEST GOY* BELL TOWER COULD YOU FIND THE SEA! COME DOWN RIGHT NOW!
AND DAVID, YOU SHOULD BE ASHAMED OF YOURSELF, ENCOURAGING MALKA IN THIS NONSENSE! YOU'RE A VERY SMART BOY, YOU KNOW THAT THE SEA IS FAR AWAY AND CAN'T BE SEEN FROM THE ROOF.
...BUT MOTHER! YOU TOLD ME YESTERDAY THAT TO GET TO AMERICA, WE ONLY NEEDED TO CROSS THE SEA!
AHHH...MY DEAR GIRL... THE SEA IS SO FAR... WE MUST FIRST RIDE A CARRIAGE ALL THE WAY TO SAIDAK.
FROM SAIDAK, WE'LL TAKE A TRAIN TO KHERSON. AND THEN ANOTHER TRAIN TO NIKOLAIEV. AND FINALLY ANOTHER TRAIN TO ODESSA.
ONCE IN ODESSA, WE'LL BOARD THE SHIP THAT WILL TAKE US TO AMERICA. NOW...
3

*GOY...A NON-JEWISH PERSON.

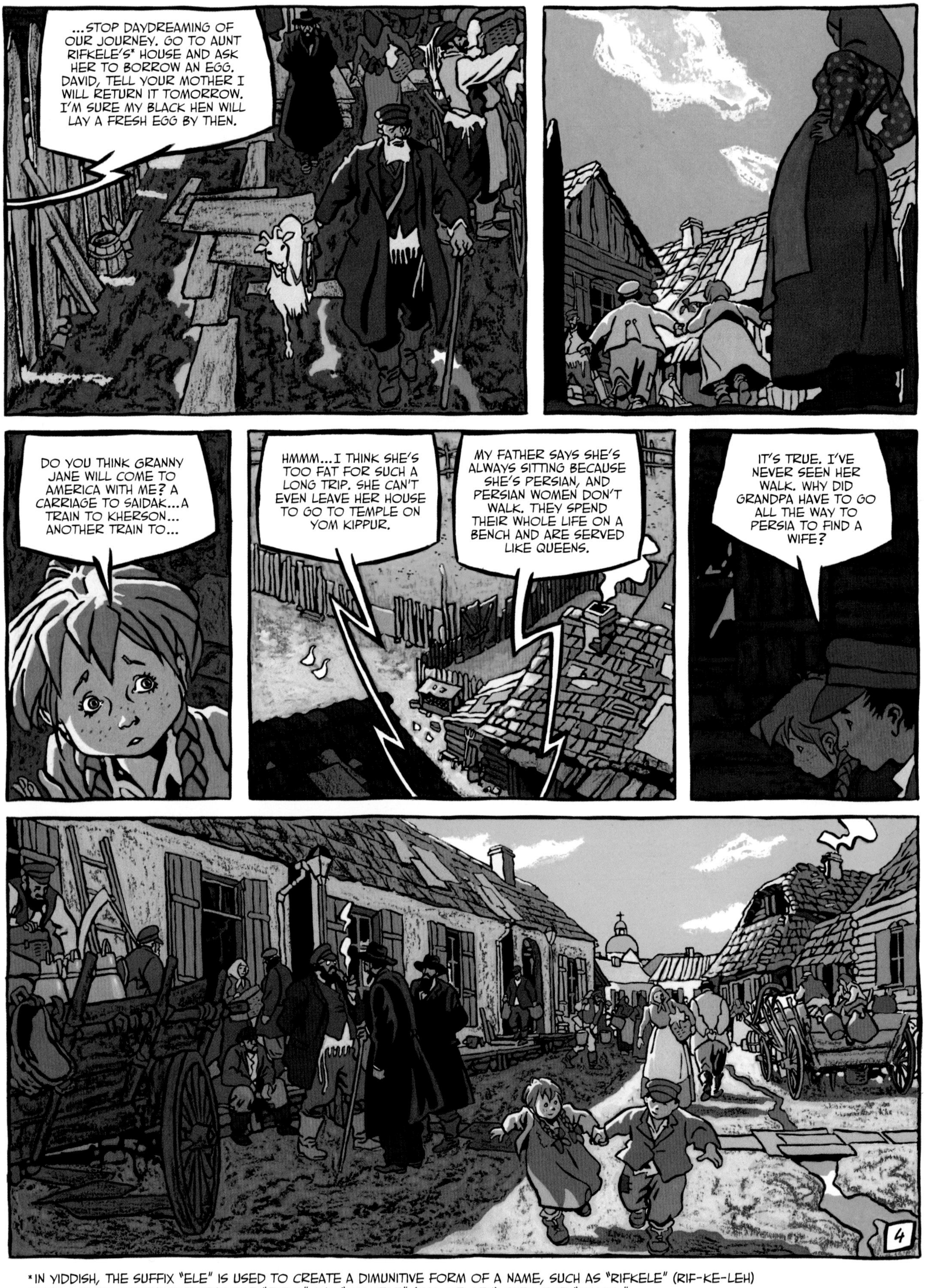
...STOP DAYDREAMING OF OUR JOURNEY. GO TO AUNT RIFKELE'S* HOUSE AND ASK HER TO BORROW AN EGG. DAVID, TELL YOUR MOTHER I WILL RETURN IT TOMORROW. I'M SURE MY BLACK HEN WILL LAY A FRESH EGG BY THEN.
DO YOU THINK GRANNY JANE WILL COME TO AMERICA WITH ME? A CARRIAGE TO SAIDAK...A TRAIN TO KHERSON... ANOTHER TRAIN TO...
HMMM...I THINK SHE'S TOO FAT FOR SUCH A LONG TRIP. SHE CAN'T EVEN LEAVE HER HOUSE TO GO TO TEMPLE ON YOM KIPPUR.
MY FATHER SAYS SHE'S ALWAYS SITTING BECAUSE SHE'S PERSIAN, AND PERSIAN WOMEN DON'T WALK. THEY SPEND THEIR WHOLE LIFE ON A BENCH AND ARE SERVED LIKE QUEENS.
IT'S TRUE. I'VE NEVER SEEN HER WALK. WHY DID GRANDPA HAVE TO GO ALL THE WAY TO PERSIA TO FIND A WIFE?

*IN YIDDISH, THE SUFFIX "ELE" IS USED TO CREATE A DIMUNITIVE FORM OF A NAME, SUCH AS "RIFKELE" (RIF-KE-LEH) BEING A TERM OF ENDEARMENT FOR "RIFKA" AND "MALKELE" (MAL-KE-LEH) USED FOR "MALKA."

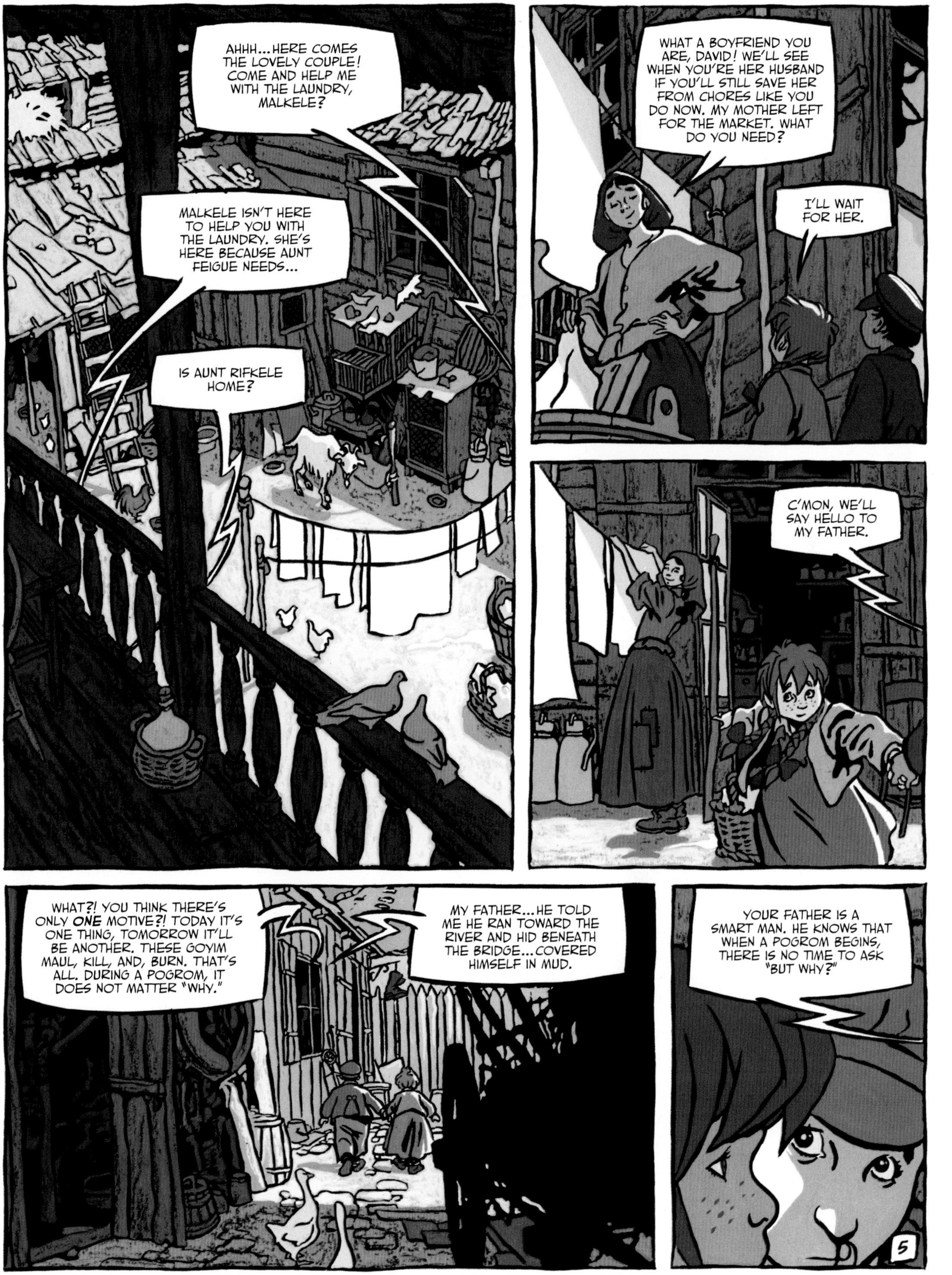
AHHH...HERE COMES THE LOVELY COUPLE! COME AND HELP ME WITH THE LAUNDRY, MALKELE?
MALKELE ISN'T HERE TO HELP YOU WITH THE LAUNDRY. SHE'S HERE BECAUSE AUNT FEIGUE NEEDS...
IS AUNT RIFKELE HOME?
WHAT A BOYFRIEND YOU ARE, DAVID! WE'LL SEE WHEN YOU'RE HER HUSBAND IF YOU'LL STILL SAVE HER FROM CHORES LIKE YOU DO NOW. MY MOTHER LEFT FOR THE MARKET. WHAT DO YOU NEED?
I'LL WAIT FOR HER.
C'MON, WE'LL SAY HELLO TO MY FATHER.
WHAT?! YOU THINK THERE'S ONLY ONE MOTIVE?! TODAY IT'S ONE THING, TOMORROW IT'LL BE ANOTHER. THESE GOYIM MAUL, KILL, AND, BURN. THAT'S ALL. DURING A POGROM, IT DOES NOT MATTER "WHY."
MY FATHER...HE TOLD ME HE RAN TOWARD THE RIVER AND HID BENEATH THE BRIDGE...COVERED HIMSELF IN MUD.
YOUR FATHER IS A SMART MAN. HE KNOWS THAT WHEN A POGROM BEGINS, THERE IS NO TIME TO ASK "BUT WHY?"
5

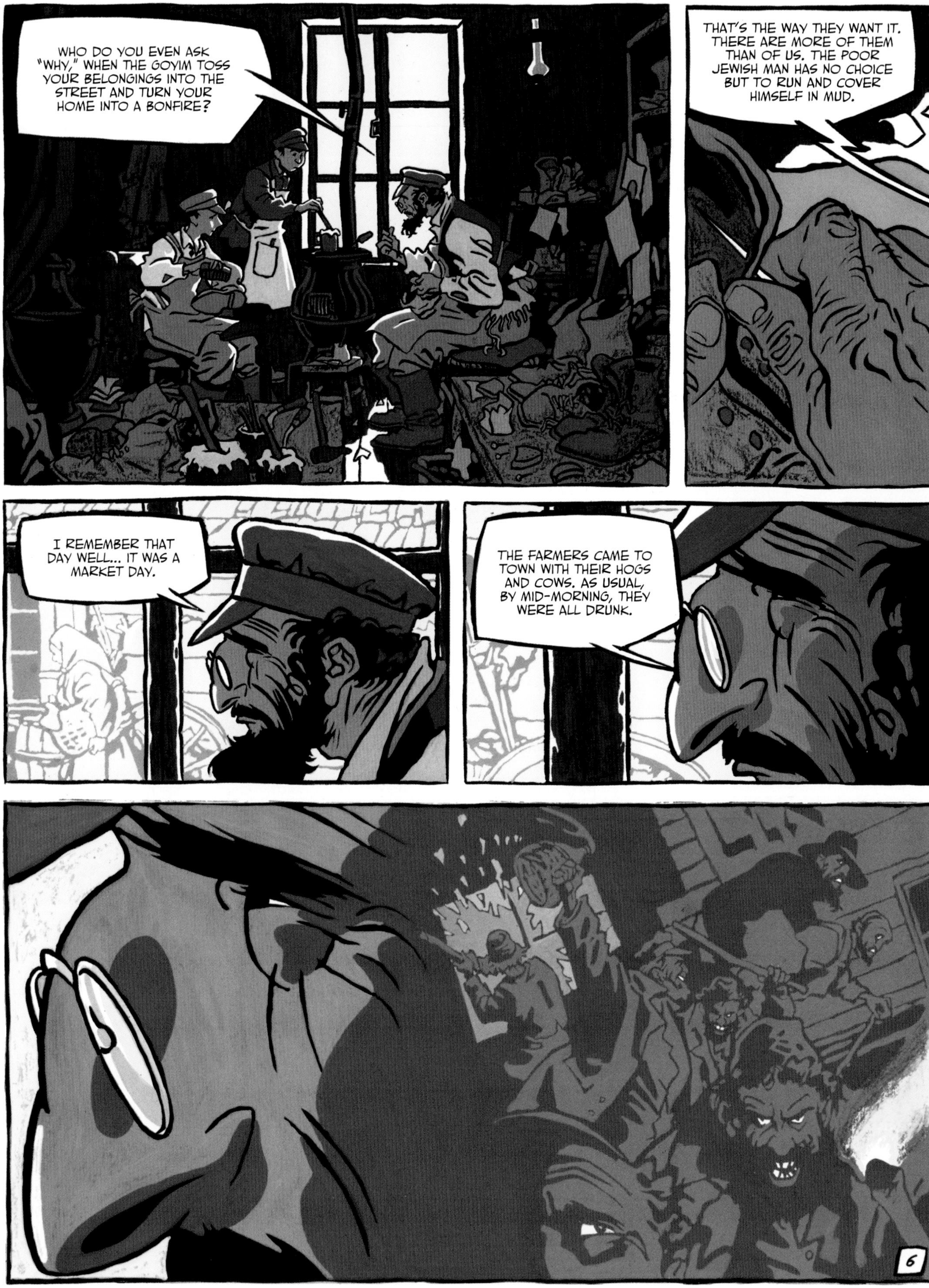
WHO DO YOU EVEN ASK "WHY," WHEN THE GOYIM TOSS YOUR BELONGINGS INTO THE STREET AND TURN YOUR HOME INTO A BONFIRE?
THAT'S THE WAY THEY WANT IT. THERE ARE MORE OF THEM THAN OF US. THE POOR JEWISH MAN HAS NO CHOICE BUT TO RUN AND COVER HIMSELF IN MUD.
I REMEMBER THAT DAY WELL... IT WAS A MARKET DAY.
THE FARMERS CAME TO TOWN WITH THEIR HOGS AND COWS. AS USUAL, BY MID-MORNING, THEY WERE ALL DRUNK.
6

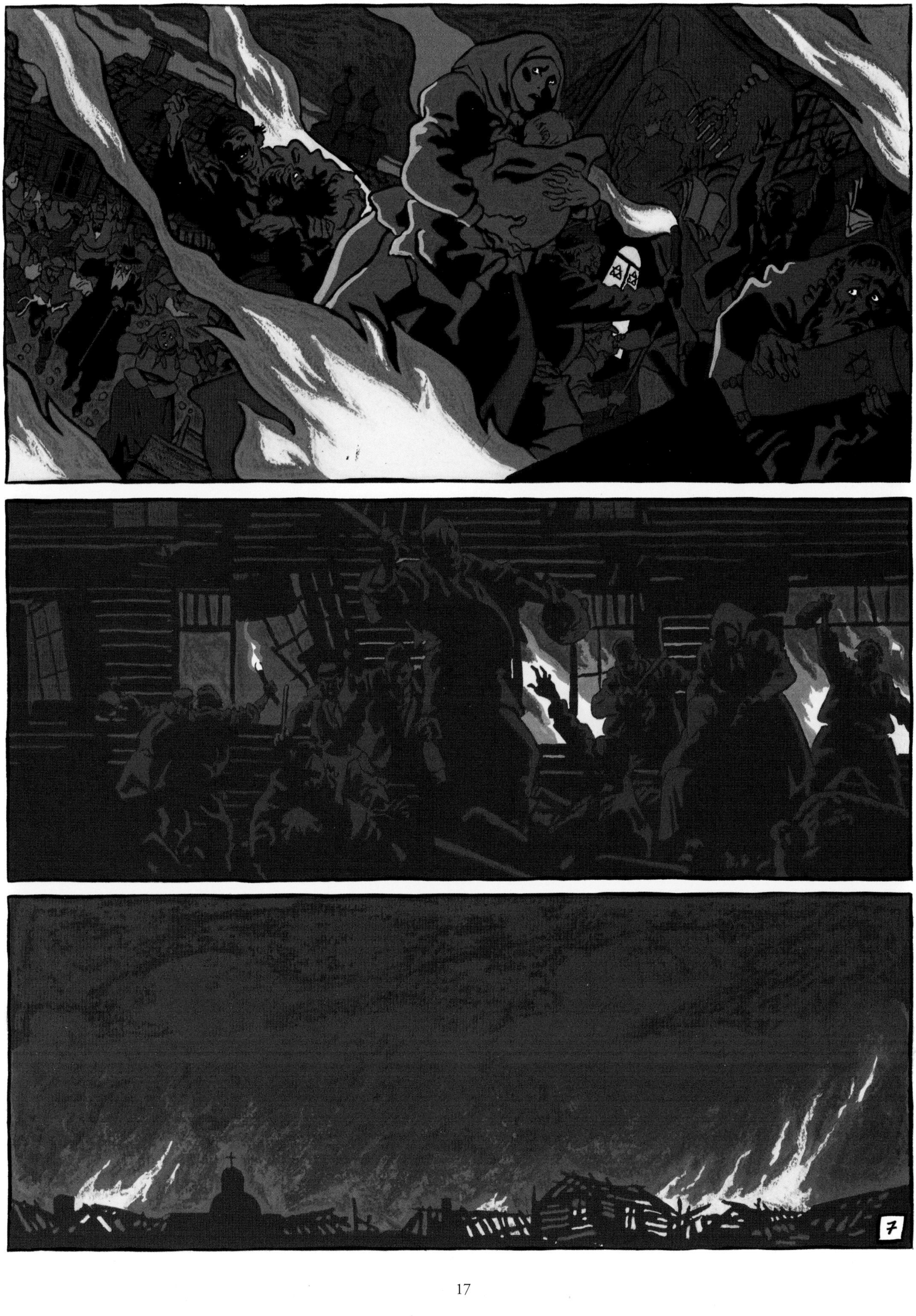
7

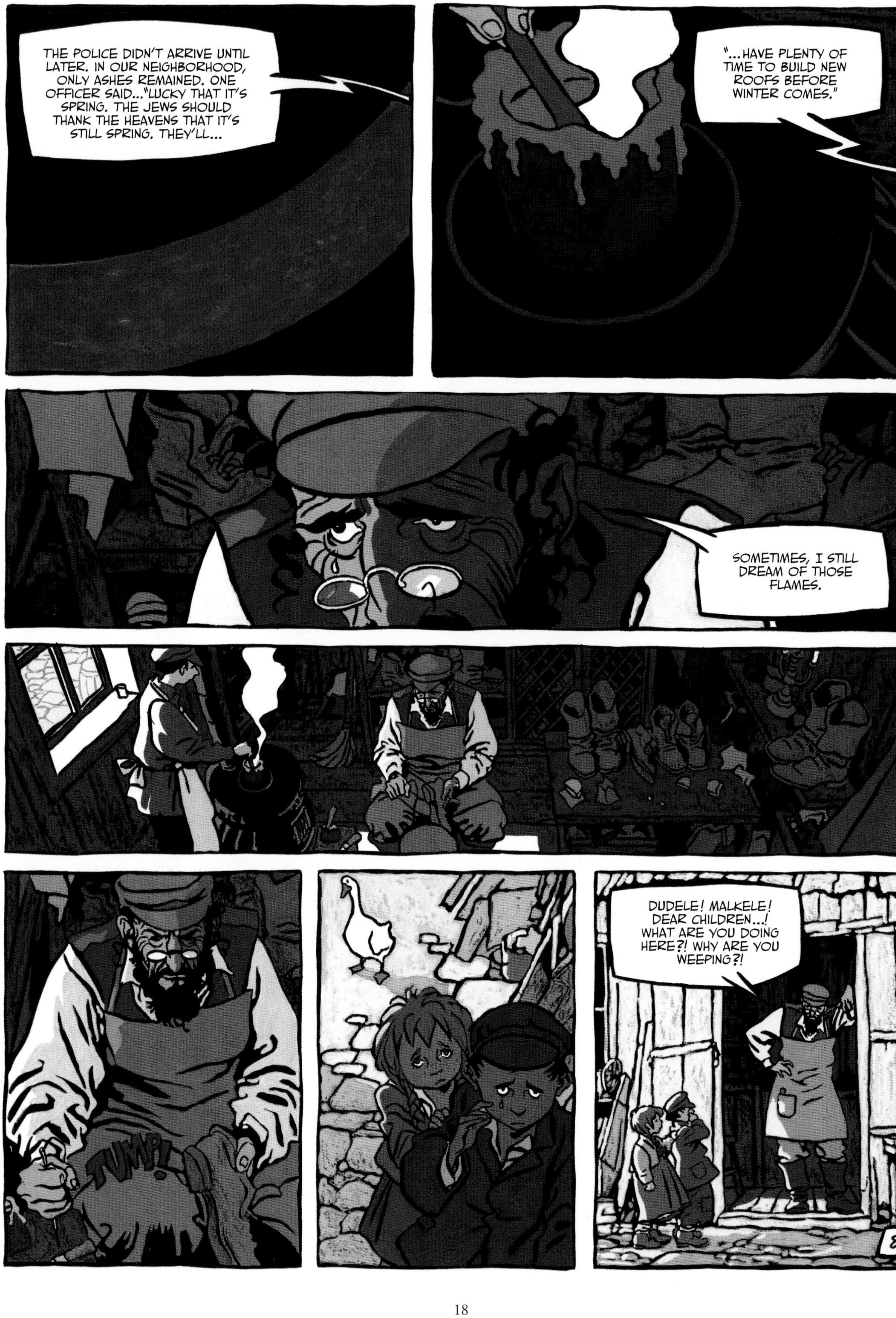
THE POLICE DIDN'T ARRIVE UNTIL LATER. IN OUR NEIGHBORHOOD, ONLY ASHES REMAINED. ONE OFFICER SAID..."LUCKY THAT IT'S SPRING. THE JEWS SHOULD THANK THE HEAVENS THAT IT'S STILL SPRING. THEY'LL...
"...HAVE PLENTY OF TIME TO BUILD NEW ROOFS BEFORE WINTER COMES."
SOMETIMES, I STILL DREAM OF THOSE FLAMES.
TUMP!
DUDELE! MALKELE! DEAR CHILDREN...! WHAT ARE YOU DOING HERE?! WHY ARE YOU WEEPING?!
8

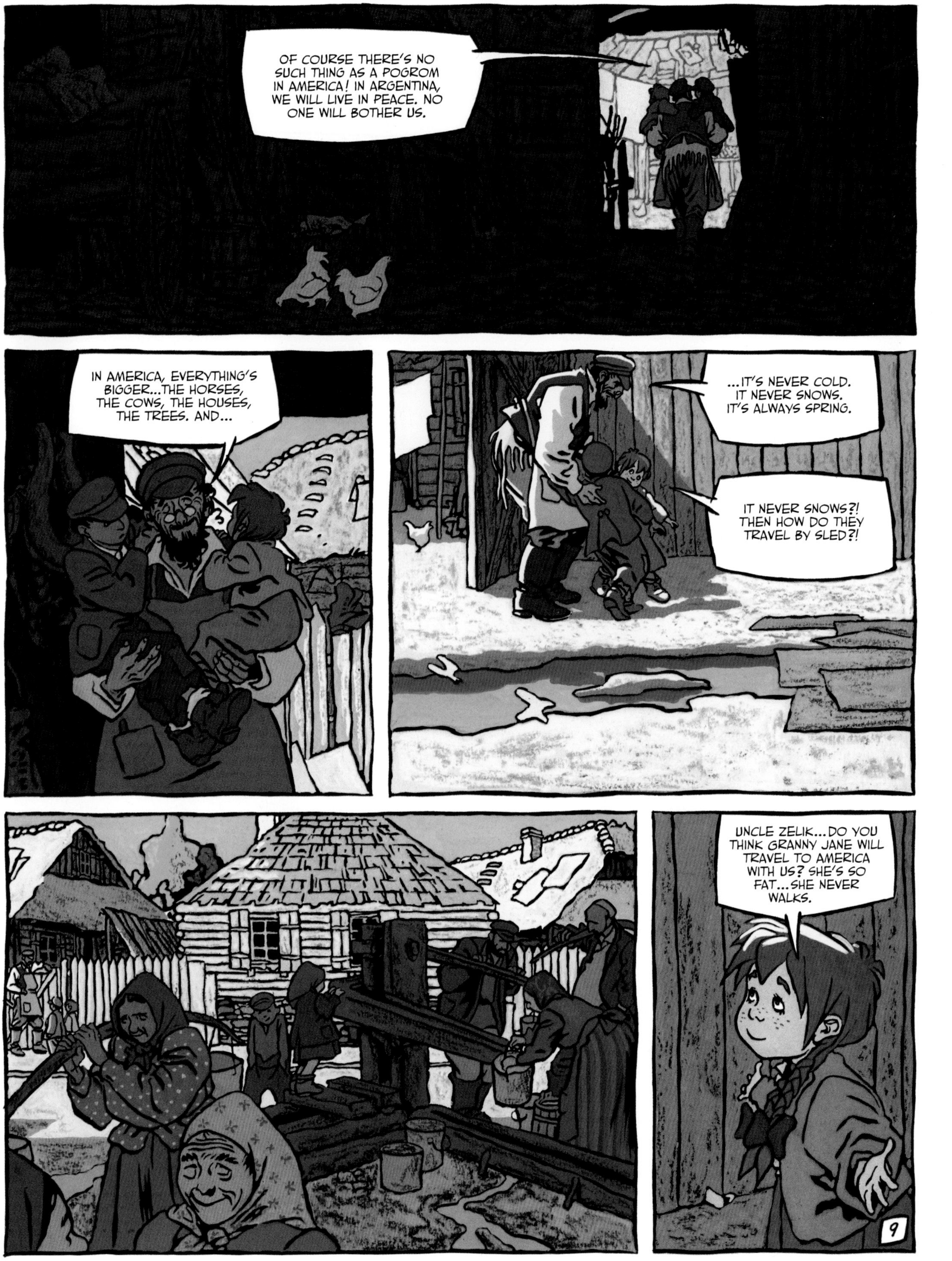
OF COURSE THERE'S NO SUCH THING AS A POGROM IN AMERICA! IN ARGENTINA, WE WILL LIVE IN PEACE. NO ONE WILL BOTHER US.
IN AMERICA, EVERYTHING'S BIGGER...THE HORSES, THE COWS, THE HOUSES, THE TREES. AND...
...IT'S NEVER COLD. IT NEVER SNOWS. IT'S ALWAYS SPRING.
IT NEVER SNOWS?! THEN HOW DO THEY TRAVEL BY SLED?!
UNCLE ZELIK...DO YOU THINK GRANNY JANE WILL TRAVEL TO AMERICA WITH US? SHE'S SO FAT...SHE NEVER WALKS.
9

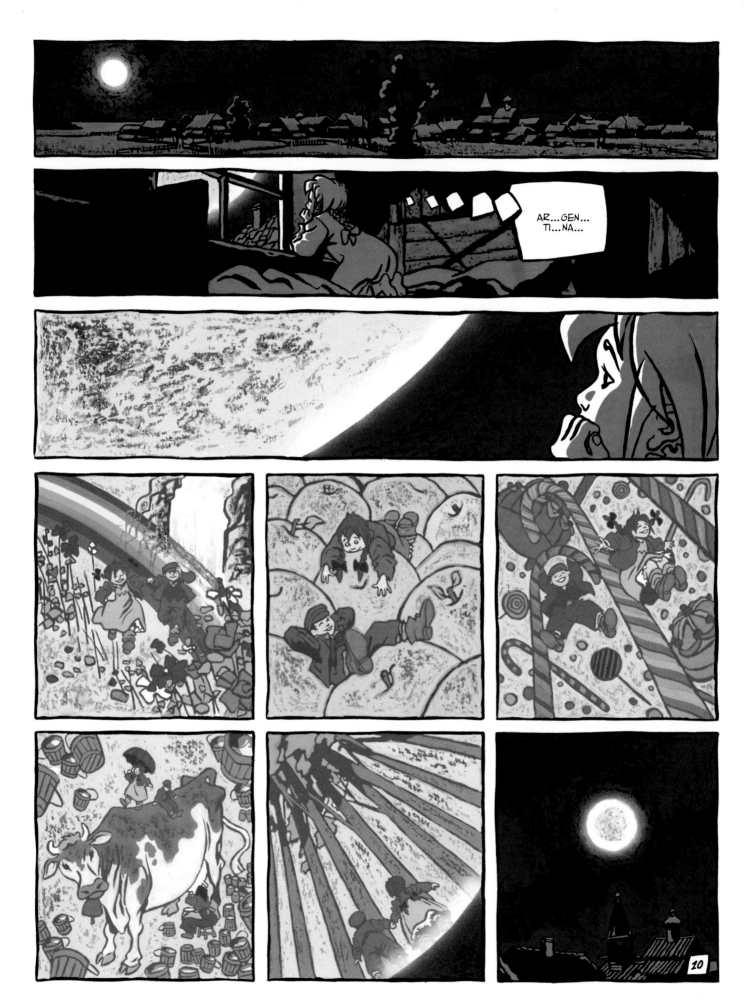

AR...GEN...
TI...NA...

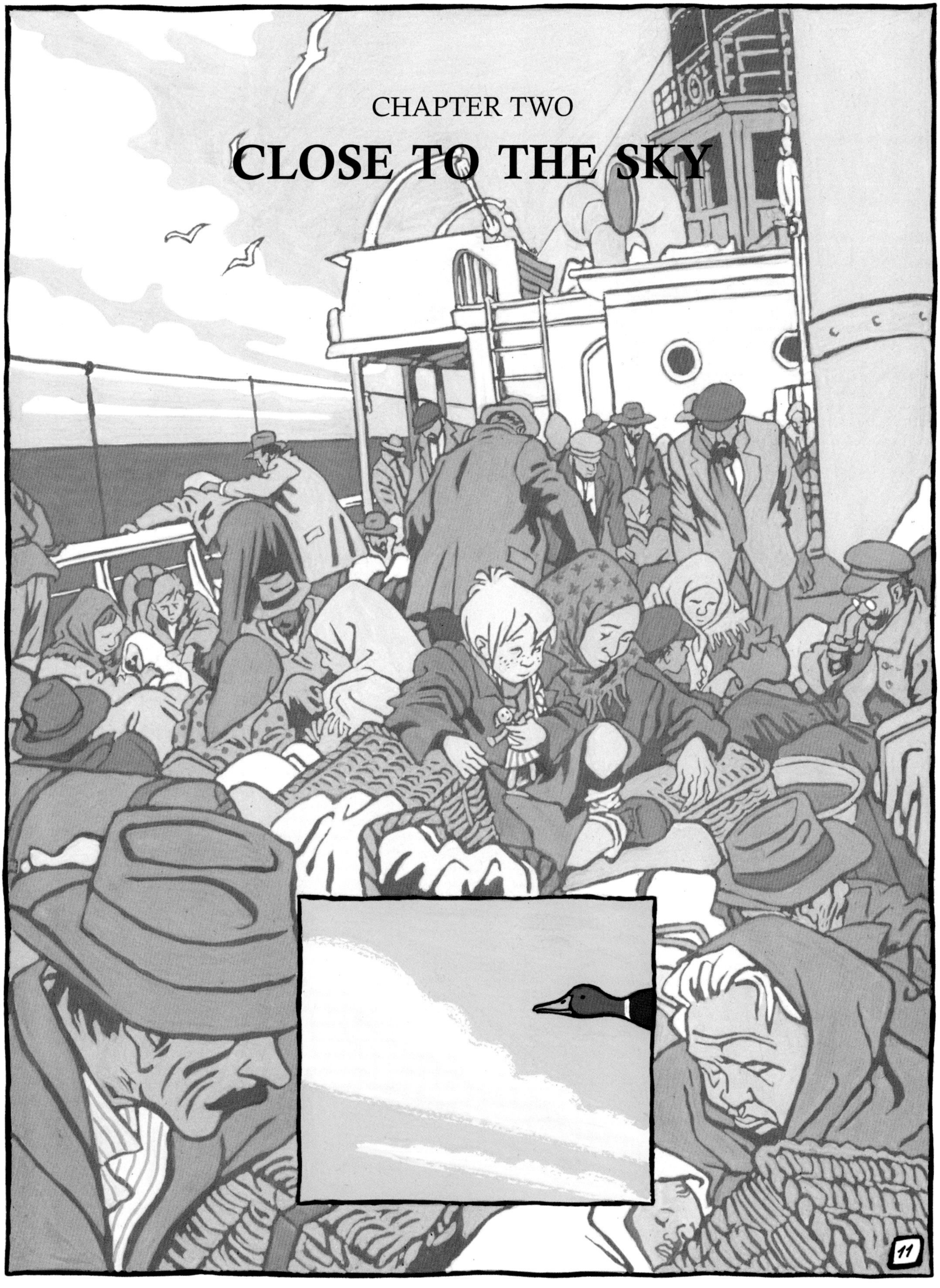
CHAPTER TWO
CLOSE TO THE SKY
11

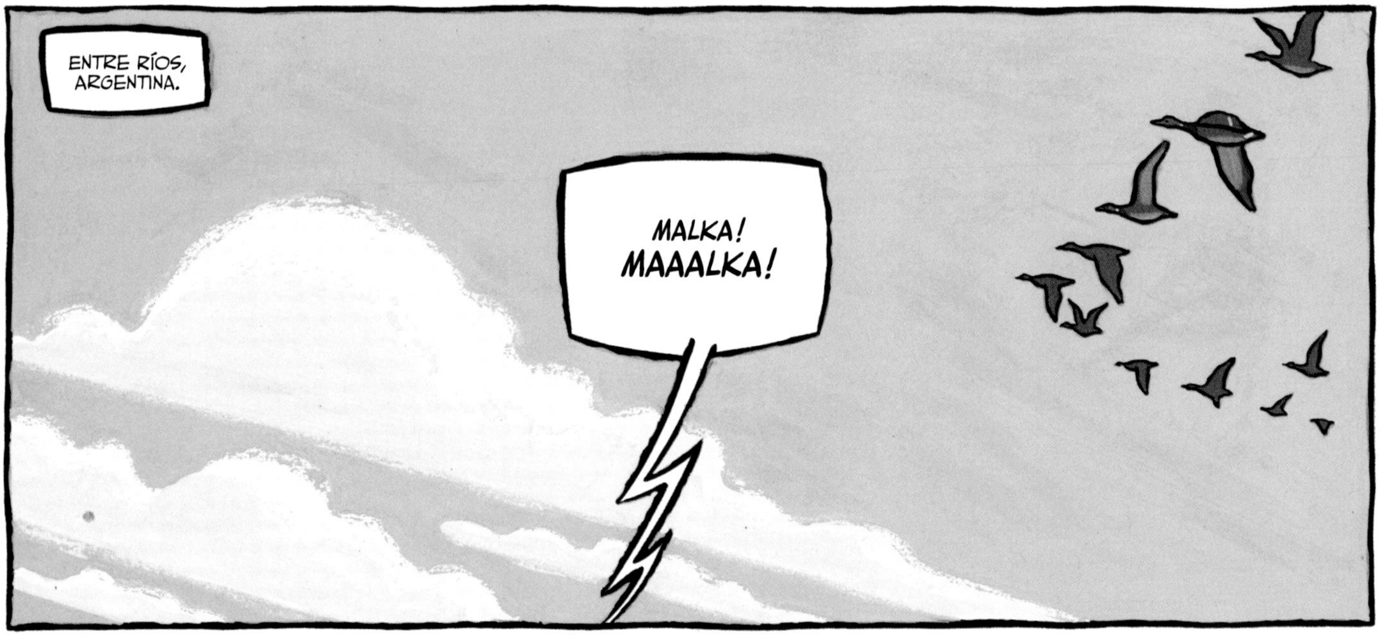
ENTRE RÍOS, ARGENTINA.
MALKA! MAAALKA!

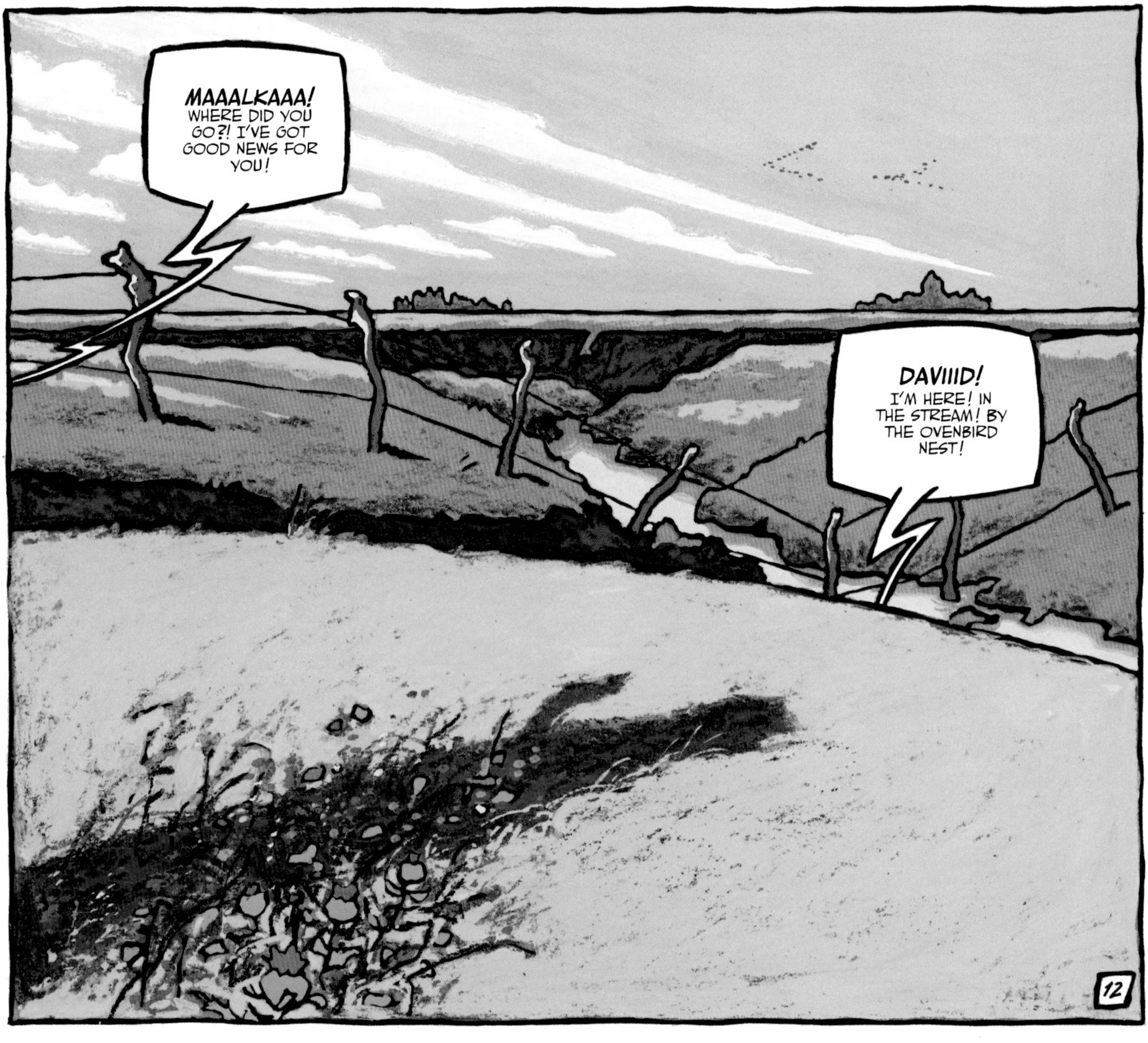
MAAALKAAA! WHERE DID YOU GO?! I'VE GOT GOOD NEWS FOR YOU!
DAVIIID! I'M HERE! IN THE STREAM! BY THE OVENBIRD NEST!
12

WHAT'S THE NEWS?

MY FATHER'S GOING TO TOWN TOMORROW!

DO YOU THINK HE WOULD...?

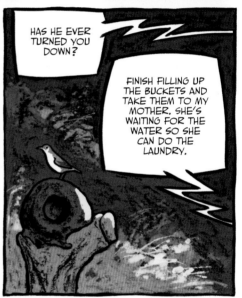

HAS HE EVER TURNED YOU DOWN?

FINISH FILLING UP THE BUCKETS AND TAKE THEM TO MY MOTHER. SHE'S WAITING FOR THE WATER SO SHE CAN DO THE LAUNDRY.

13

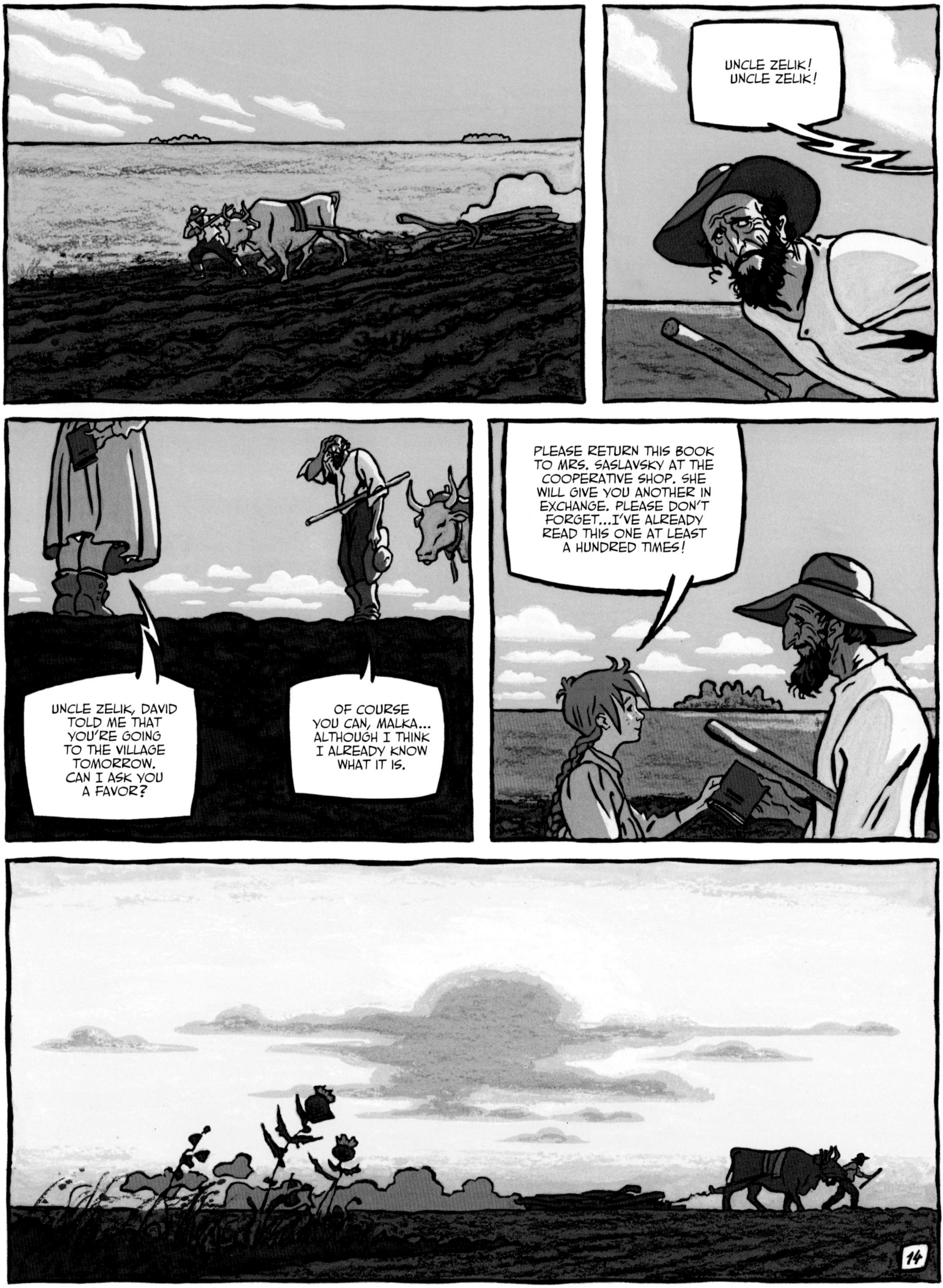
UNCLE ZELIK!
UNCLE ZELIK!
UNCLE ZELIK, DAVID TOLD ME THAT YOU'RE GOING TO THE VILLAGE TOMORROW. CAN I ASK YOU A FAVOR?
OF COURSE YOU CAN, MALKA... ALTHOUGH I THINK I ALREADY KNOW WHAT IT IS.
PLEASE RETURN THIS BOOK TO MRS. SASLAVSKY AT THE COOPERATIVE SHOP. SHE WILL GIVE YOU ANOTHER IN EXCHANGE. PLEASE DON'T FORGET...I'VE ALREADY READ THIS ONE AT LEAST A HUNDRED TIMES!
14

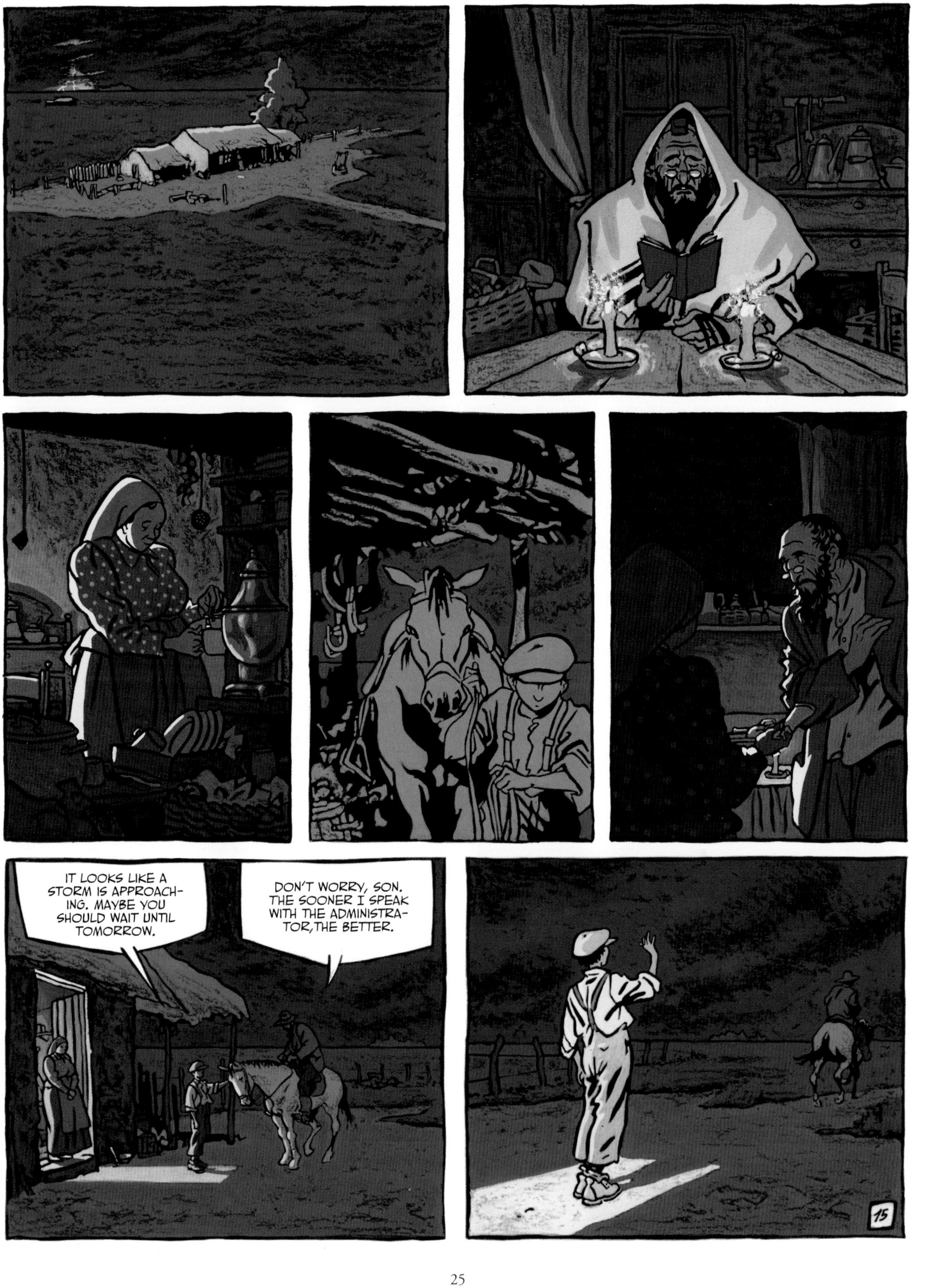
IT LOOKS LIKE A STORM IS APPROACHING. MAYBE YOU SHOULD WAIT UNTIL TOMORROW.
DON'T WORRY, SON. THE SOONER I SPEAK WITH THE ADMINISTRATOR, THE BETTER.
15

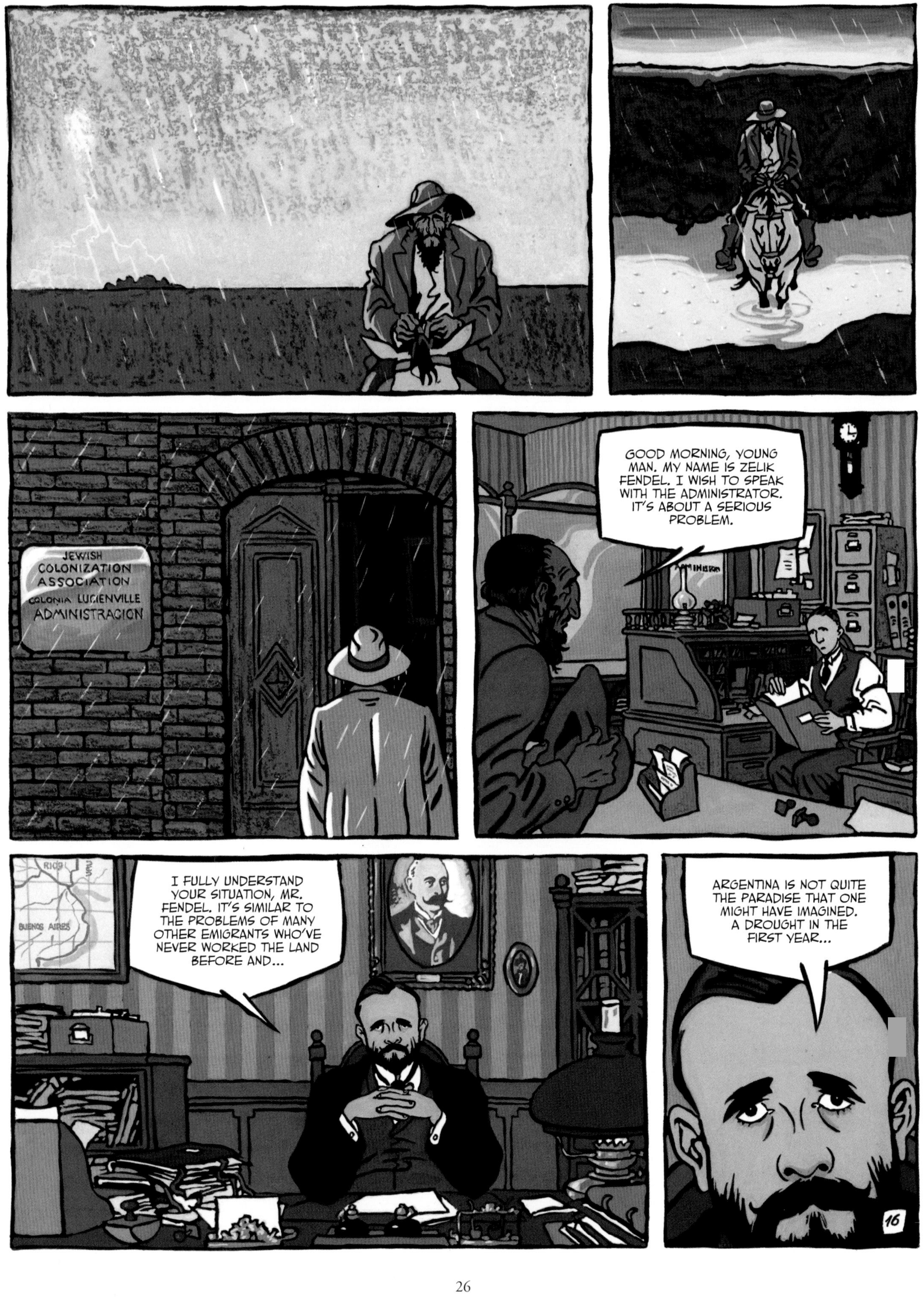
JEWISH COLONIZATION ASSOCIATION
COLONIA LUCIENVILLE
ADMINISTRACION
GOOD MORNING, YOUNG MAN. MY NAME IS ZELIK FENDEL. I WISH TO SPEAK WITH THE ADMINISTRATOR. IT'S ABOUT A SERIOUS PROBLEM.
BUENOS AIRES
I FULLY UNDERSTAND YOUR SITUATION, MR. FENDEL. IT'S SIMILAR TO THE PROBLEMS OF MANY OTHER EMIGRANTS WHO'VE NEVER WORKED THE LAND BEFORE AND...
ARGENTINA IS NOT QUITE THE PARADISE THAT ONE MIGHT HAVE IMAGINED. A DROUGHT IN THE FIRST YEAR...
16

...THE PLAGUE OF LOCUSTS THE FOLLOWING YEAR...THE POOR QUALITY OF THE SEEDS...NONE OF THESE THINGS ARE YOUR FAULT. I KNOW, I KNOW VERY WELL. WHAT CAN BE DONE IN THE FACE OF SO MUCH MISFORTUNE?

I THINK IF YOU COULD GRANT ME A LOAN, NEXT YEAR I WILL BE ABLE TO...

MR. FENDEL, PLEASE. YOU KNOW THAT OUR ORGANIZATION HAS ALREADY PROVIDED YOU WITH A PARCEL OF LAND...

...A HOUSE, A PLOW, AND AN OX...NOT TO MENTION THE TRAVEL EXPENSES FOR YOUR VOYAGE AND A SCHOOL FOR THE CHILDREN...

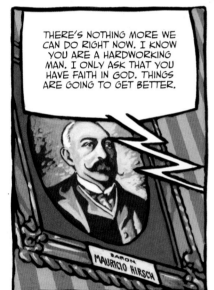

THERE'S NOTHING MORE WE CAN DO RIGHT NOW. I KNOW YOU ARE A HARDWORKING MAN. I ONLY ASK THAT YOU HAVE FAITH IN GOD. THINGS ARE GOING TO GET BETTER.

BARON MAURICIO HIRSCH

I'M SORRY, MALKELE... TODAY, I CANNOT ASK MRS. SASLAVSKY FOR A NEW BOOK...TODAY, I DO NOT HAVE THE STRENGTH... I DO NOT HAVE THE WORDS...I CANNOT...

17

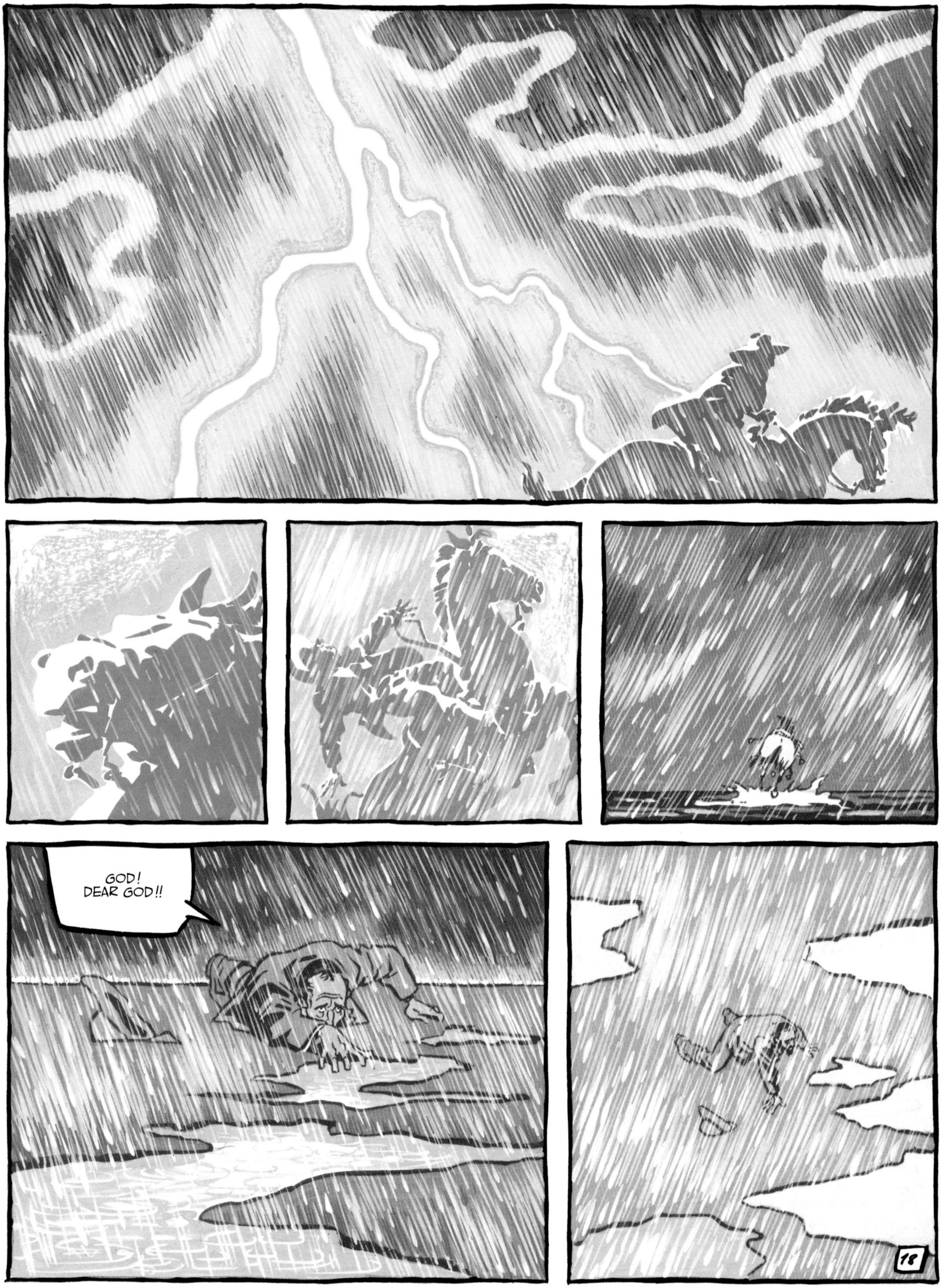
GOD!
DEAR GOD!!
18

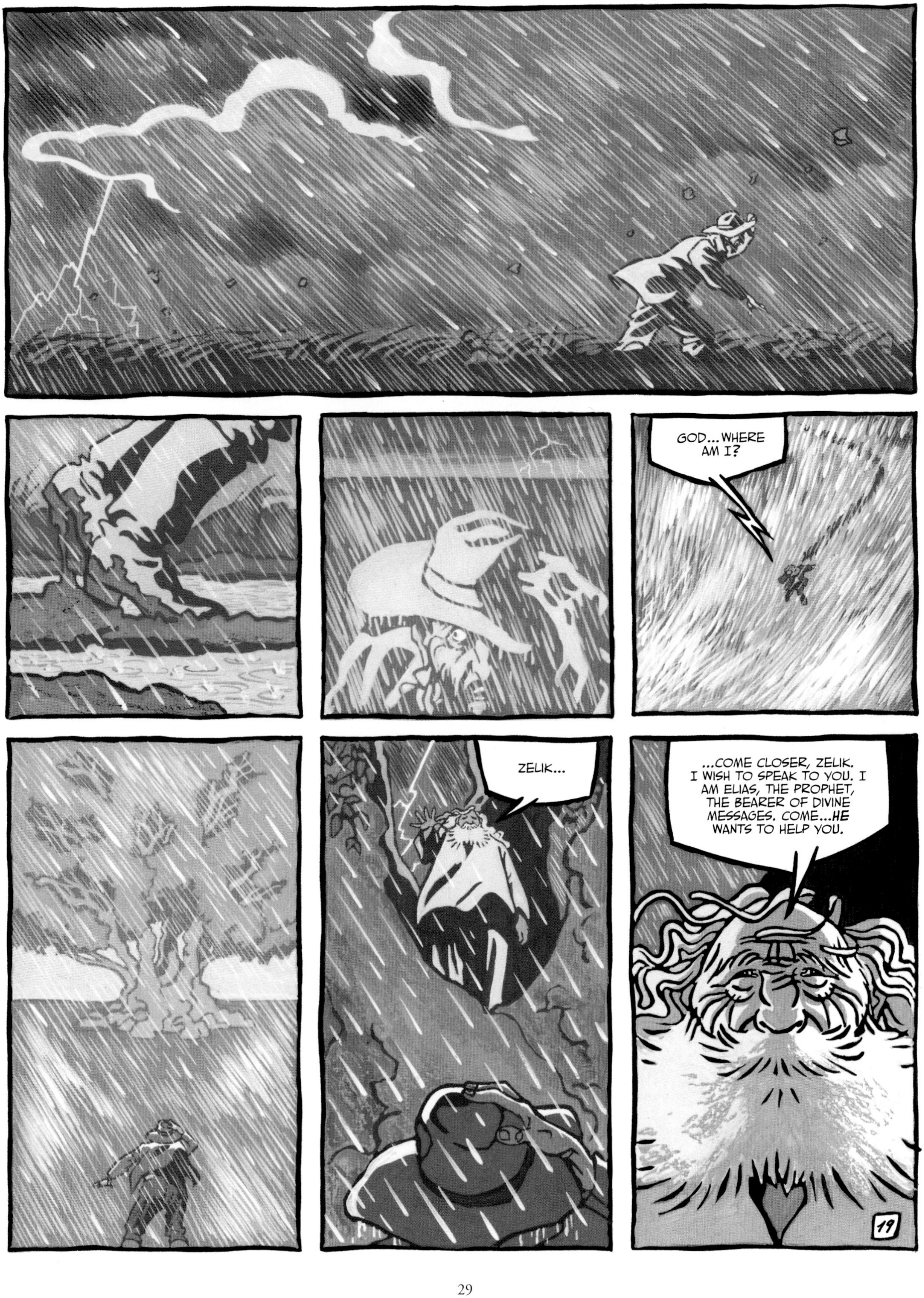
GOD...WHERE AM I?
ZELIK...
...COME CLOSER, ZELIK. I WISH TO SPEAK TO YOU. I AM ELIAS, THE PROPHET, THE BEARER OF DIVINE MESSAGES. COME...HE WANTS TO HELP YOU.
19

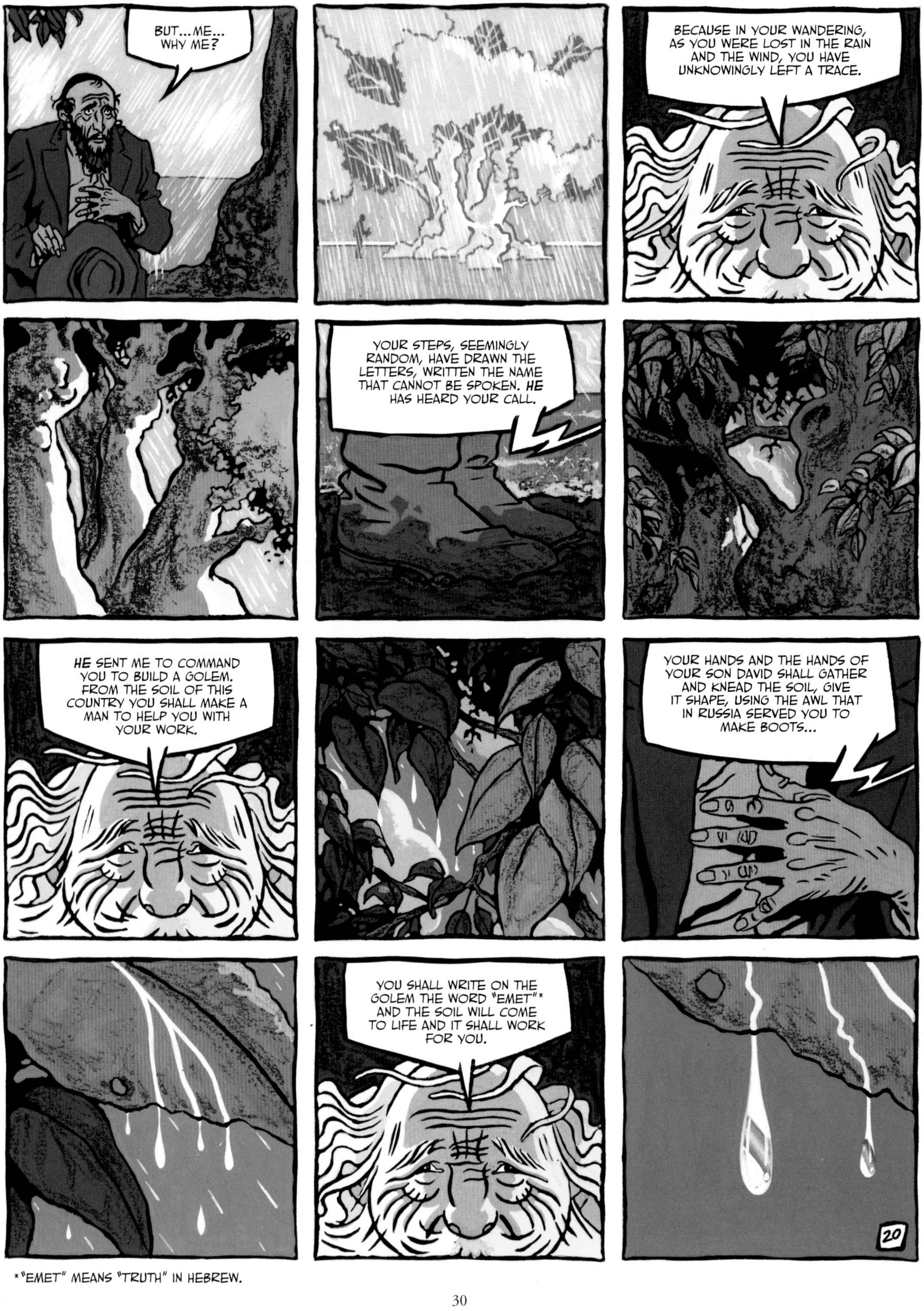

BUT... ME... WHY ME?
BECAUSE IN YOUR WANDERING, AS YOU WERE LOST IN THE RAIN AND THE WIND, YOU HAVE UNKNOWINGLY LEFT A TRACE.
YOUR STEPS, SEEMINGLY RANDOM, HAVE DRAWN THE LETTERS, WRITTEN THE NAME THAT CANNOT BE SPOKEN. HE HAS HEARD YOUR CALL.
HE SENT ME TO COMMAND YOU TO BUILD A GOLEM. FROM THE SOIL OF THIS COUNTRY YOU SHALL MAKE A MAN TO HELP YOU WITH YOUR WORK.
YOUR HANDS AND THE HANDS OF YOUR SON DAVID SHALL GATHER AND KNEAD THE SOIL, GIVE IT SHAPE, USING THE AWL THAT IN RUSSIA SERVED YOU TO MAKE BOOTS...
YOU SHALL WRITE ON THE GOLEM THE WORD "EMET"* AND THE SOIL WILL COME TO LIFE AND IT SHALL WORK FOR YOU.
20

* "EMET" MEANS "TRUTH" IN HEBREW.

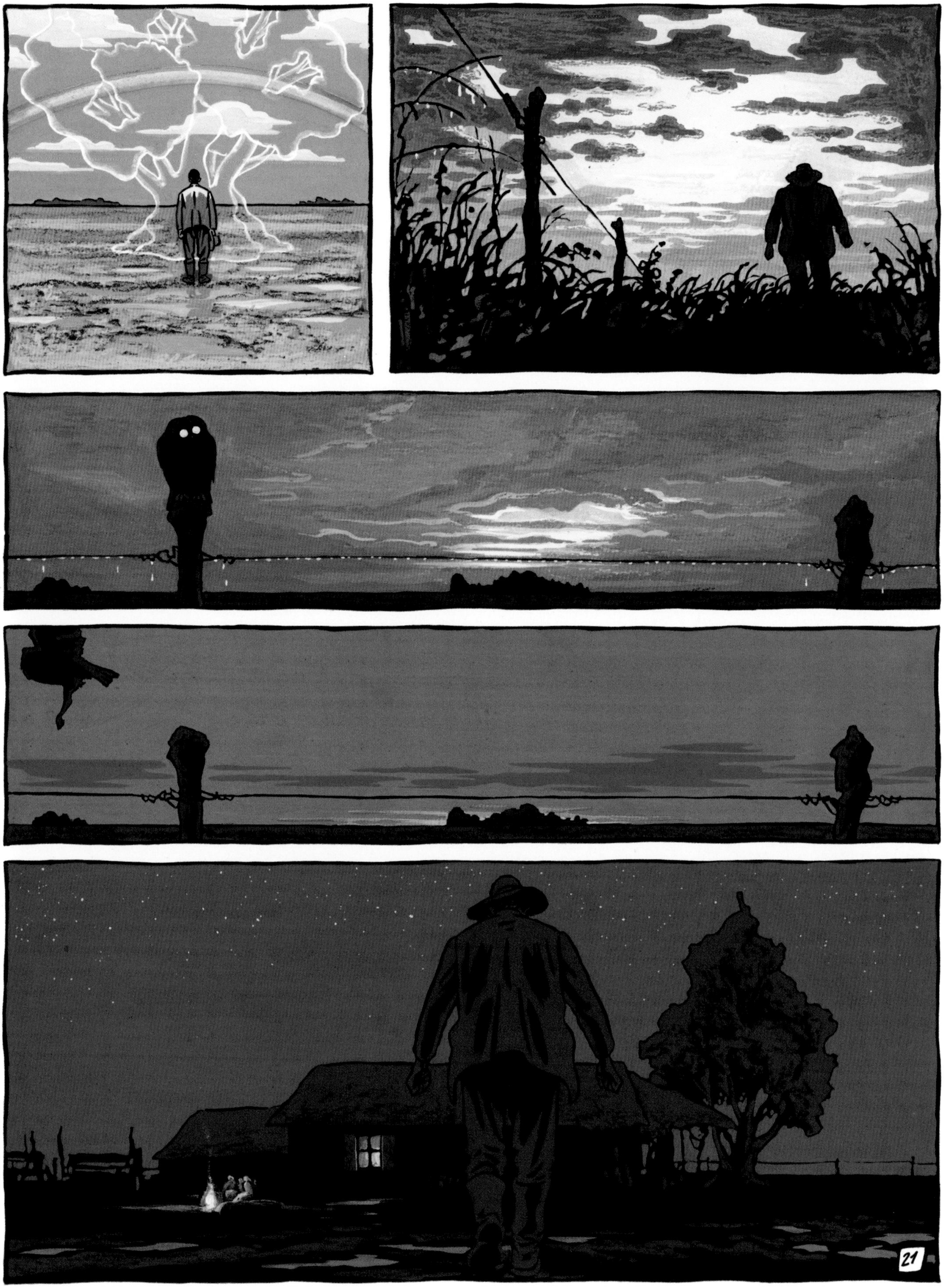
21

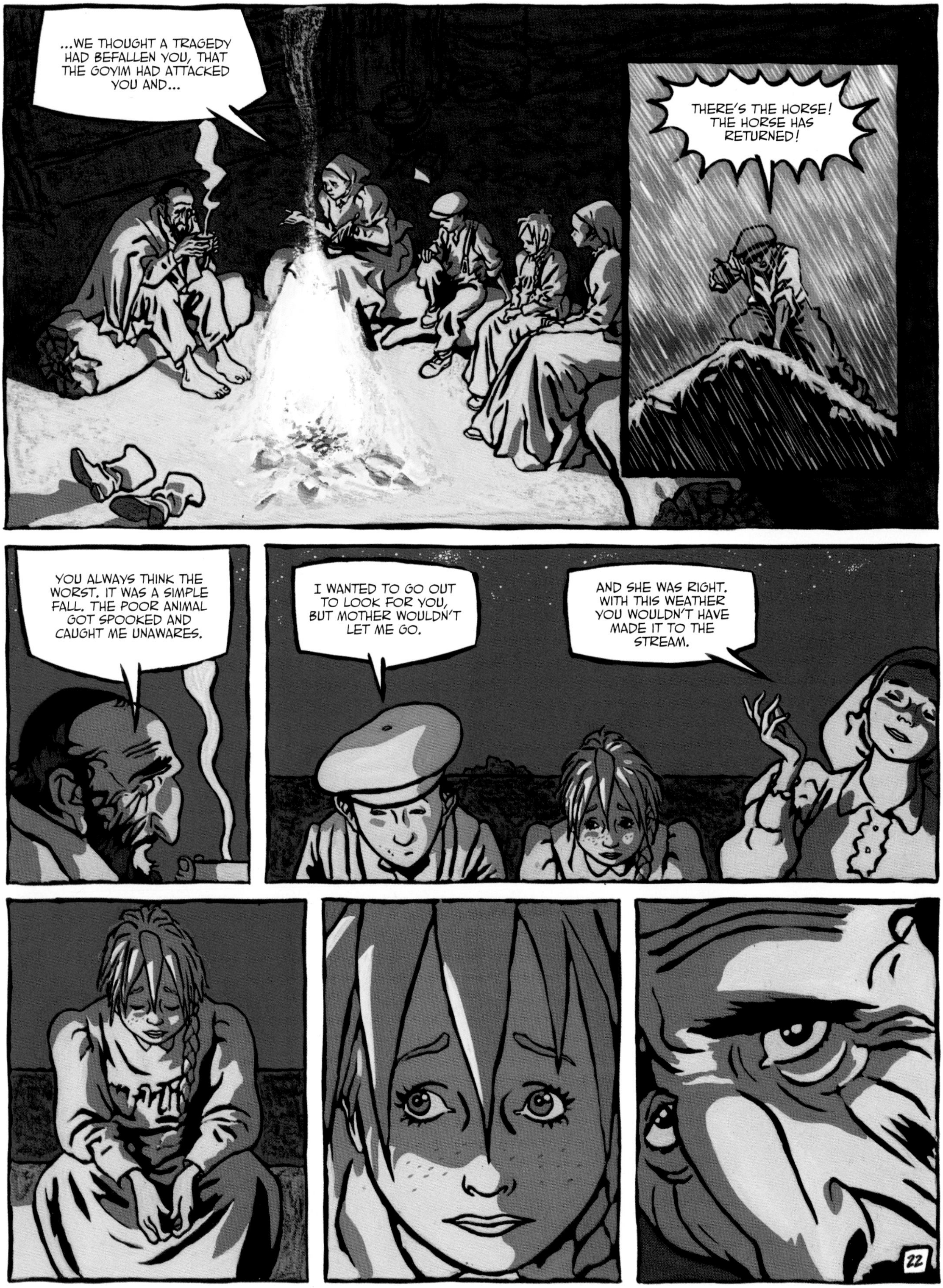
...WE THOUGHT A TRAGEDY HAD BEFALLEN YOU, THAT THE GOYIM HAD ATTACKED YOU AND...
THERE'S THE HORSE! THE HORSE HAS RETURNED!
YOU ALWAYS THINK THE WORST. IT WAS A SIMPLE FALL. THE POOR ANIMAL GOT SPOOKED AND CAUGHT ME UNAWARES.
I WANTED TO GO OUT TO LOOK FOR YOU, BUT MOTHER WOULDN'T LET ME GO.
AND SHE WAS RIGHT. WITH THIS WEATHER YOU WOULDN'T HAVE MADE IT TO THE STREAM.
22

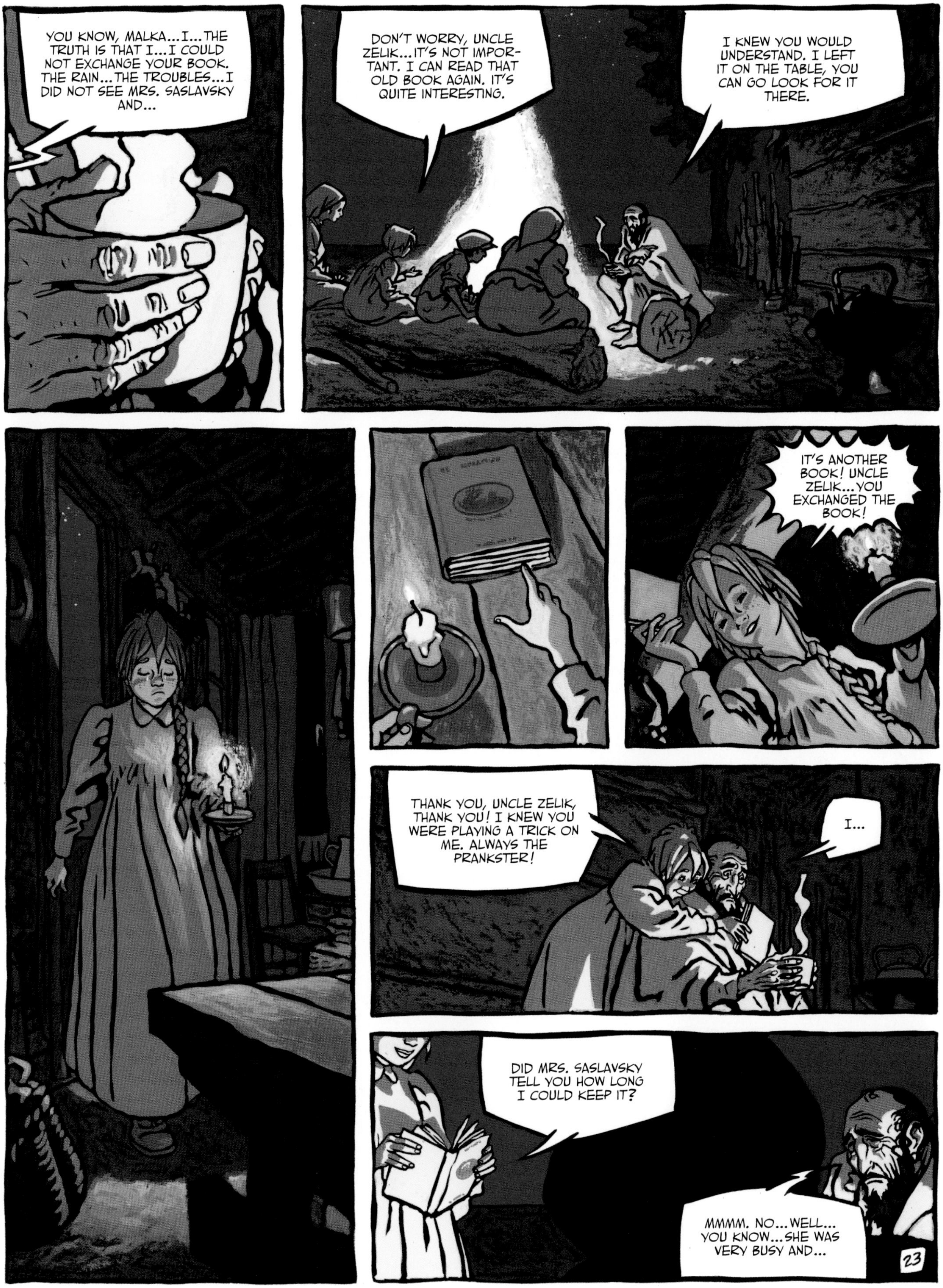

YOU KNOW, MALKA...I...THE TRUTH IS THAT I...I COULD NOT EXCHANGE YOUR BOOK. THE RAIN...THE TROUBLES...I DID NOT SEE MRS. SASLAVSKY AND...
DON'T WORRY, UNCLE ZELIK...IT'S NOT IMPORTANT. I CAN READ THAT OLD BOOK AGAIN. IT'S QUITE INTERESTING.
I KNEW YOU WOULD UNDERSTAND. I LEFT IT ON THE TABLE, YOU CAN GO LOOK FOR IT THERE.
IT'S ANOTHER BOOK! UNCLE ZELIK...YOU EXCHANGED THE BOOK!
THANK YOU, UNCLE ZELIK, THANK YOU! I KNEW YOU WERE PLAYING A TRICK ON ME. ALWAYS THE PRANKSTER!
I...
DID MRS. SASLAVSKY TELL YOU HOW LONG I COULD KEEP IT?
MMMM. NO...WELL... YOU KNOW...SHE WAS VERY BUSY AND...
23

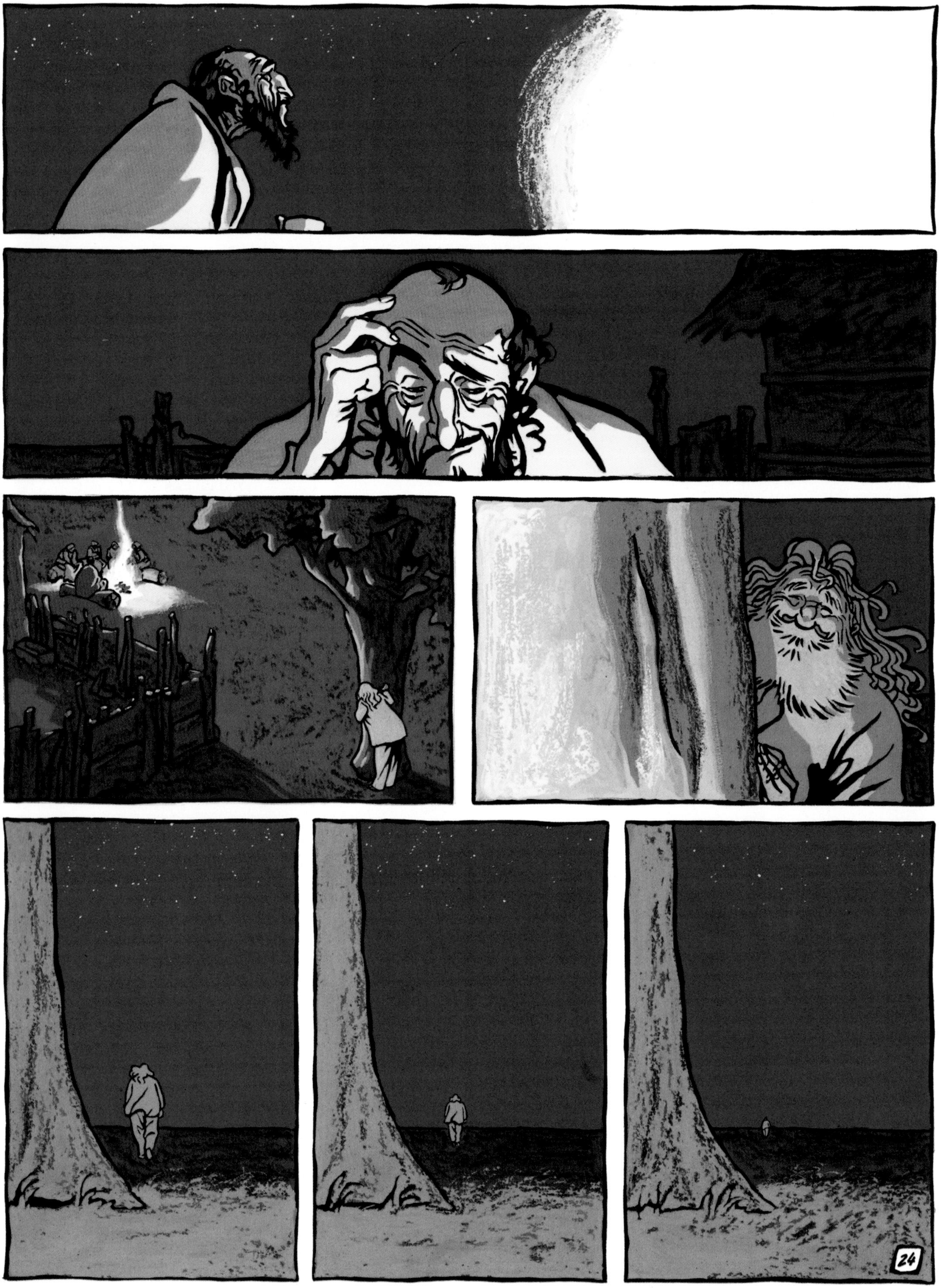
24

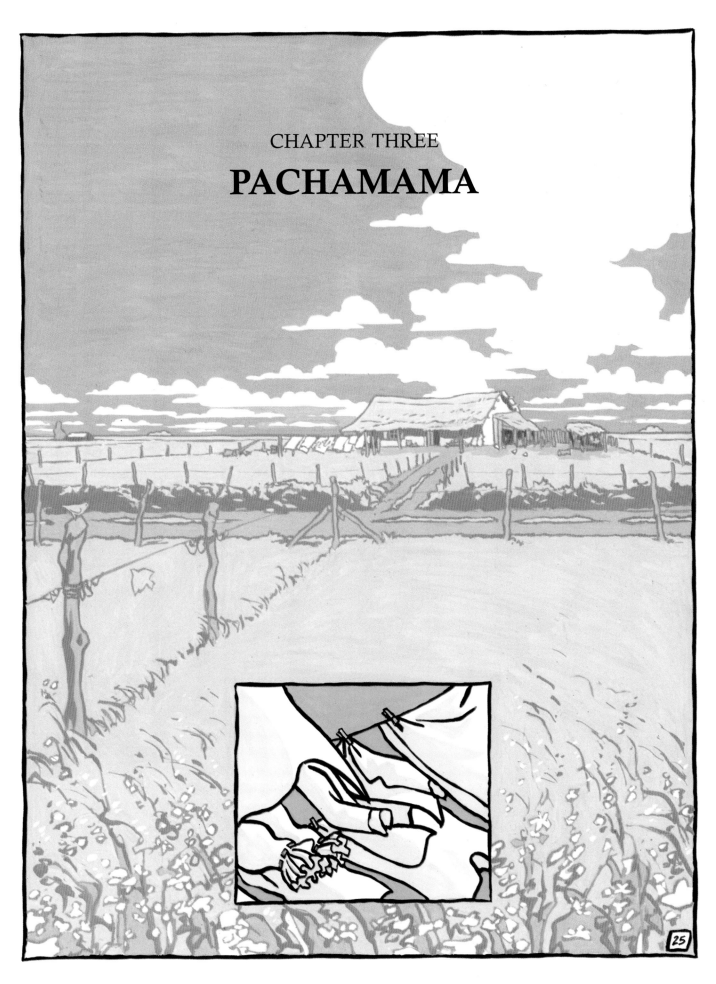

CHAPTER THREE

PACHAMAMA

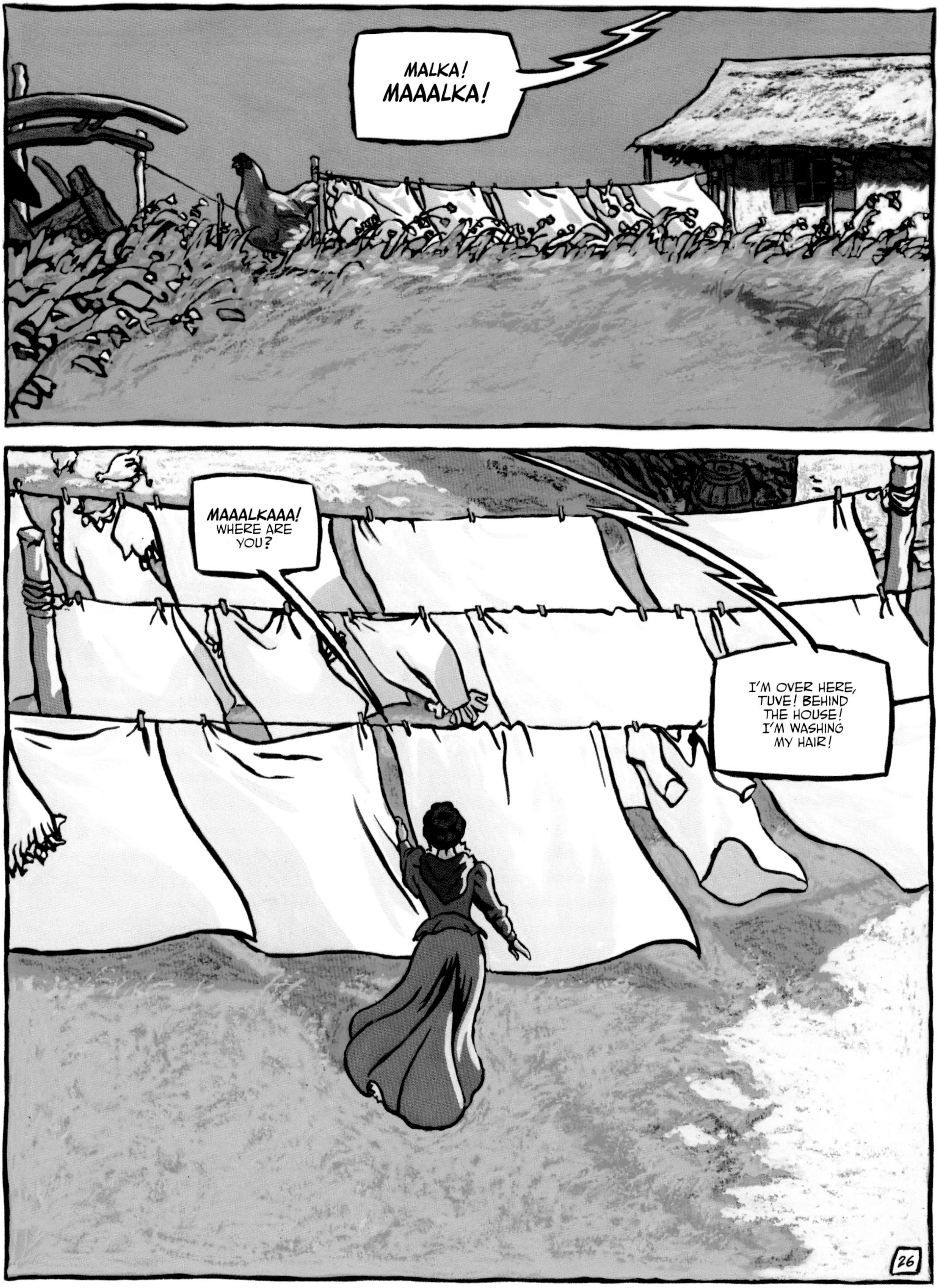
MALKA! MAAALKA!
MAAALKAAA! WHERE ARE YOU?
I'M OVER HERE, TUVE! BEHIND THE HOUSE! I'M WASHING MY HAIR!
26

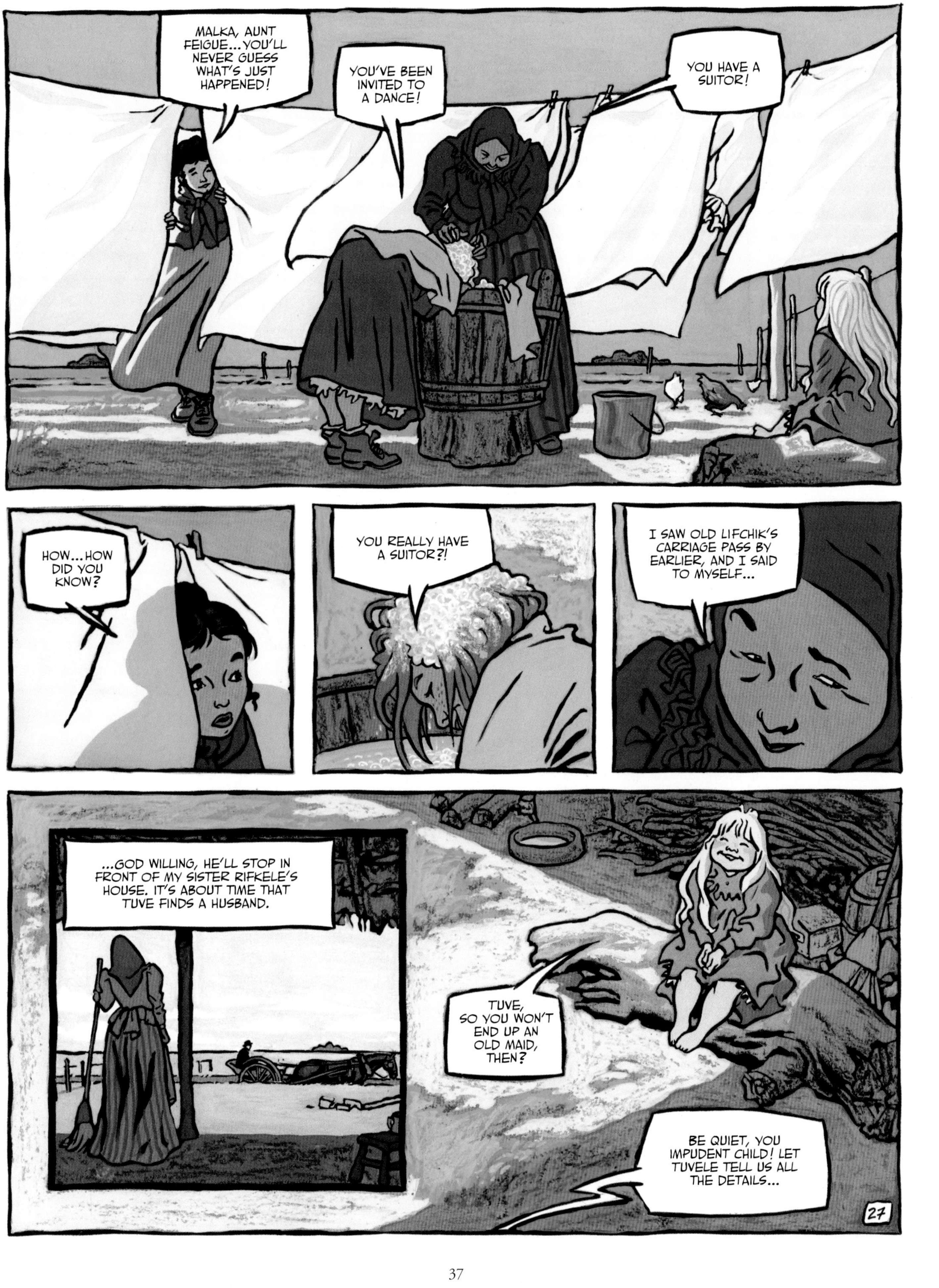
MALKA, AUNT FEIGUE...YOU'LL NEVER GUESS WHAT'S JUST HAPPENED!
YOU'VE BEEN INVITED TO A DANCE!
YOU HAVE A SUITOR!
HOW...HOW DID YOU KNOW?
YOU REALLY HAVE A SUITOR?!
I SAW OLD LIFCHIK'S CARRIAGE PASS BY EARLIER, AND I SAID TO MYSELF...
...GOD WILLING, HE'LL STOP IN FRONT OF MY SISTER RIFKELE'S HOUSE. IT'S ABOUT TIME THAT TUVE FINDS A HUSBAND.
TUVE, SO YOU WON'T END UP AN OLD MAID, THEN?
BE QUIET, YOU IMPUDENT CHILD! LET TUVELE TELL US ALL THE DETAILS...
27

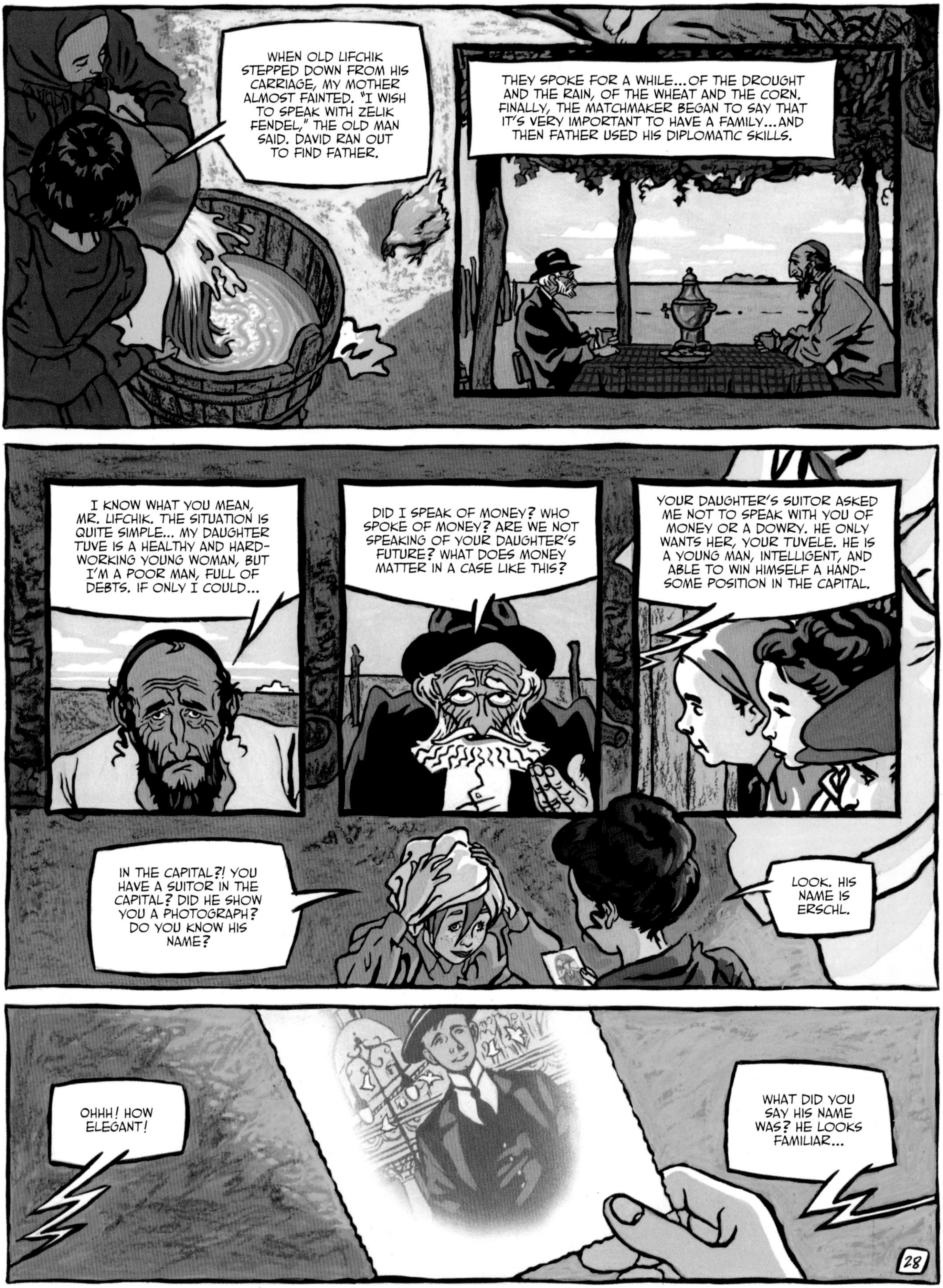
WHEN OLD LIFCHIK STEPPED DOWN FROM HIS CARRIAGE, MY MOTHER ALMOST FAINTED. "I WISH TO SPEAK WITH ZELIK FENDEL," THE OLD MAN SAID. DAVID RAN OUT TO FIND FATHER.
THEY SPOKE FOR A WHILE... OF THE DROUGHT AND THE RAIN, OF THE WHEAT AND THE CORN. FINALLY, THE MATCHMAKER BEGAN TO SAY THAT IT'S VERY IMPORTANT TO HAVE A FAMILY... AND THEN FATHER USED HIS DIPLOMATIC SKILLS.
I KNOW WHAT YOU MEAN, MR. LIFCHIK. THE SITUATION IS QUITE SIMPLE... MY DAUGHTER TUVE IS A HEALTHY AND HARD-WORKING YOUNG WOMAN, BUT I'M A POOR MAN, FULL OF DEBTS. IF ONLY I COULD...
DID I SPEAK OF MONEY? WHO SPOKE OF MONEY? ARE WE NOT SPEAKING OF YOUR DAUGHTER'S FUTURE? WHAT DOES MONEY MATTER IN A CASE LIKE THIS?
YOUR DAUGHTER'S SUITOR ASKED ME NOT TO SPEAK WITH YOU OF MONEY OR A DOWRY. HE ONLY WANTS HER, YOUR TUVELE. HE IS A YOUNG MAN, INTELLIGENT, AND ABLE TO WIN HIMSELF A HANDSOME POSITION IN THE CAPITAL.
IN THE CAPITAL?! YOU HAVE A SUITOR IN THE CAPITAL? DID HE SHOW YOU A PHOTOGRAPH? DO YOU KNOW HIS NAME?
LOOK. HIS NAME IS ERSCHL.
OHHH! HOW ELEGANT!
WHAT DID YOU SAY HIS NAME WAS? HE LOOKS FAMILIAR...
28

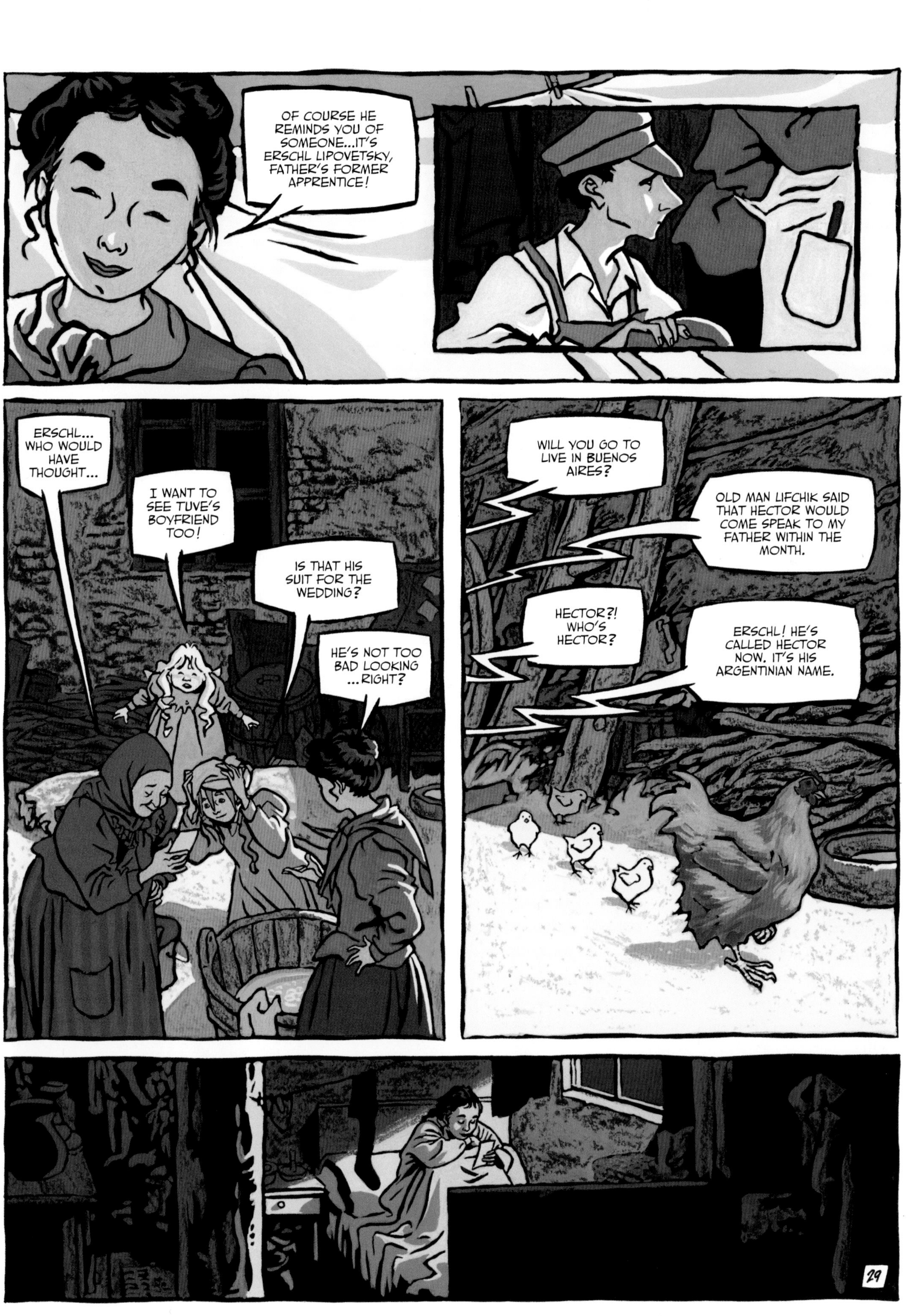
OF COURSE HE REMINDS YOU OF SOMEONE...IT'S ERSCHL LIPOVETSKY, FATHER'S FORMER APPRENTICE!
ERSCHL... WHO WOULD HAVE THOUGHT...
I WANT TO SEE TUVE'S BOYFRIEND TOO!
IS THAT HIS SUIT FOR THE WEDDING?
HE'S NOT TOO BAD LOOKING ...RIGHT?
WILL YOU GO TO LIVE IN BUENOS AIRES?
OLD MAN LIFCHIK SAID THAT HECTOR WOULD COME SPEAK TO MY FATHER WITHIN THE MONTH.
HECTOR?! WHO'S HECTOR?
ERSCHL! HE'S CALLED HECTOR NOW. IT'S HIS ARGENTINIAN NAME.
29

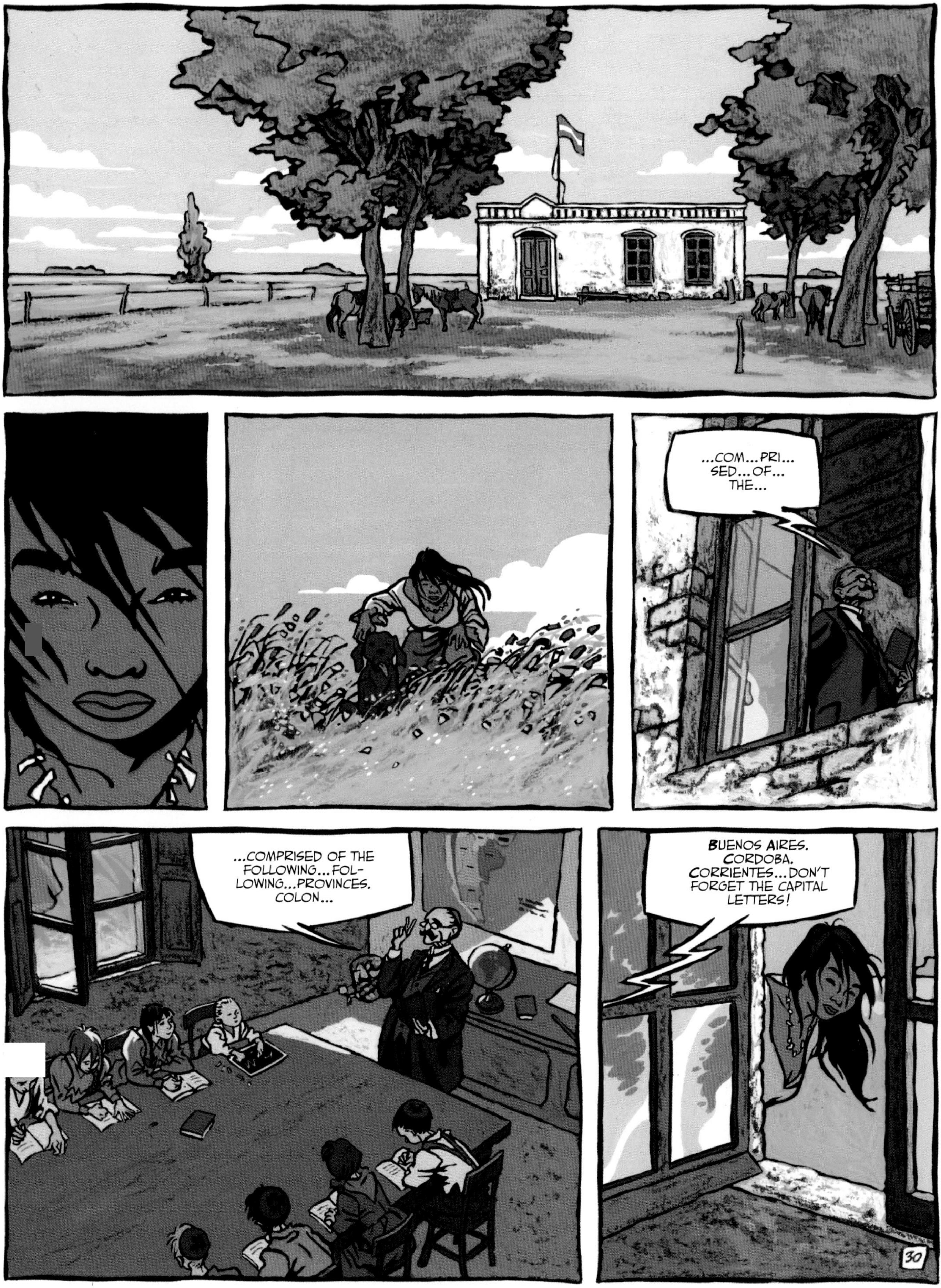
...COM...PRI...
SED...OF...
THE...
...COMPRISED OF THE FOLLOWING...FOL-LOWING...PROVINCES. COLON...
BUENOS AIRES. CORDOBA. CORRIENTES...DON'T FORGET THE CAPITAL LETTERS!
30

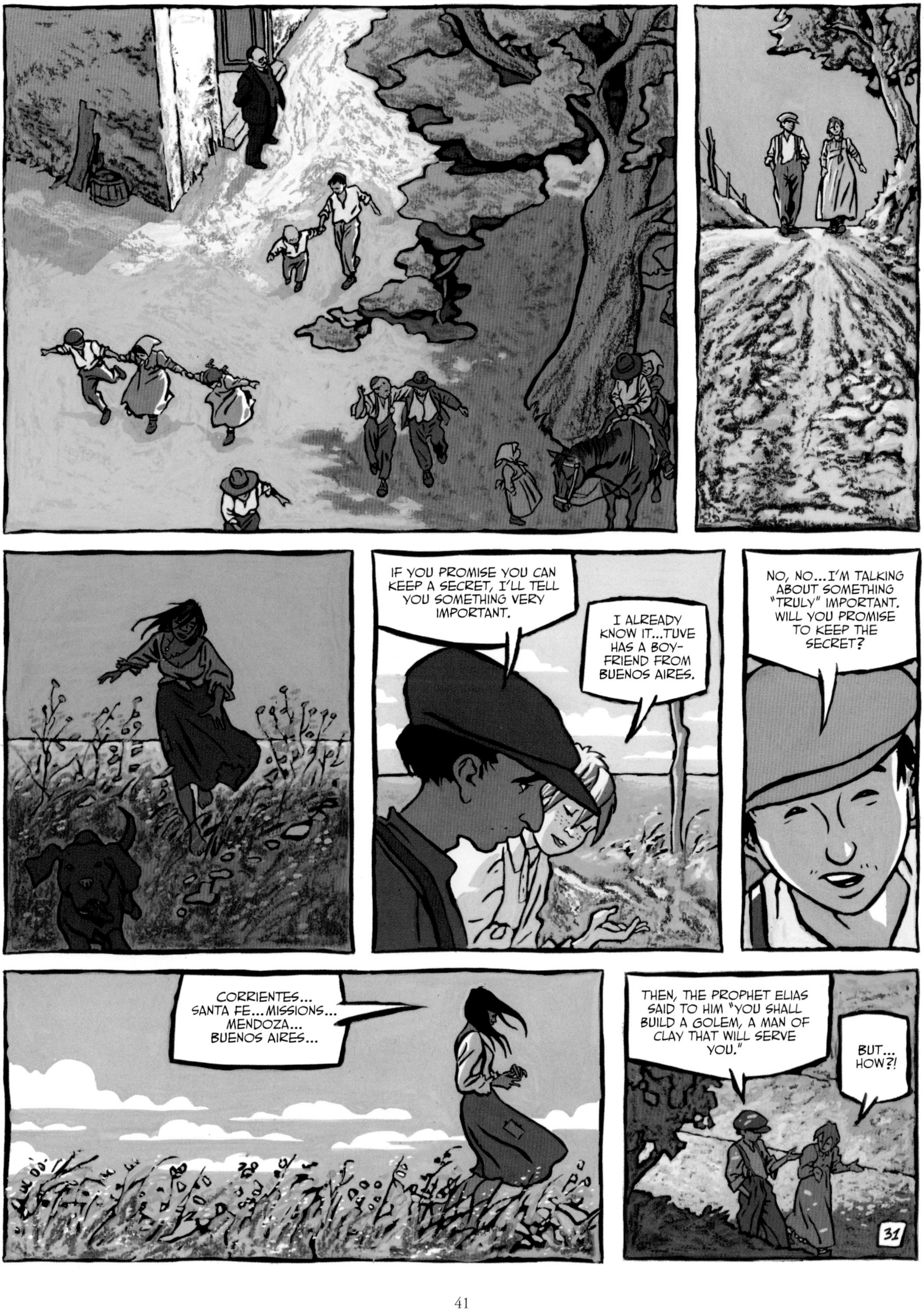
IF YOU PROMISE YOU CAN KEEP A SECRET, I'LL TELL YOU SOMETHING VERY IMPORTANT.
I ALREADY KNOW IT...TUVE HAS A BOY-FRIEND FROM BUENOS AIRES.
NO, NO...I'M TALKING ABOUT SOMETHING "TRULY" IMPORTANT. WILL YOU PROMISE TO KEEP THE SECRET?
CORRIENTES... SANTA FE...MISSIONS... MENDOZA... BUENOS AIRES...
THEN, THE PROPHET ELIAS SAID TO HIM "YOU SHALL BUILD A GOLEM, A MAN OF CLAY THAT WILL SERVE YOU."
BUT... HOW?!
31

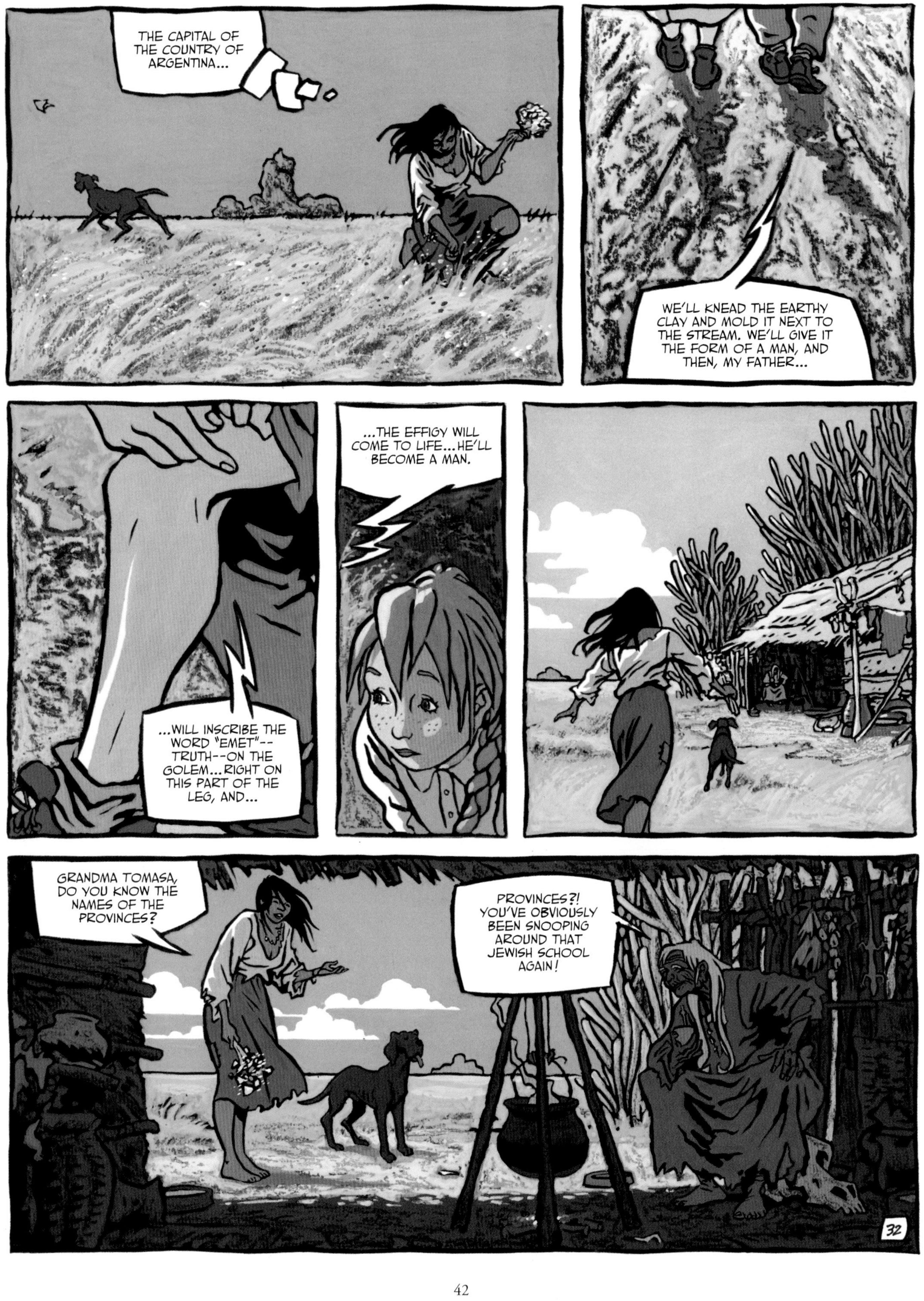

THE CAPITAL OF THE COUNTRY OF ARGENTINA...
WE'LL KNEAD THE EARTHY CLAY AND MOLD IT NEXT TO THE STREAM. WE'LL GIVE IT THE FORM OF A MAN, AND THEN, MY FATHER...
...WILL INSCRIBE THE WORD "EMET"--TRUTH--ON THE GOLEM...RIGHT ON THIS PART OF THE LEG, AND...
...THE EFFIGY WILL COME TO LIFE...HE'LL BECOME A MAN.
GRANDMA TOMASA, DO YOU KNOW THE NAMES OF THE PROVINCES?
PROVINCES?! YOU'VE OBVIOUSLY BEEN SNOOPING AROUND THAT JEWISH SCHOOL AGAIN!
32

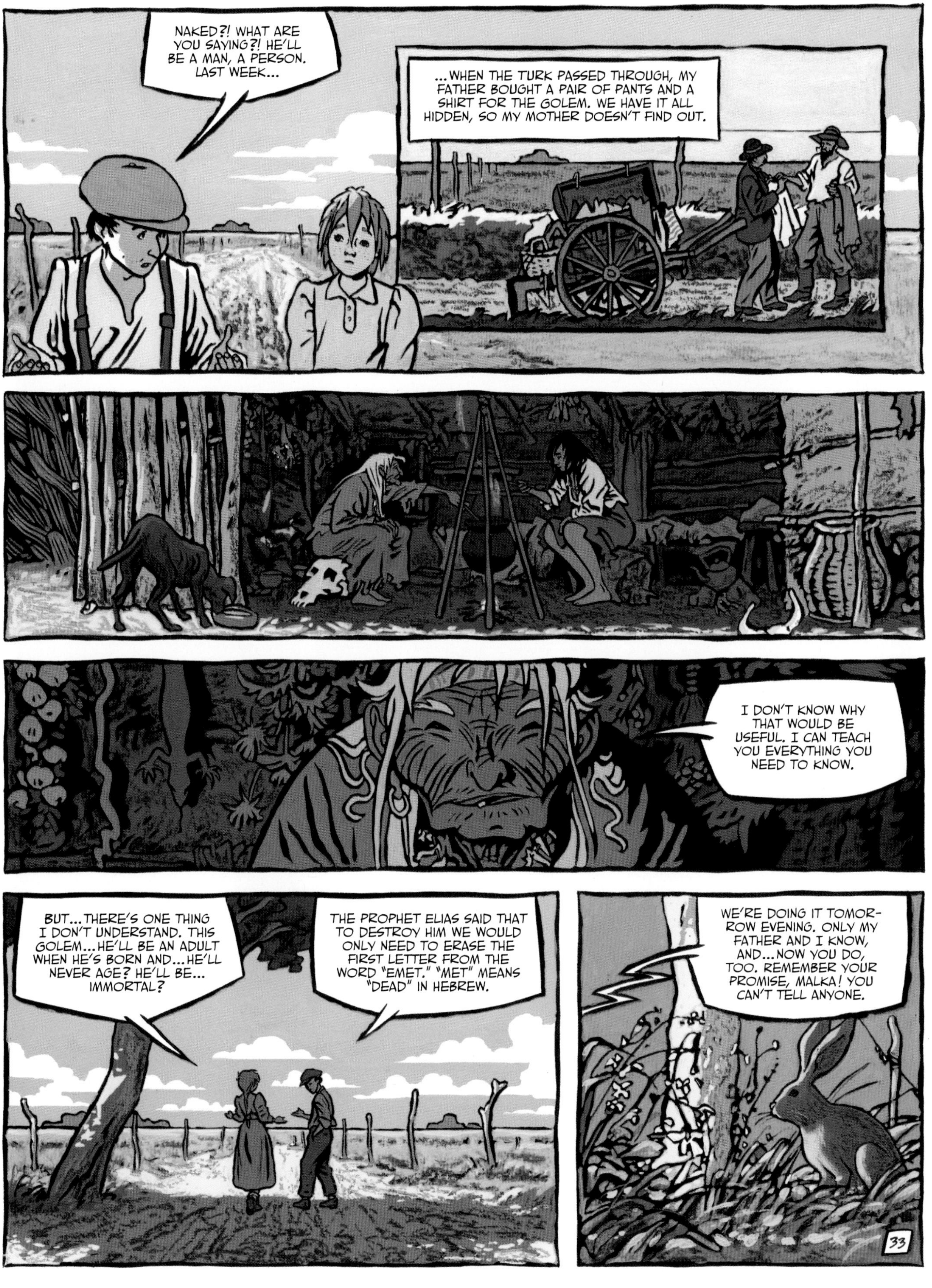
NAKED?! WHAT ARE YOU SAYING?! HE'LL BE A MAN, A PERSON. LAST WEEK...
...WHEN THE TURK PASSED THROUGH, MY FATHER BOUGHT A PAIR OF PANTS AND A SHIRT FOR THE GOLEM. WE HAVE IT ALL HIDDEN, SO MY MOTHER DOESN'T FIND OUT.
I DON'T KNOW WHY THAT WOULD BE USEFUL. I CAN TEACH YOU EVERYTHING YOU NEED TO KNOW.
BUT...THERE'S ONE THING I DON'T UNDERSTAND. THIS GOLEM...HE'LL BE AN ADULT WHEN HE'S BORN AND...HE'LL NEVER AGE? HE'LL BE... IMMORTAL?
THE PROPHET ELIAS SAID THAT TO DESTROY HIM WE WOULD ONLY NEED TO ERASE THE FIRST LETTER FROM THE WORD "EMET." "MET" MEANS "DEAD" IN HEBREW.
WE'RE DOING IT TOMORROW EVENING. ONLY MY FATHER AND I KNOW, AND...NOW YOU DO, TOO. REMEMBER YOUR PROMISE, MALKA! YOU CAN'T TELL ANYONE.
33

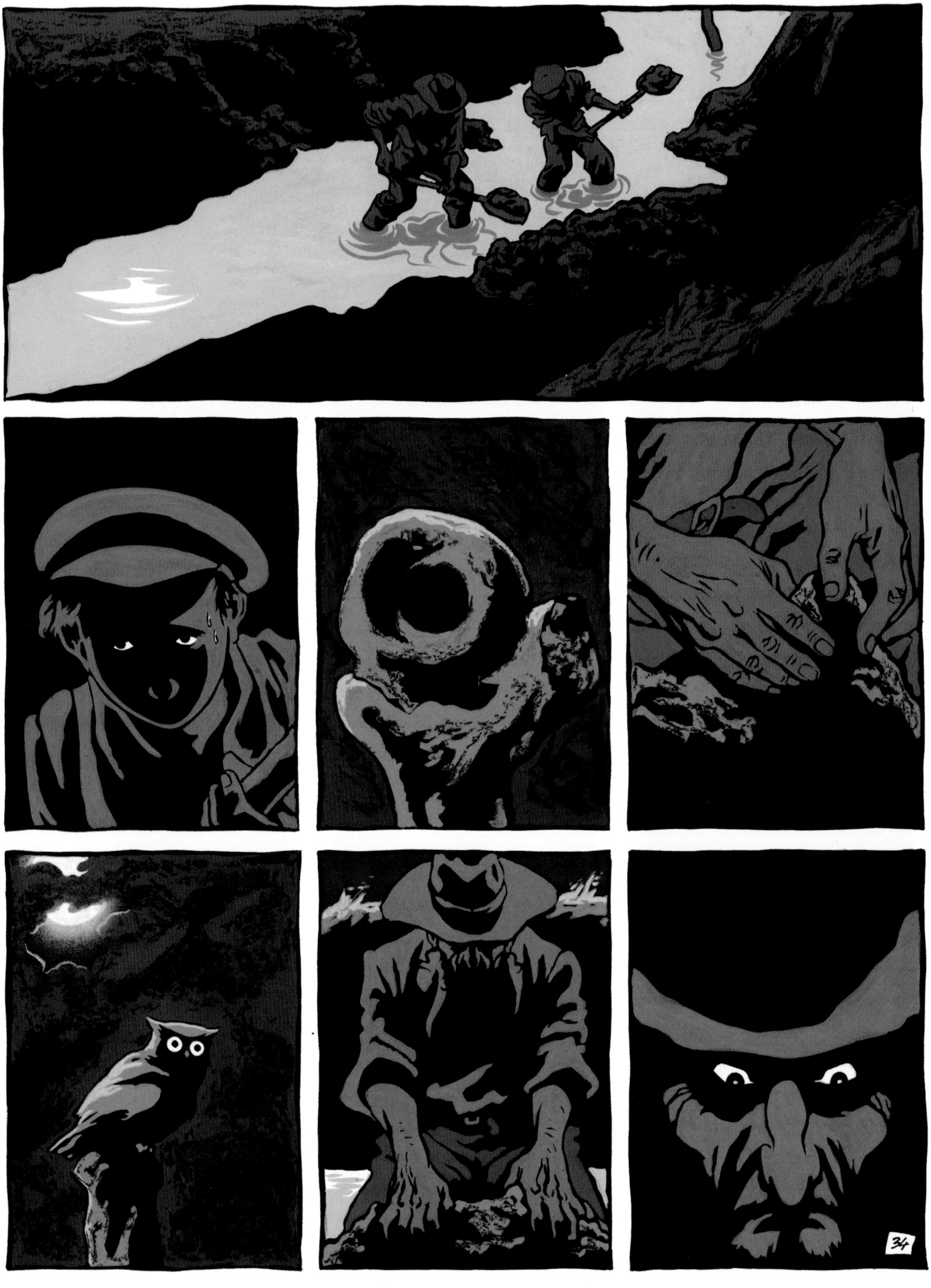
34

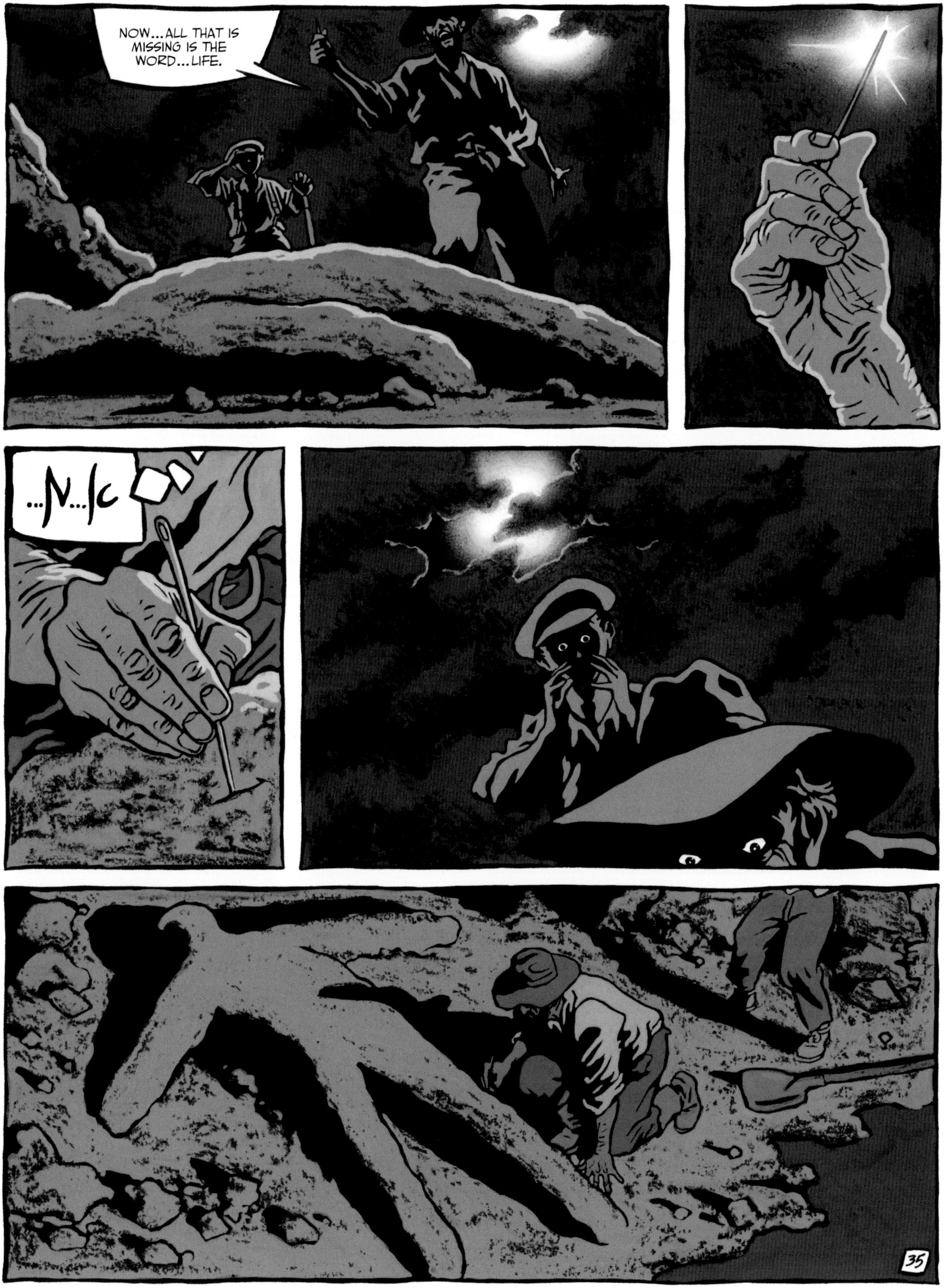
NOW...ALL THAT IS MISSING IS THE WORD...LIFE.
...N...Ic
35

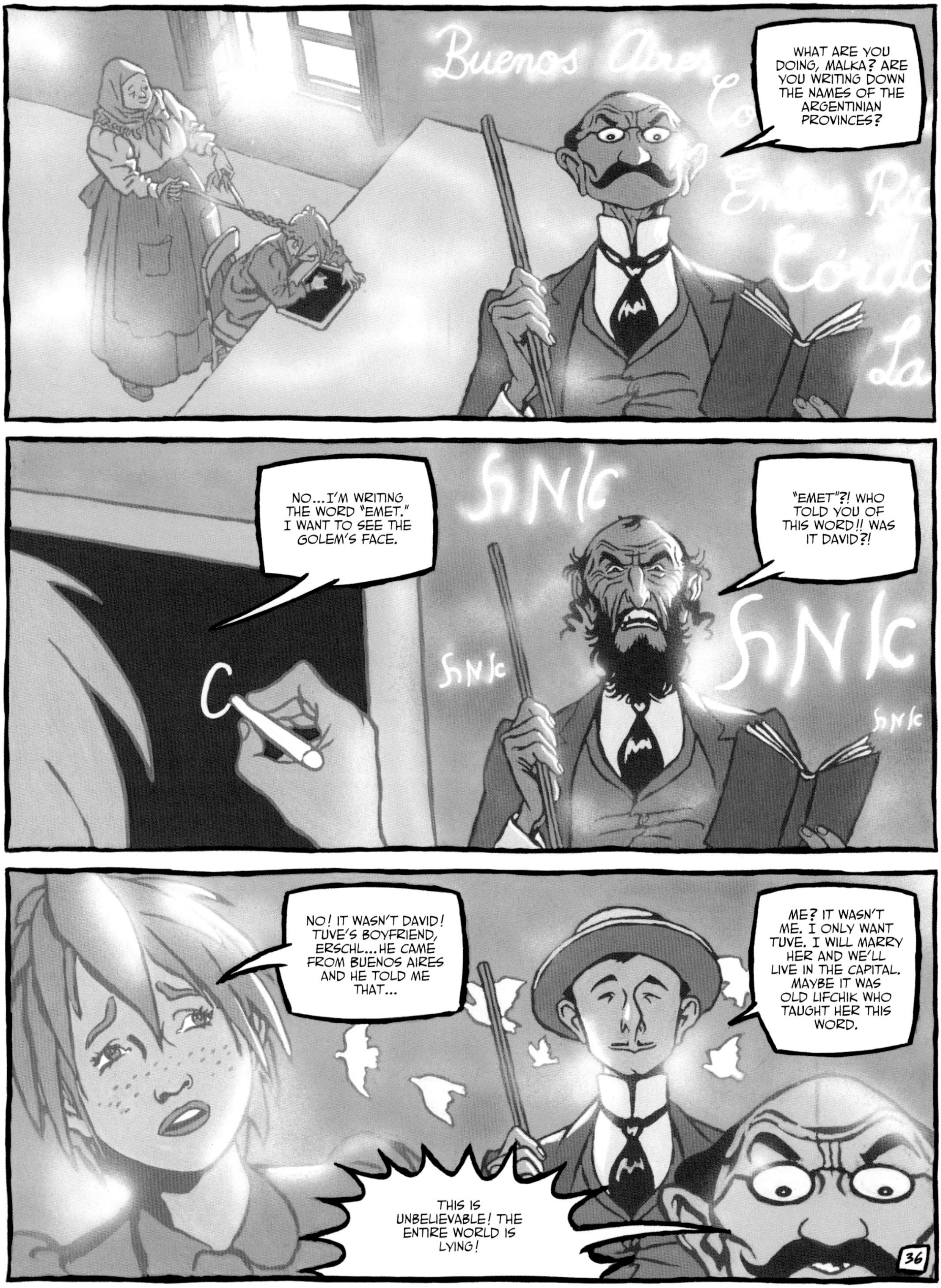

Buenos Aires
WHAT ARE YOU DOING, MALKA? ARE YOU WRITING DOWN THE NAMES OF THE ARGENTINIAN PROVINCES?
NO...I'M WRITING THE WORD "EMET." I WANT TO SEE THE GOLEM'S FACE.
"EMET"?! WHO TOLD YOU OF THIS WORD!! WAS IT DAVID?!
NO! IT WASN'T DAVID! TUVE'S BOYFRIEND, ERSCHL...HE CAME FROM BUENOS AIRES AND HE TOLD ME THAT...
ME? IT WASN'T ME. I ONLY WANT TUVE. I WILL MARRY HER AND WE'LL LIVE IN THE CAPITAL. MAYBE IT WAS OLD LIFCHIK WHO TAUGHT HER THIS WORD.
THIS IS UNBELIEVABLE! THE ENTIRE WORLD IS LYING!
36

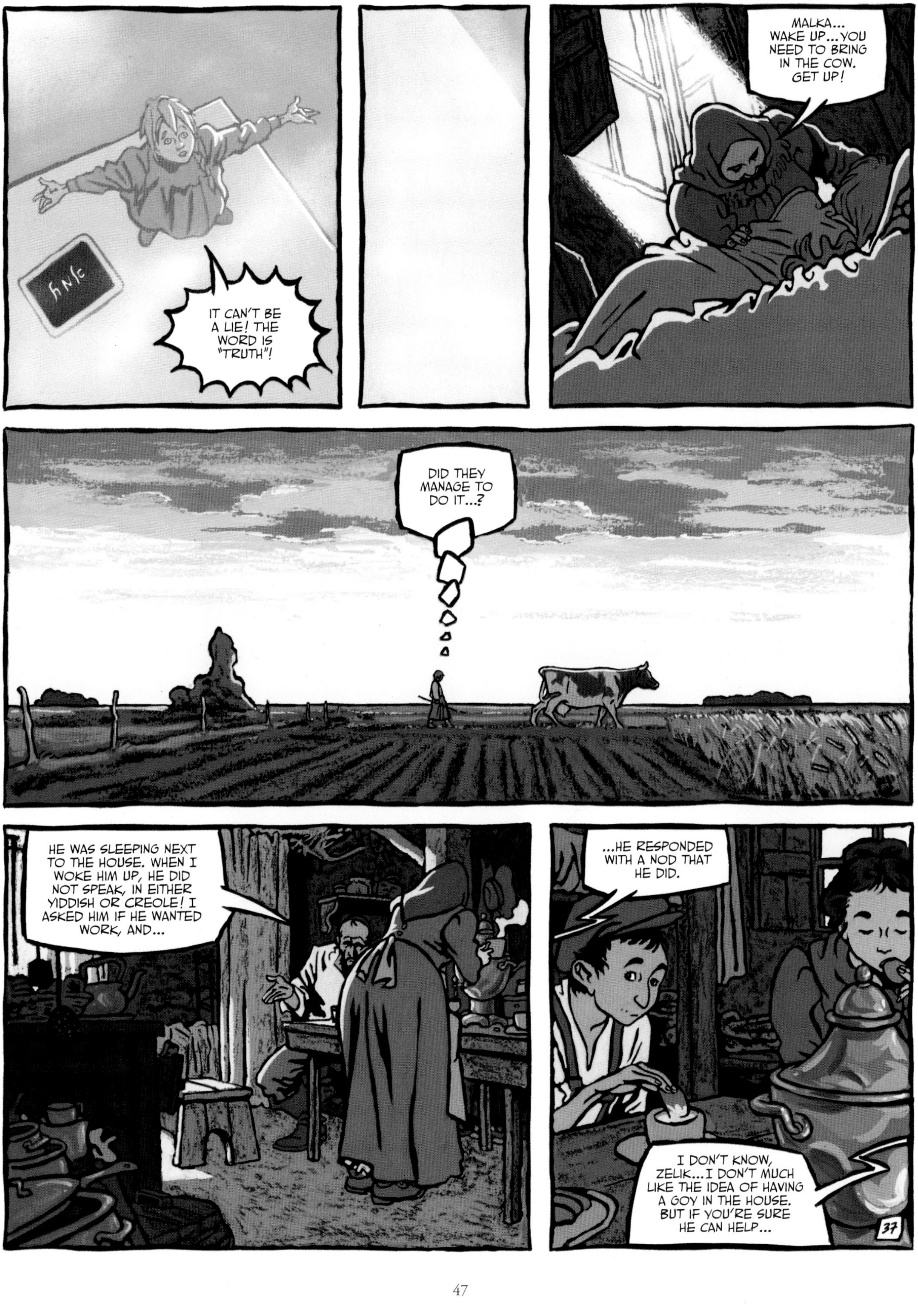
IT CAN'T BE A LIE! THE WORD IS "TRUTH"!
MALKA... WAKE UP...YOU NEED TO BRING IN THE COW. GET UP!
DID THEY MANAGE TO DO IT...?
HE WAS SLEEPING NEXT TO THE HOUSE. WHEN I WOKE HIM UP, HE DID NOT SPEAK, IN EITHER YIDDISH OR CREOLE! I ASKED HIM IF HE WANTED WORK, AND...
...HE RESPONDED WITH A NOD THAT HE DID.
I DON'T KNOW, ZELIK...I DON'T MUCH LIKE THE IDEA OF HAVING A GOY IN THE HOUSE. BUT IF YOU'RE SURE HE CAN HELP...
37

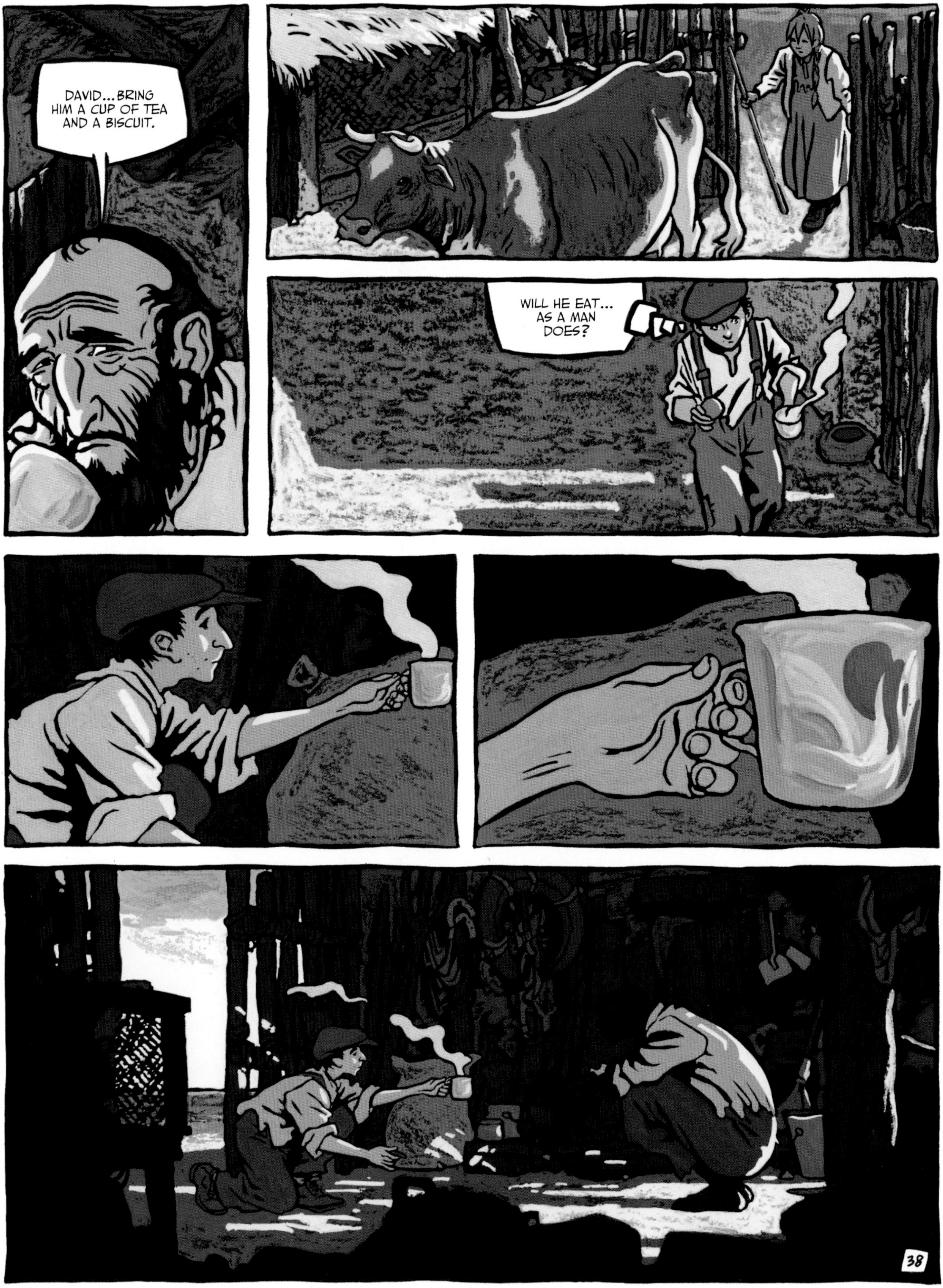
DAVID... BRING HIM A CUP OF TEA AND A BISCUIT.
WILL HE EAT... AS A MAN DOES?
38

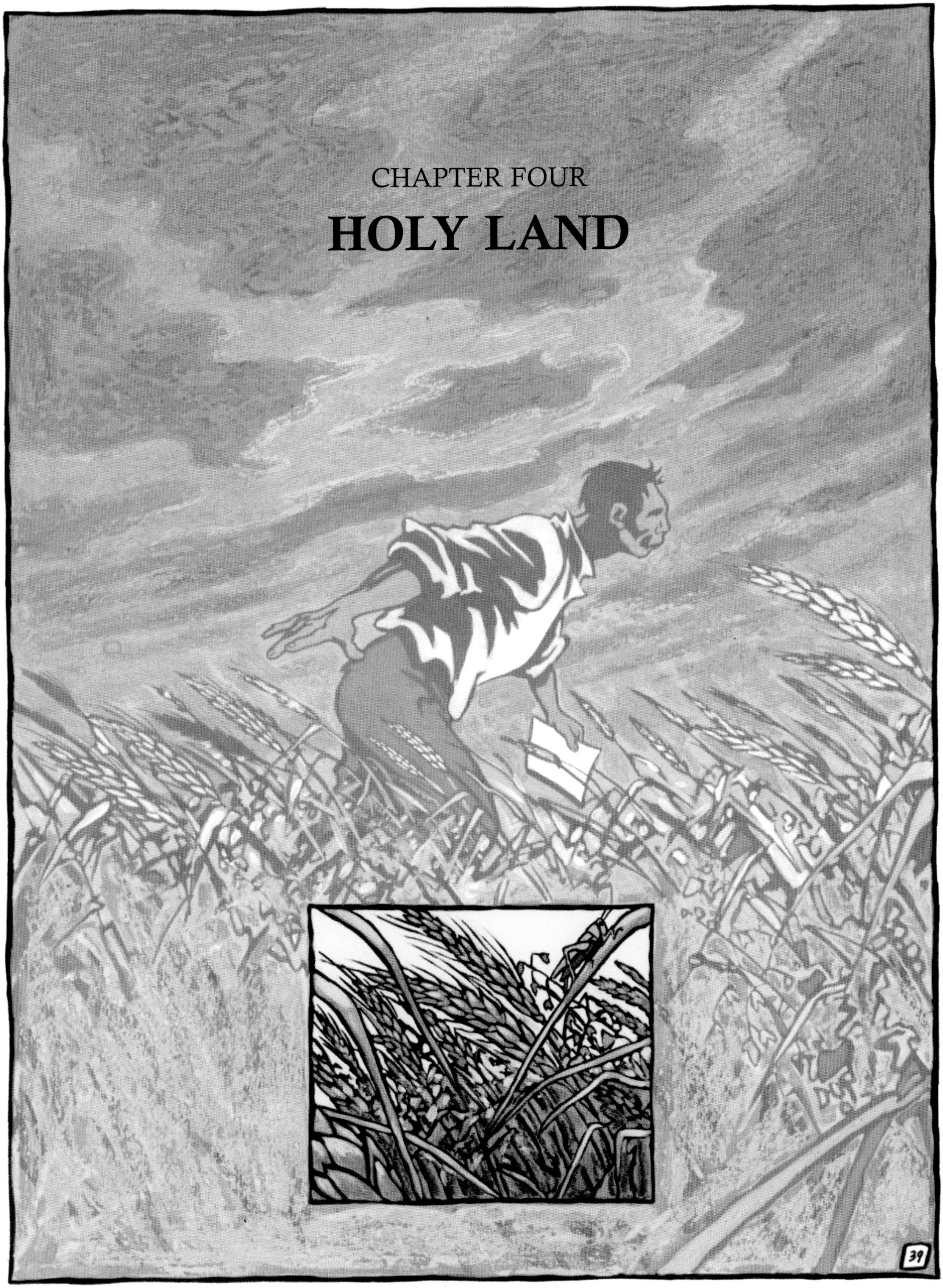
CHAPTER FOUR
HOLY LAND
39

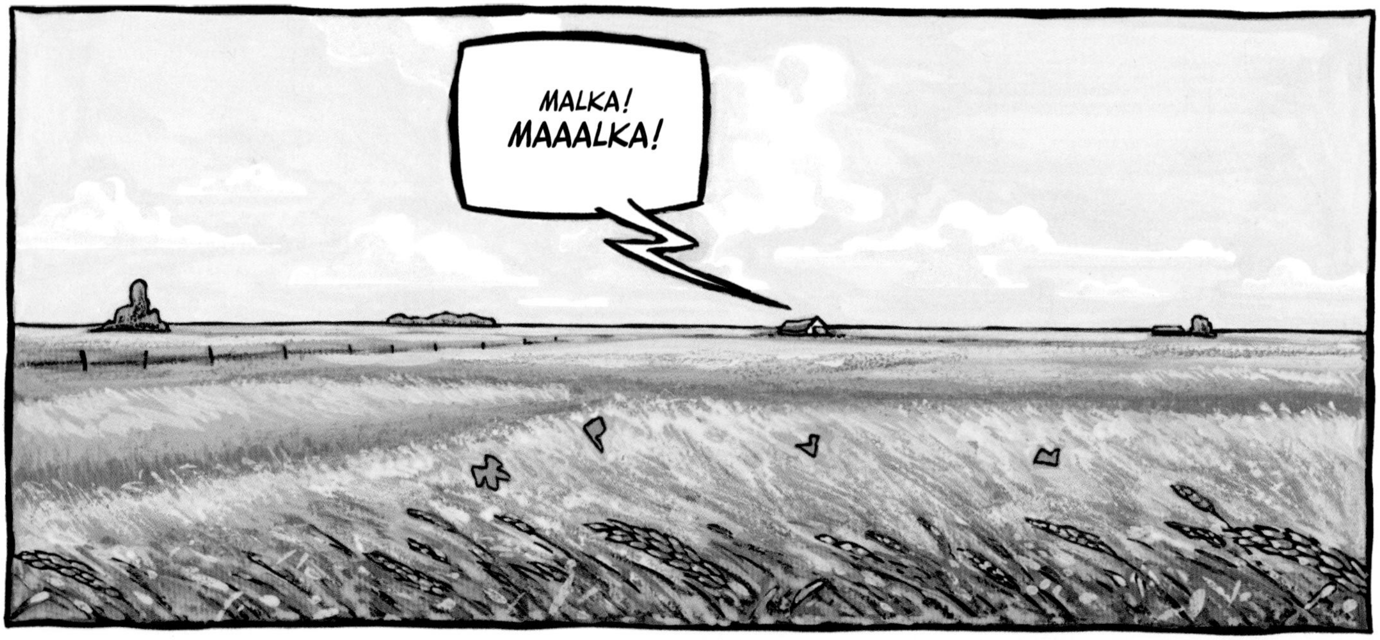
MALKA! MAAALKA!

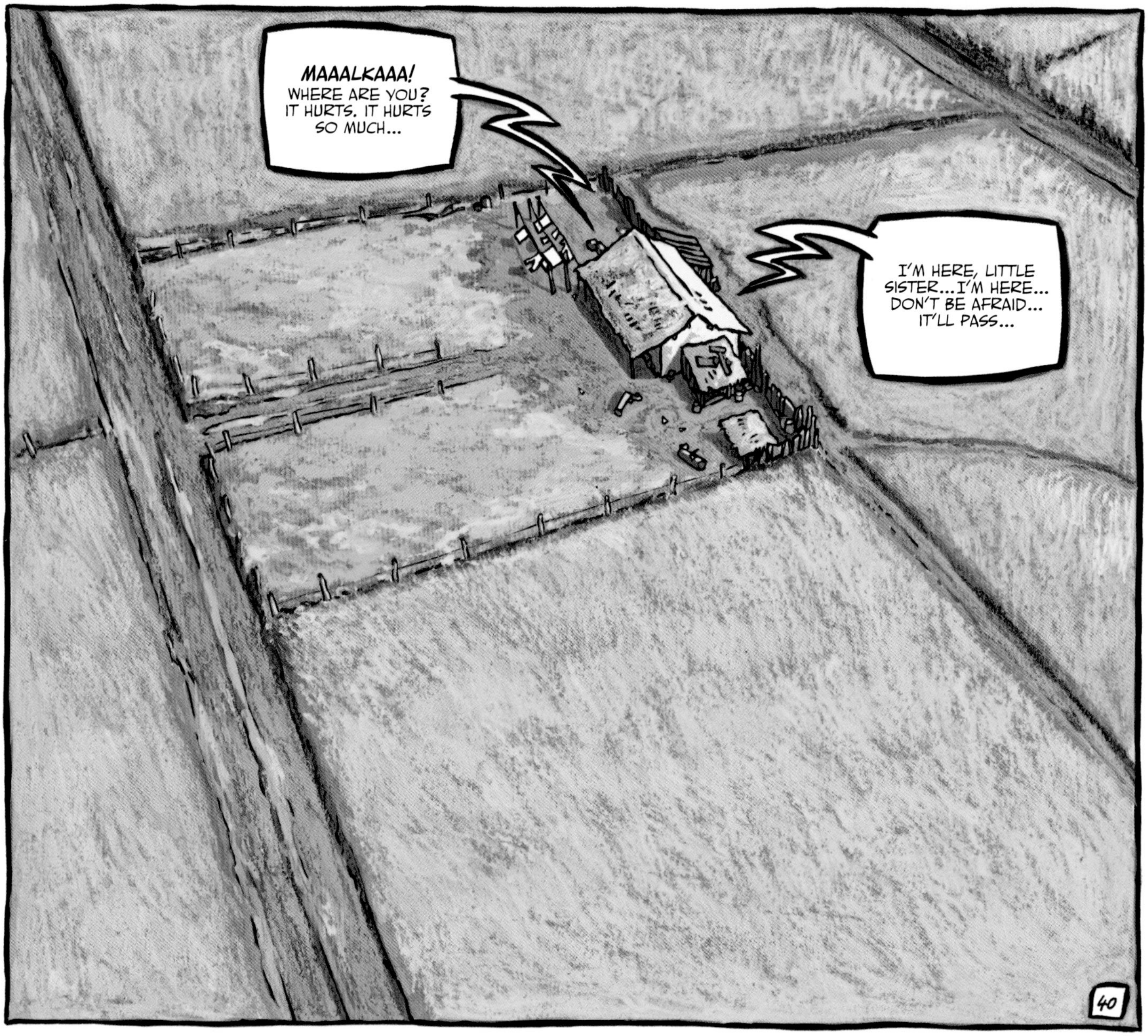
MAAALKAAA! WHERE ARE YOU? IT HURTS. IT HURTS SO MUCH...
I'M HERE, LITTLE SISTER...I'M HERE... DON'T BE AFRAID... IT'LL PASS...
40

IT HURTS...

RELAX...DOCTOR YARCHO WILL COME TO CURE YOU...RELAX...

ZELIK...

SHLOIME...! FEIGUE...! WHAT'S WRONG?!

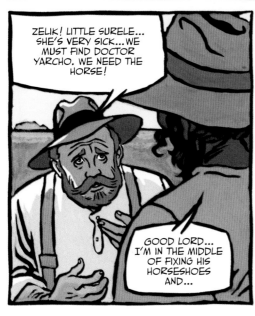

ZELIK! LITTLE SURELE... SHE'S VERY SICK...WE MUST FIND DOCTOR YARCHO. WE NEED THE HORSE!

GOOD LORD... I'M IN THE MIDDLE OF FIXING HIS HORSESHOES AND...

WHAT'S GOING ON?!

SHLOIME NEEDS TO GO GET DOCTOR YARCHO, BUT THE HORSE IS IN NO CONDITION TO RUN INTO TOWN...BUT MAYBE...

41

MALKA, I'M COLD...

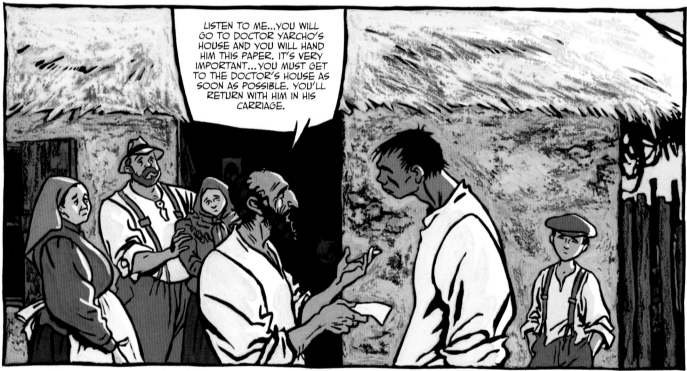

LISTEN TO ME...YOU WILL GO TO DOCTOR YARCHO'S HOUSE AND YOU WILL HAND HIM THIS PAPER. IT'S VERY IMPORTANT...YOU MUST GET TO THE DOCTOR'S HOUSE AS SOON AS POSSIBLE. YOU'LL RETURN WITH HIM IN HIS CARRIAGE.

NOW...RUN! AND MAY GOD PROTECT YOU!

42

53

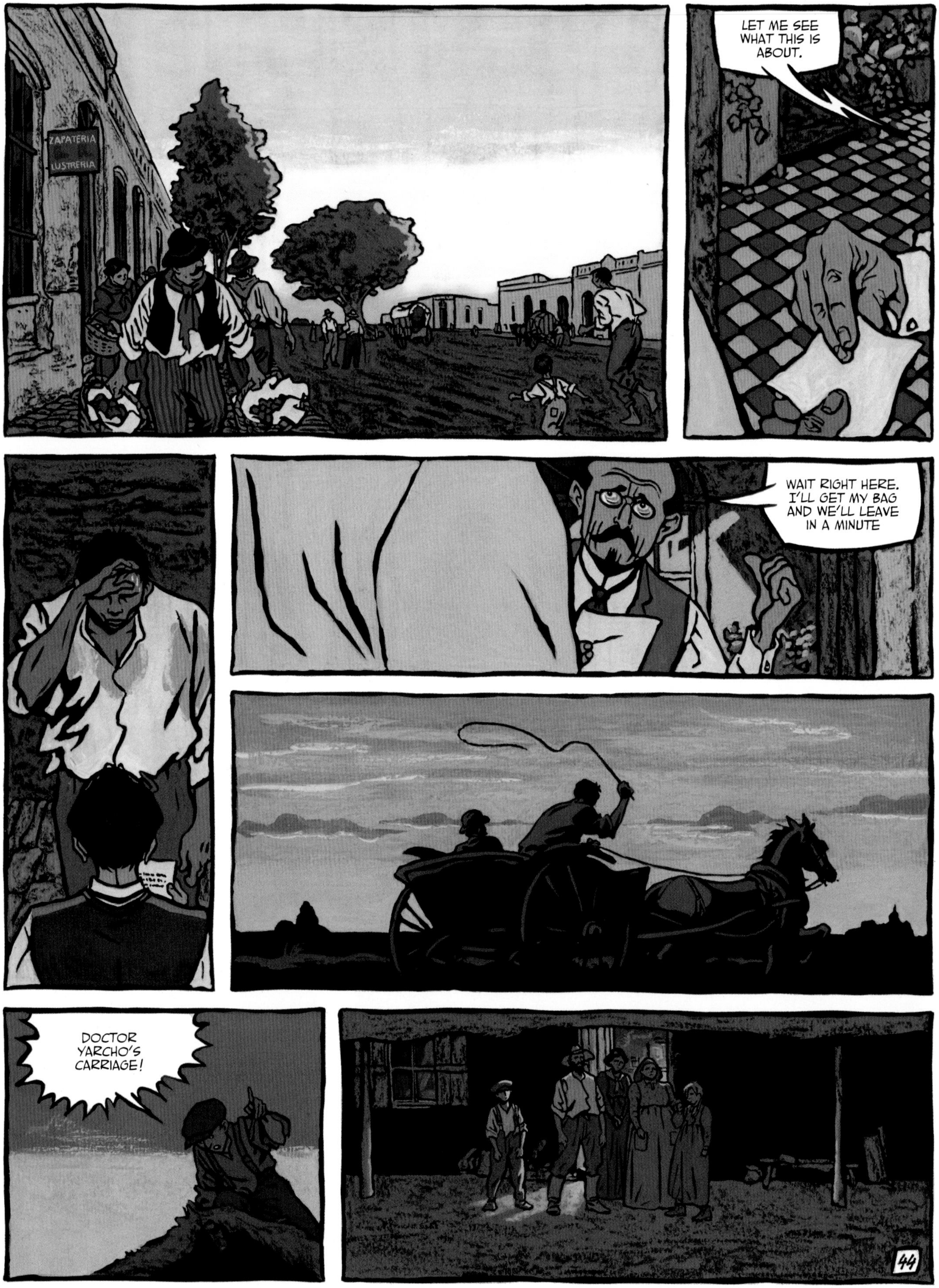
ZAPATERIA
LUSTRERIA
LET ME SEE WHAT THIS IS ABOUT.
WAIT RIGHT HERE. I'LL GET MY BAG AND WE'LL LEAVE IN A MINUTE
DOCTOR YARCHO'S CARRIAGE!
44

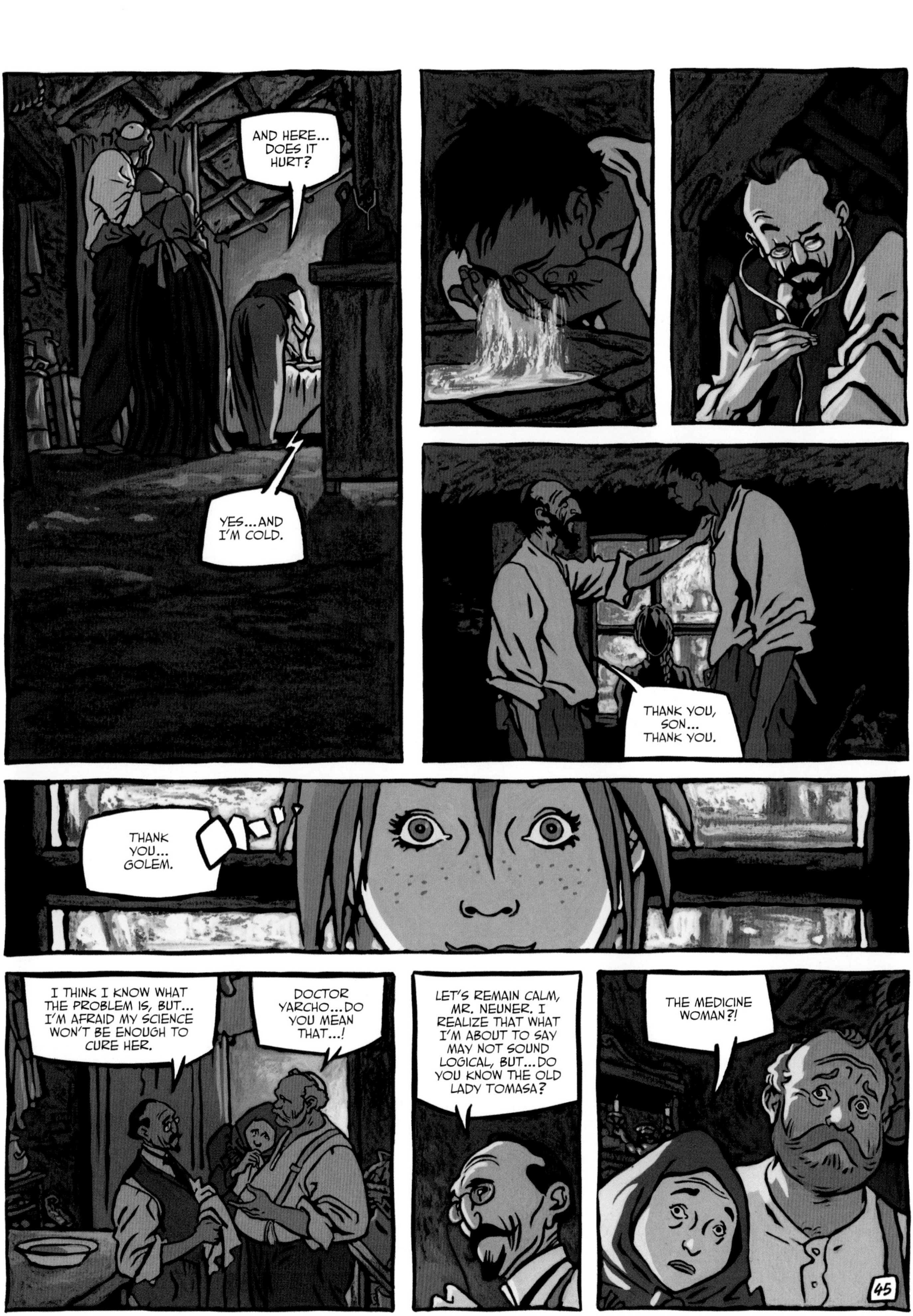
AND HERE... DOES IT HURT?
YES...AND I'M COLD.
THANK YOU, SON... THANK YOU.
THANK YOU... GOLEM.
I THINK I KNOW WHAT THE PROBLEM IS, BUT... I'M AFRAID MY SCIENCE WON'T BE ENOUGH TO CURE HER.
DOCTOR YARCHO...DO YOU MEAN THAT...!
LET'S REMAIN CALM, MR. NEUNER. I REALIZE THAT WHAT I'M ABOUT TO SAY MAY NOT SOUND LOGICAL, BUT...DO YOU KNOW THE OLD LADY TOMASA?
THE MEDICINE WOMAN?!
45

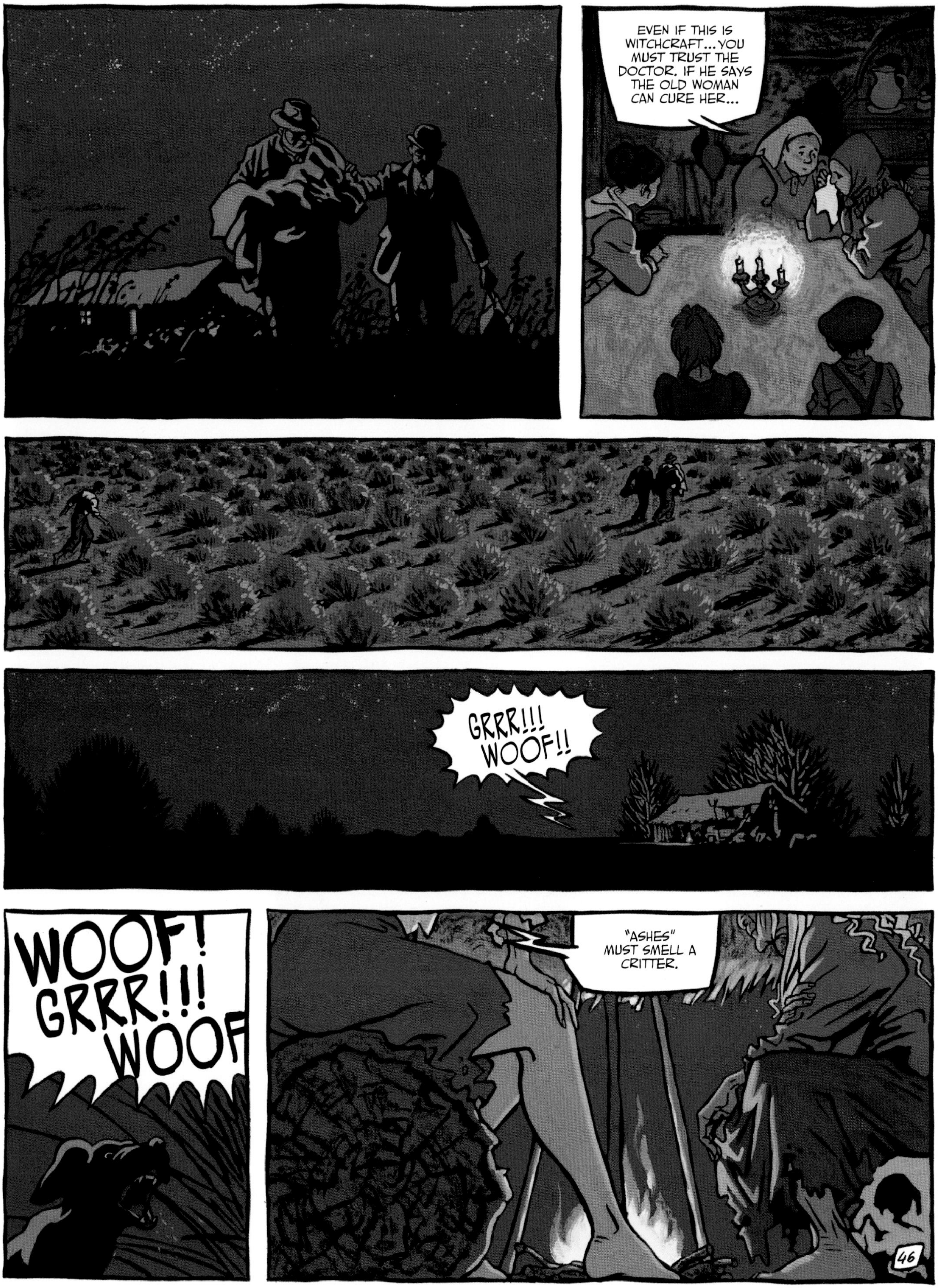
EVEN IF THIS IS WITCHCRAFT...YOU MUST TRUST THE DOCTOR. IF HE SAYS THE OLD WOMAN CAN CURE HER...
GRRR!!! WOOF!!
WOOF! GRRR!!! WOOF
"ASHES" MUST SMELL A CRITTER.
46

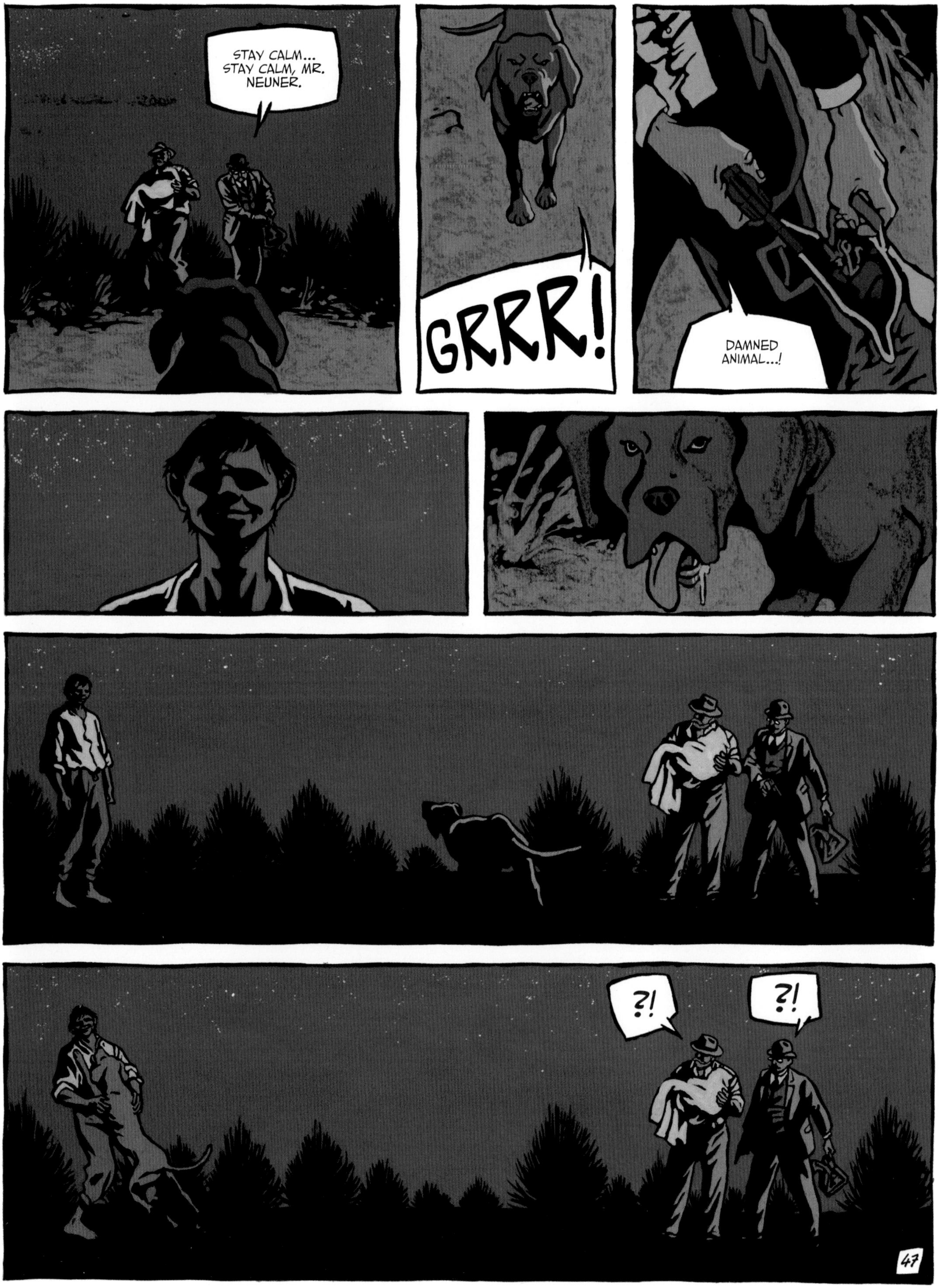
STAY CALM... STAY CALM, MR. NEUNER.
GRRR!
DAMNED ANIMAL...!
?!
?!
47

GOOD EVENING, TOMASA. I BRING YOU A GIRL WHO'S VERY SICK...

THIS POOR CREATURE HAS A SEVERE BLOCKAGE. WE MUST CLEAR THE "EMPACHO."*

*ARGENTINIAN NATURAL HEALERS PRACTICE A FORM OF ACUPRESSURE TO CLEAR DYSPEPSIA.

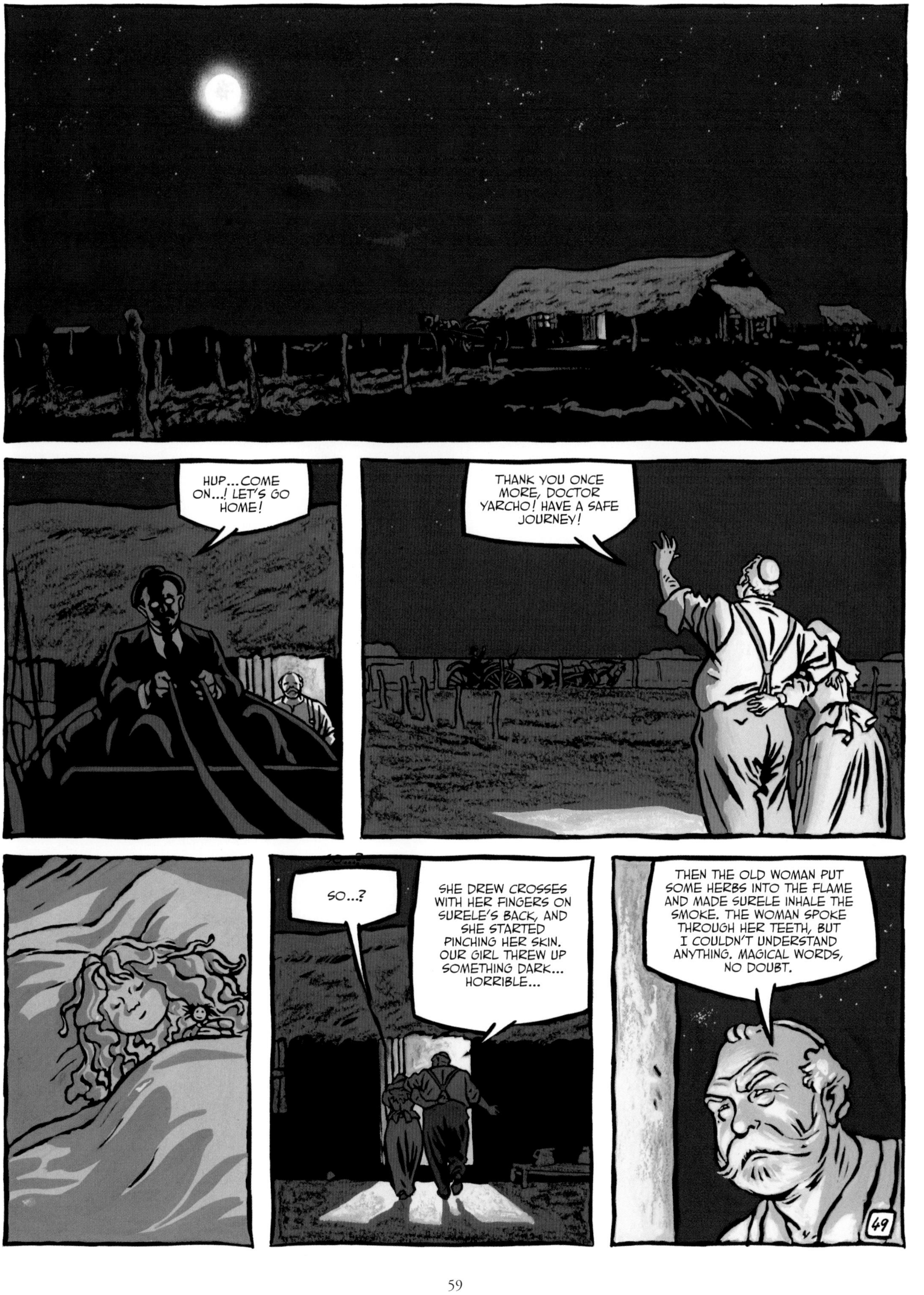
HUP...COME ON...! LET'S GO HOME!
THANK YOU ONCE MORE, DOCTOR YARCHO! HAVE A SAFE JOURNEY!
SO...?
SHE DREW CROSSES WITH HER FINGERS ON SURELE'S BACK, AND SHE STARTED PINCHING HER SKIN. OUR GIRL THREW UP SOMETHING DARK... HORRIBLE...
THEN THE OLD WOMAN PUT SOME HERBS INTO THE FLAME AND MADE SURELE INHALE THE SMOKE. THE WOMAN SPOKE THROUGH HER TEETH, BUT I COULDN'T UNDERSTAND ANYTHING. MAGICAL WORDS, NO DOUBT.
49

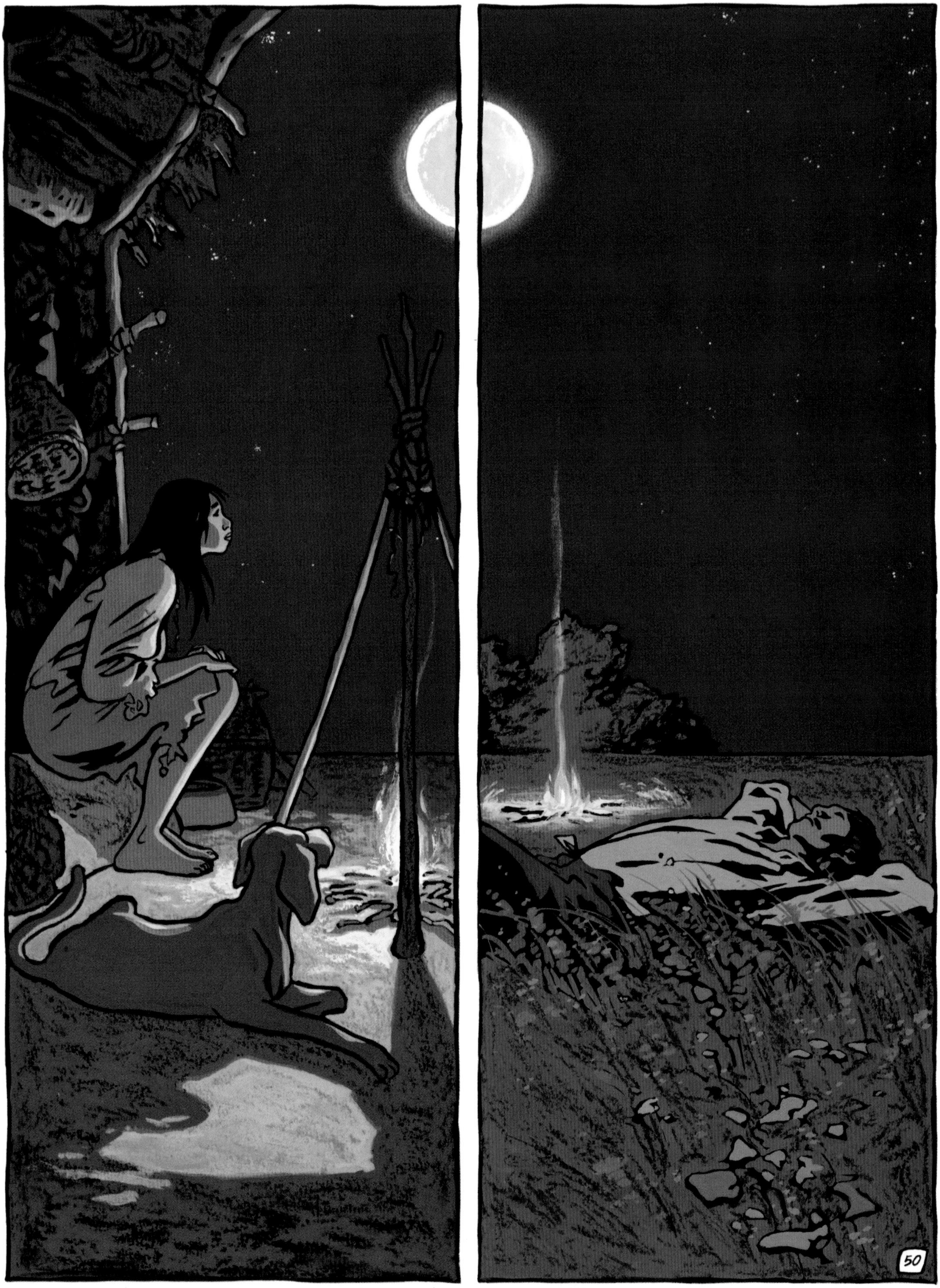
50

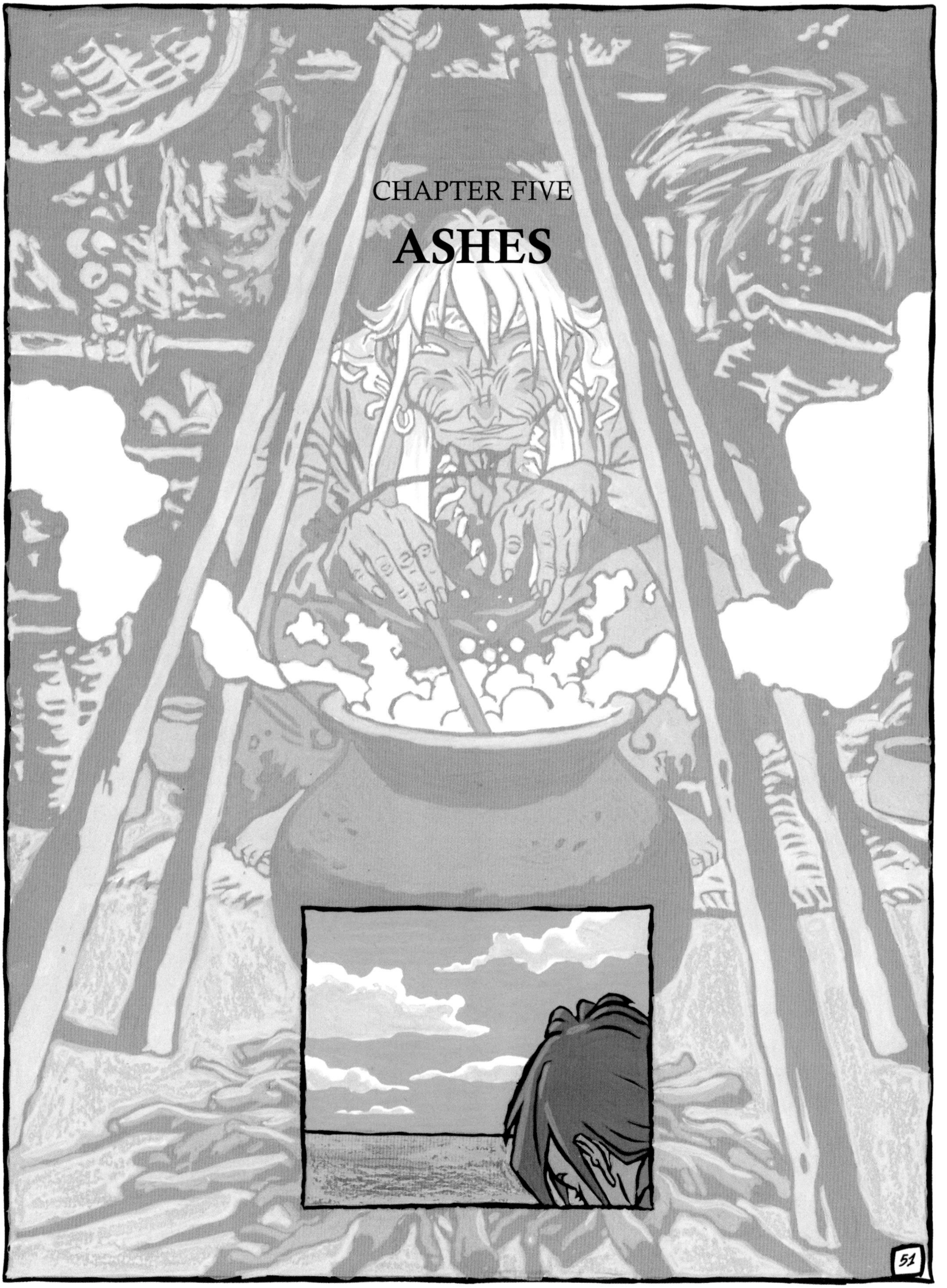
CHAPTER FIVE
ASHES
51

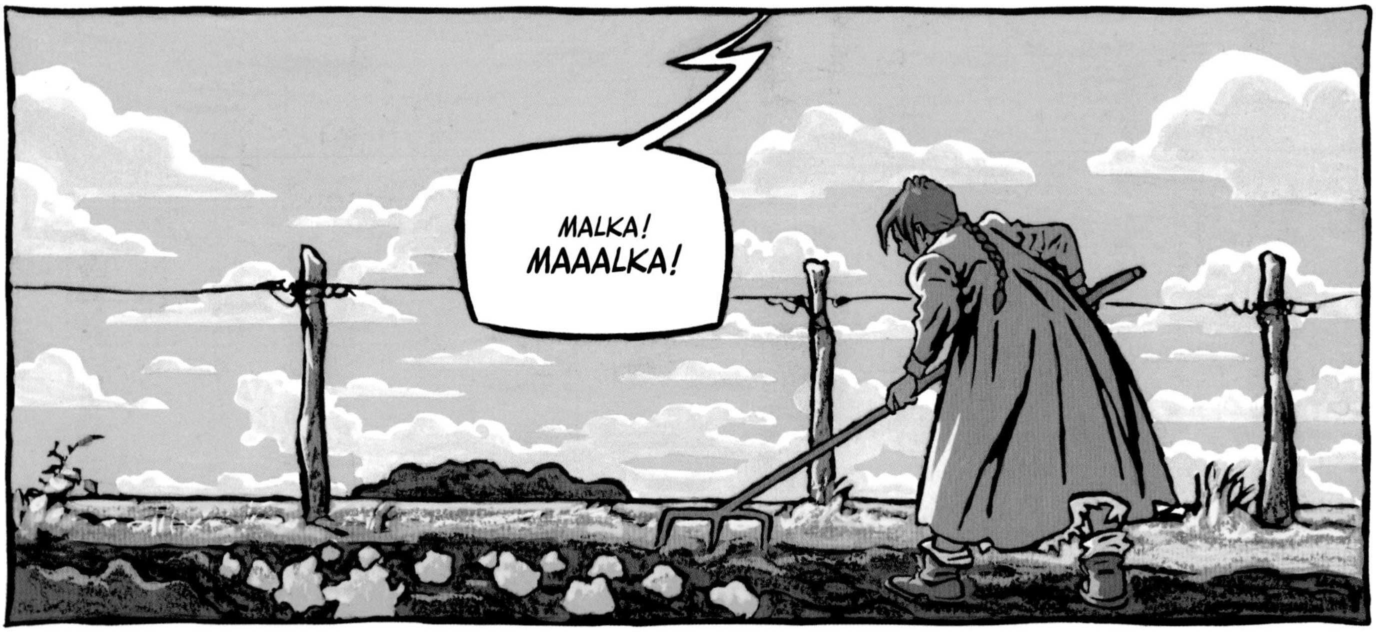
MALKA!
MAAALKA!

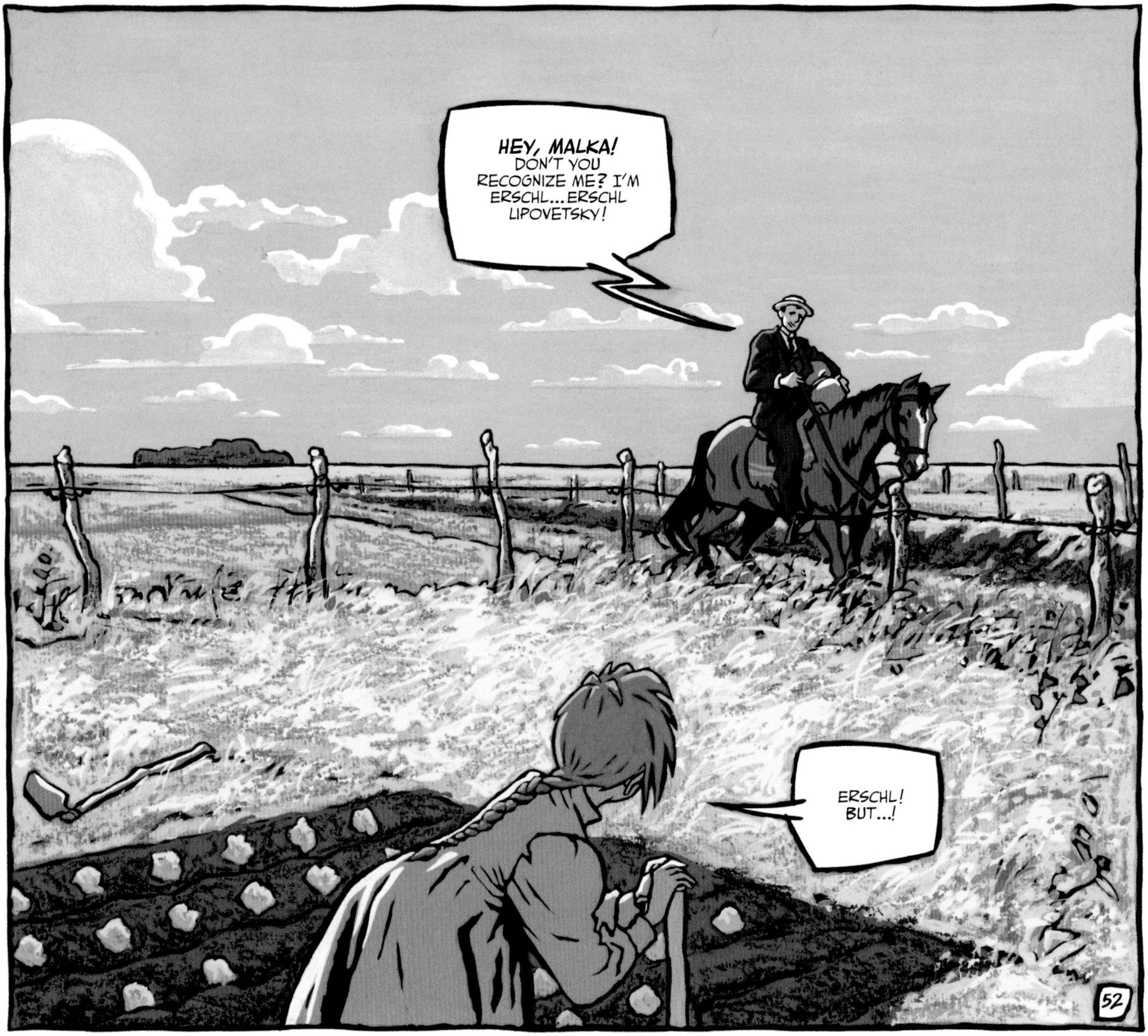
HEY, MALKA! DON'T YOU RECOGNIZE ME? I'M ERSCHL...ERSCHL LIPOVETSKY!
ERSCHL! BUT...!
52

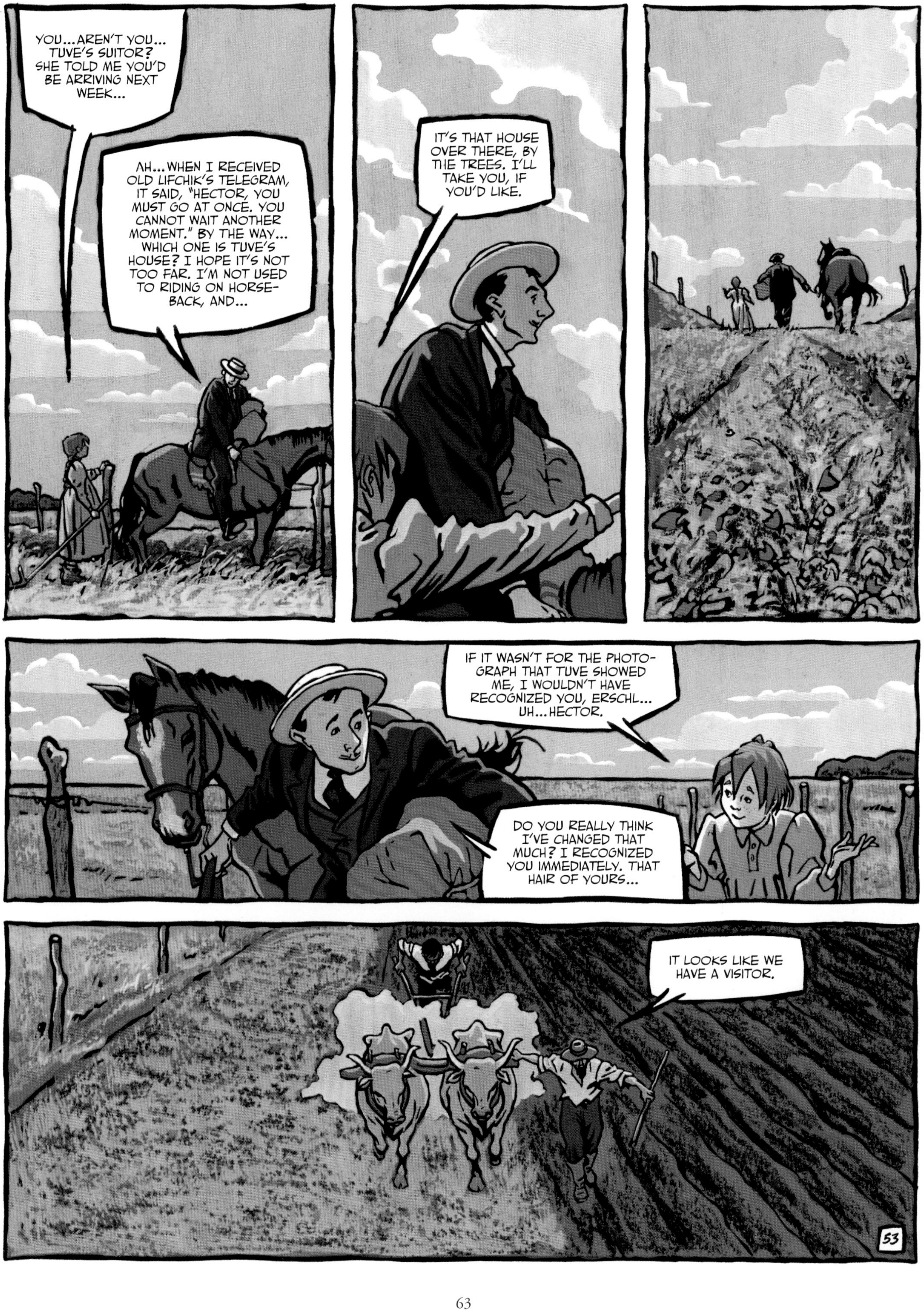
YOU...AREN'T YOU... TUVE'S SUITOR? SHE TOLD ME YOU'D BE ARRIVING NEXT WEEK...
AH...WHEN I RECEIVED OLD LIFCHIK'S TELEGRAM, IT SAID, "HECTOR, YOU MUST GO AT ONCE. YOU CANNOT WAIT ANOTHER MOMENT." BY THE WAY... WHICH ONE IS TUVE'S HOUSE? I HOPE IT'S NOT TOO FAR. I'M NOT USED TO RIDING ON HORSE-BACK, AND...
IT'S THAT HOUSE OVER THERE, BY THE TREES. I'LL TAKE YOU, IF YOU'D LIKE.
IF IT WASN'T FOR THE PHOTOGRAPH THAT TUVE SHOWED ME, I WOULDN'T HAVE RECOGNIZED YOU, ERSCHL... UH...HECTOR.
DO YOU REALLY THINK I'VE CHANGED THAT MUCH? I RECOGNIZED YOU IMMEDIATELY. THAT HAIR OF YOURS...
IT LOOKS LIKE WE HAVE A VISITOR.
53

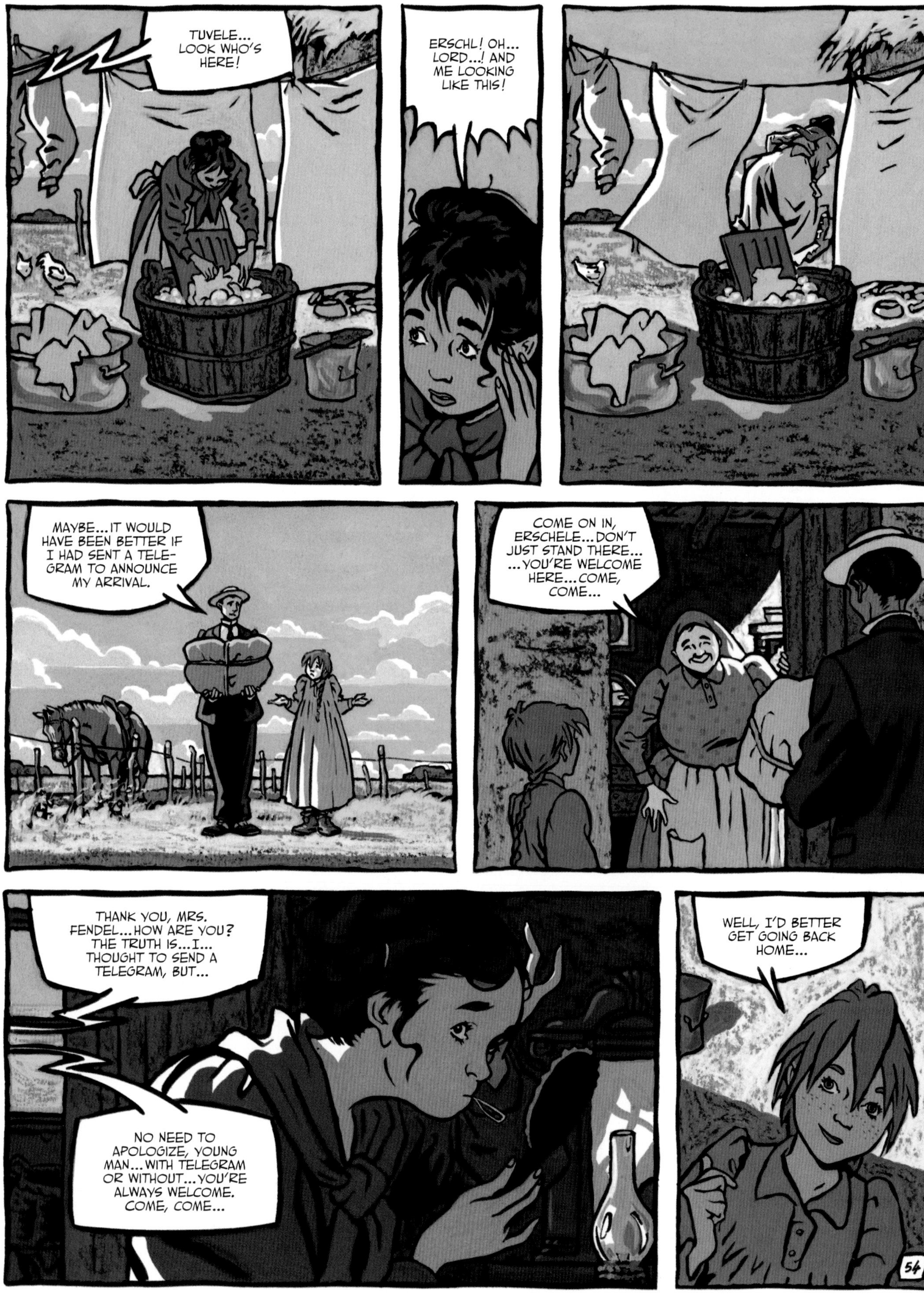
TUVELE... LOOK WHO'S HERE!
ERSCHL! OH... LORD...! AND ME LOOKING LIKE THIS!
MAYBE...IT WOULD HAVE BEEN BETTER IF I HAD SENT A TELE-GRAM TO ANNOUNCE MY ARRIVAL.
COME ON IN, ERSCHELE...DON'T JUST STAND THERE... ...YOU'RE WELCOME HERE...COME, COME...
THANK YOU, MRS. FENDEL...HOW ARE YOU? THE TRUTH IS...I... THOUGHT TO SEND A TELEGRAM, BUT...
NO NEED TO APOLOGIZE, YOUNG MAN...WITH TELEGRAM OR WITHOUT...YOU'RE ALWAYS WELCOME. COME, COME...
WELL, I'D BETTER GET GOING BACK HOME...
54

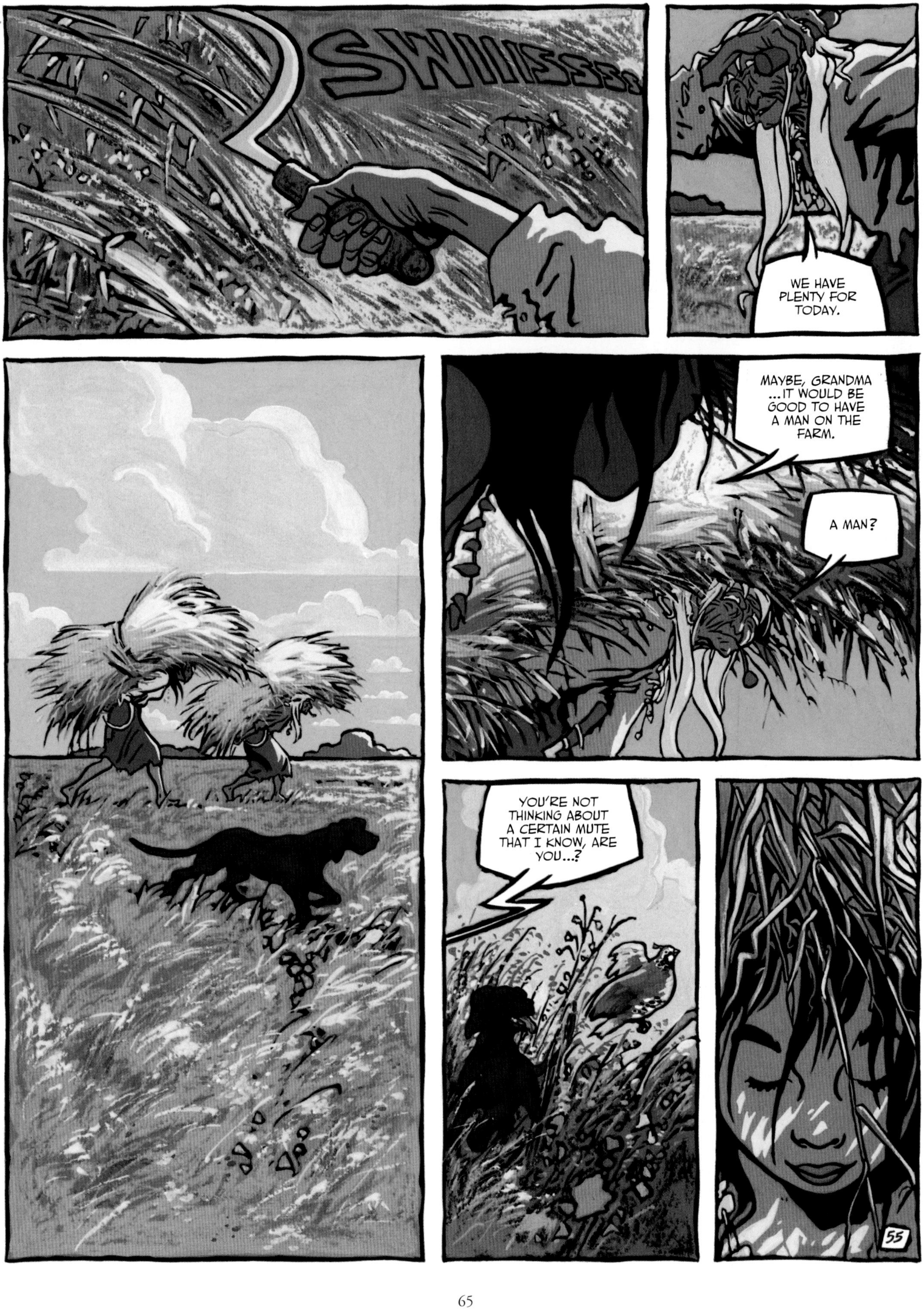
SWIIISSSS
WE HAVE PLENTY FOR TODAY.
MAYBE, GRANDMA ...IT WOULD BE GOOD TO HAVE A MAN ON THE FARM.
A MAN?
YOU'RE NOT THINKING ABOUT A CERTAIN MUTE THAT I KNOW, ARE YOU...?
55

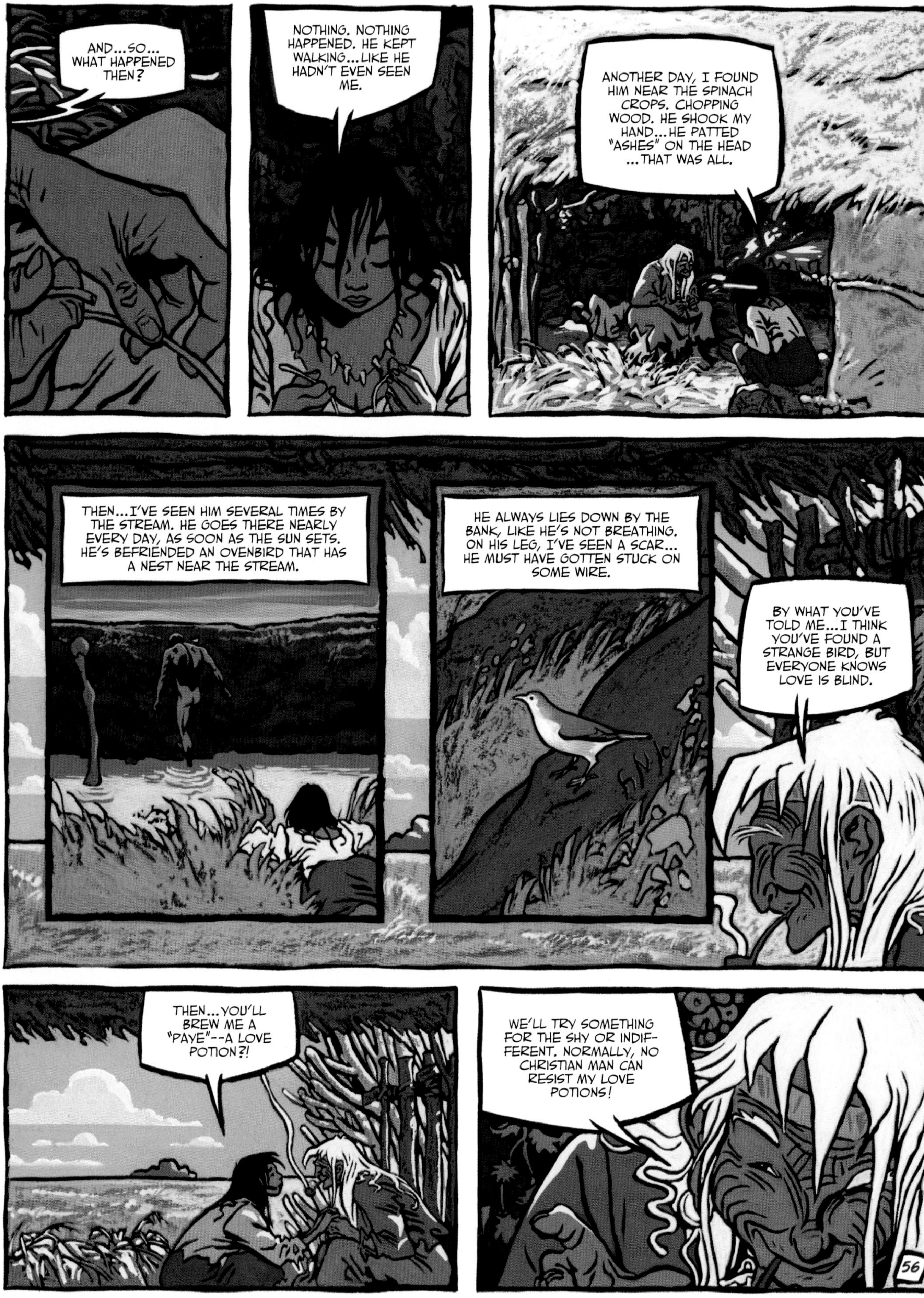
AND...SO... WHAT HAPPENED THEN?
NOTHING. NOTHING HAPPENED. HE KEPT WALKING...LIKE HE HADN'T EVEN SEEN ME.
ANOTHER DAY, I FOUND HIM NEAR THE SPINACH CROPS. CHOPPING WOOD. HE SHOOK MY HAND...HE PATTED "ASHES" ON THE HEAD ...THAT WAS ALL.
THEN...I'VE SEEN HIM SEVERAL TIMES BY THE STREAM. HE GOES THERE NEARLY EVERY DAY, AS SOON AS THE SUN SETS. HE'S BEFRIENDED AN OVENBIRD THAT HAS A NEST NEAR THE STREAM.
HE ALWAYS LIES DOWN BY THE BANK, LIKE HE'S NOT BREATHING. ON HIS LEG, I'VE SEEN A SCAR... HE MUST HAVE GOTTEN STUCK ON SOME WIRE.
BY WHAT YOU'VE TOLD ME...I THINK YOU'VE FOUND A STRANGE BIRD, BUT EVERYONE KNOWS LOVE IS BLIND.
THEN...YOU'LL BREW ME A "PAYE"--A LOVE POTION?!
WE'LL TRY SOMETHING FOR THE SHY OR INDIF-FERENT. NORMALLY, NO CHRISTIAN MAN CAN RESIST MY LOVE POTIONS!
56

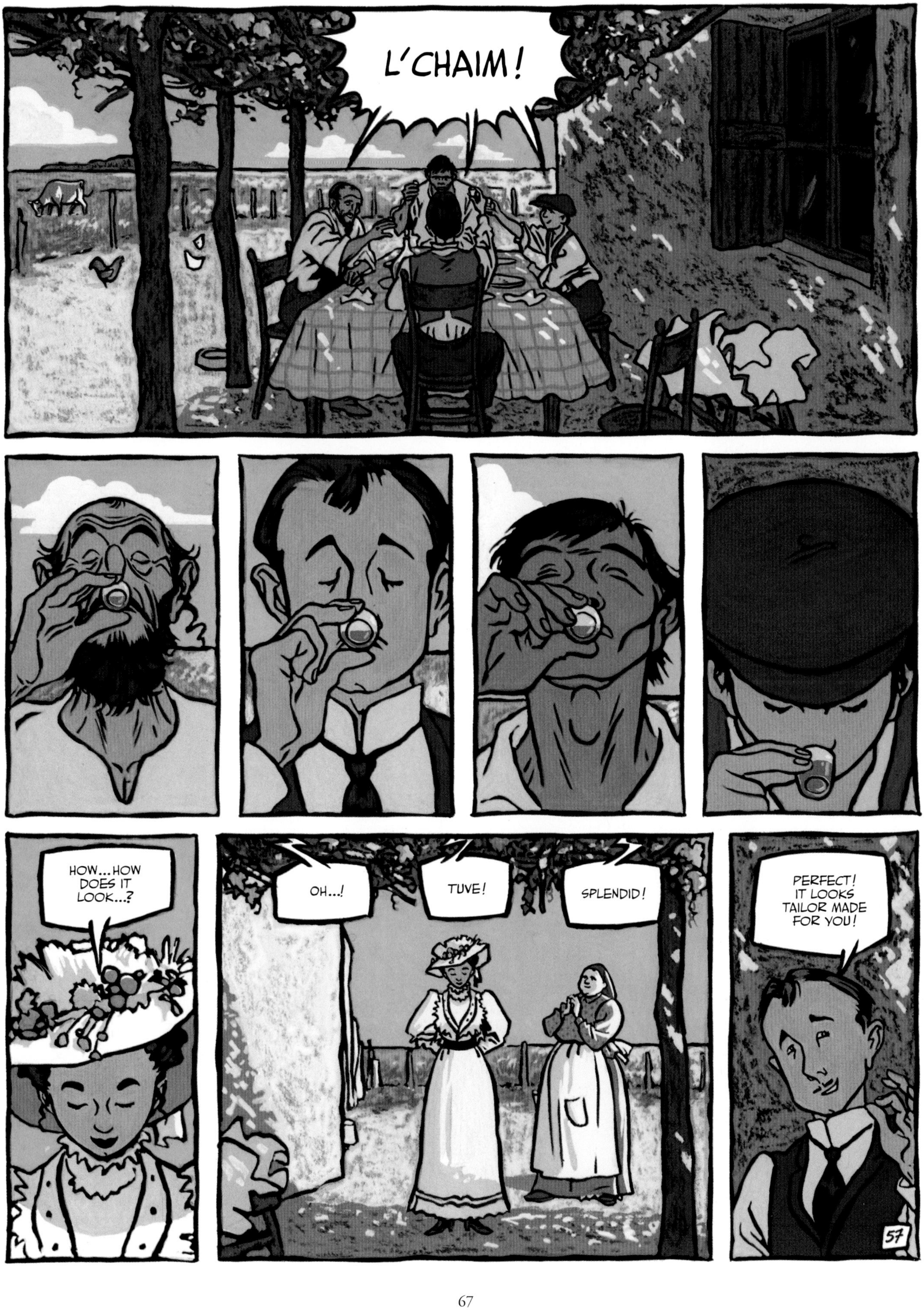

L'CHAIM!
HOW... HOW DOES IT LOOK...?
OH...!
TUVE!
SPLENDID!
PERFECT! IT LOOKS TAILOR MADE FOR YOU!
57

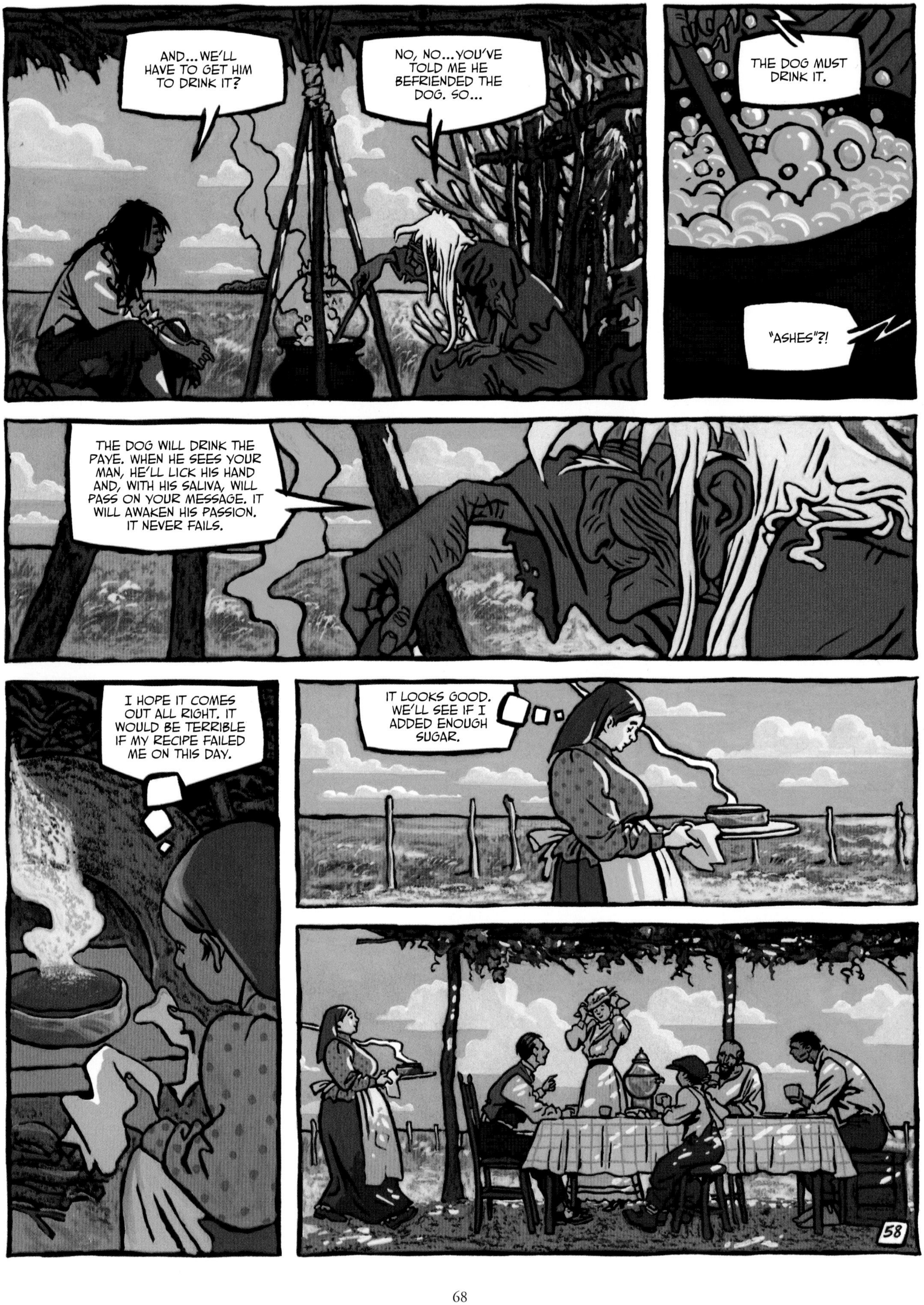
AND...WE'LL HAVE TO GET HIM TO DRINK IT?
NO, NO...YOU'VE TOLD ME HE BEFRIENDED THE DOG. SO...
THE DOG MUST DRINK IT.
"ASHES"?!
THE DOG WILL DRINK THE PAYE. WHEN HE SEES YOUR MAN, HE'LL LICK HIS HAND AND, WITH HIS SALIVA, WILL PASS ON YOUR MESSAGE. IT WILL AWAKEN HIS PASSION. IT NEVER FAILS.
I HOPE IT COMES OUT ALL RIGHT. IT WOULD BE TERRIBLE IF MY RECIPE FAILED ME ON THIS DAY.
IT LOOKS GOOD. WE'LL SEE IF I ADDED ENOUGH SUGAR.
58

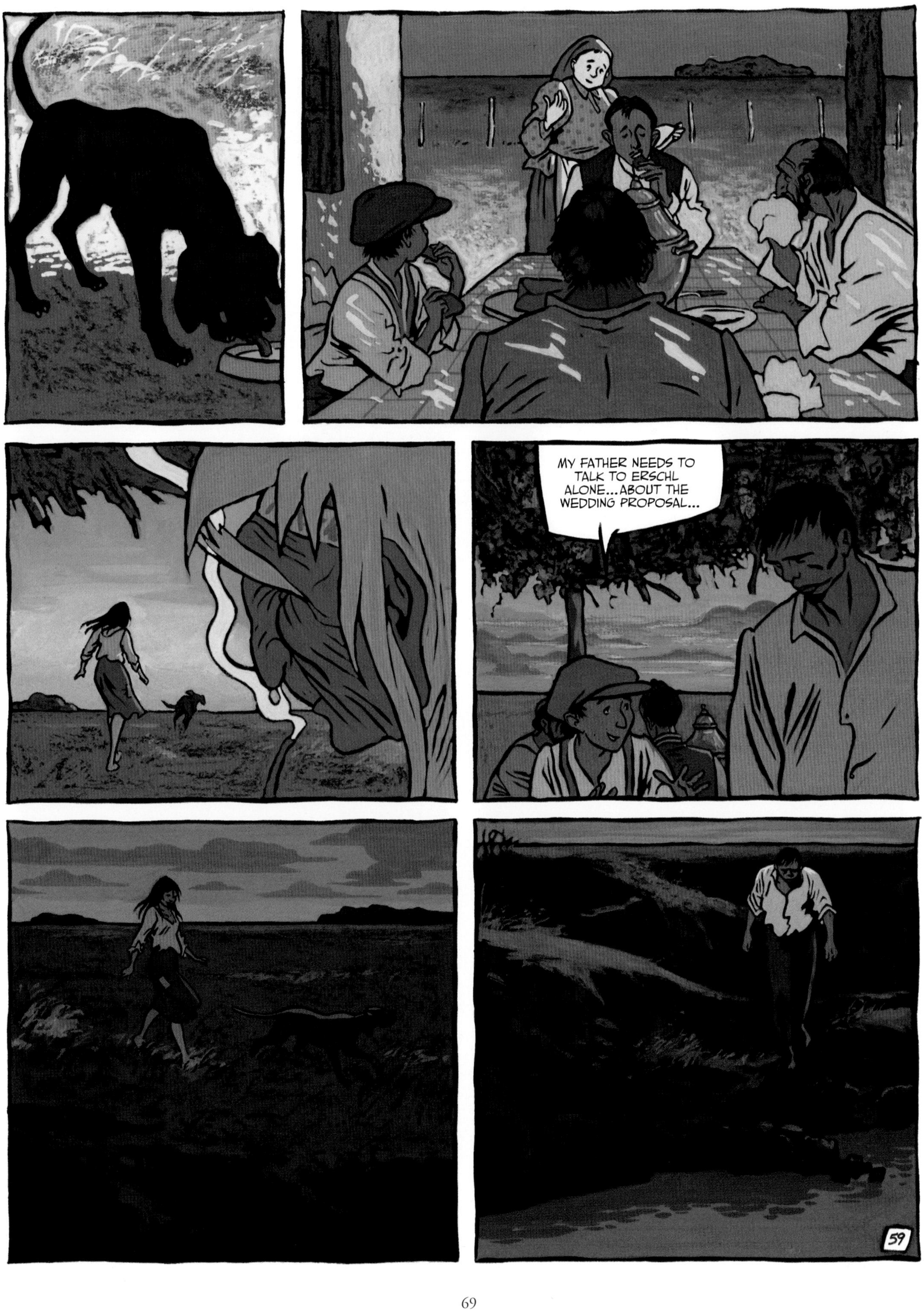
MY FATHER NEEDS TO TALK TO ERSCHL ALONE...ABOUT THE WEDDING PROPOSAL...
59

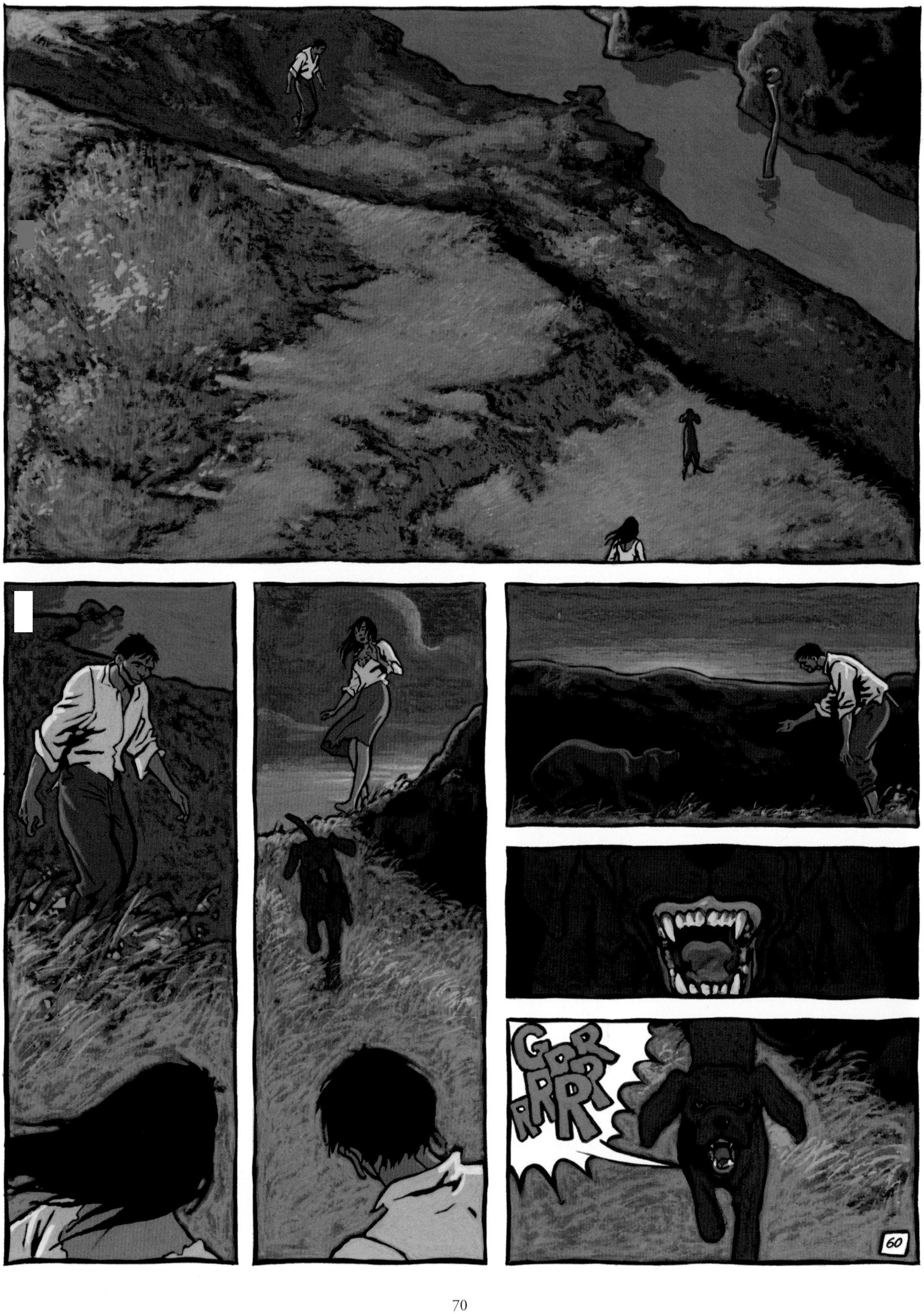
GRRRRRR
60

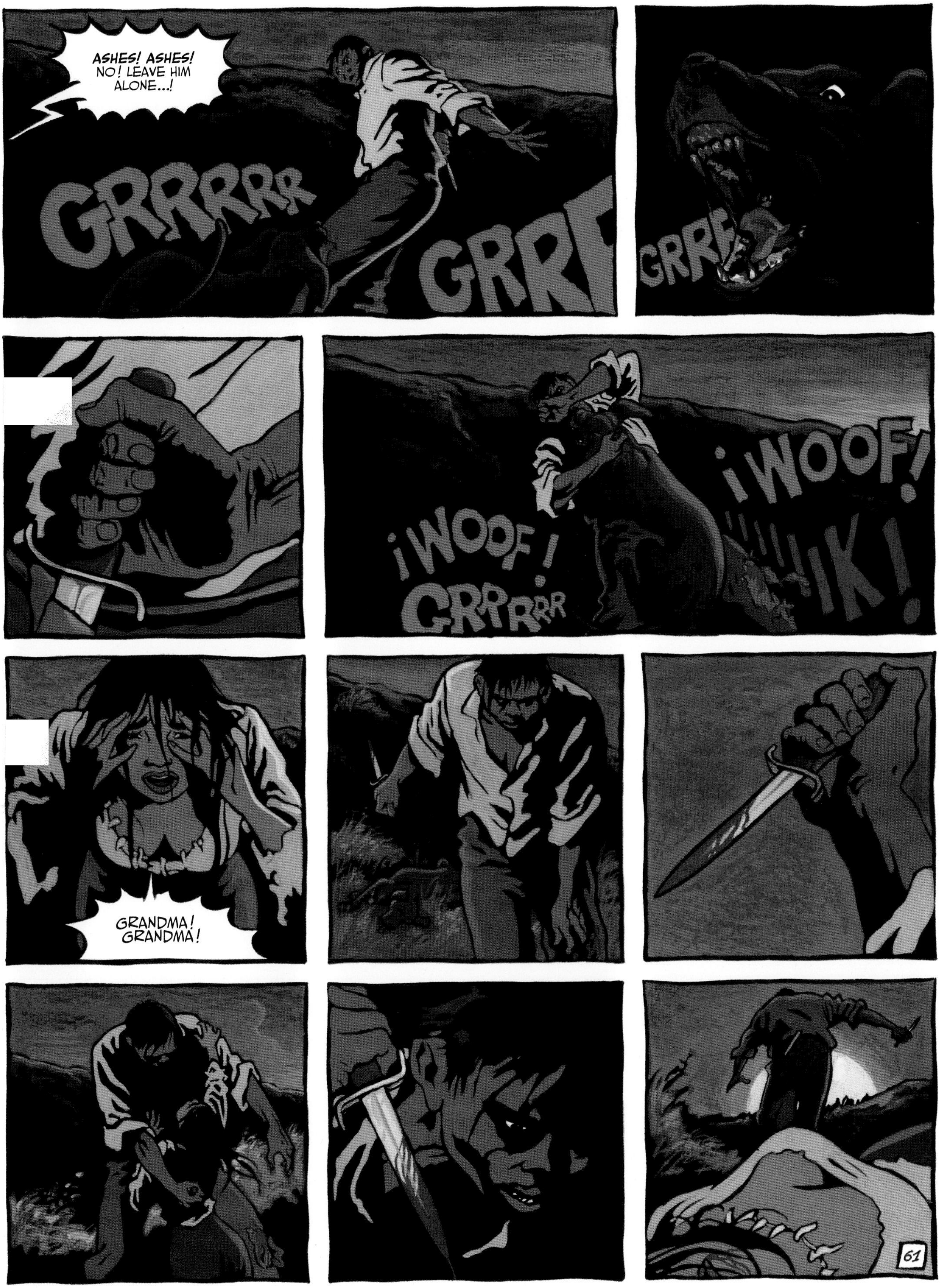
ASHES! ASHES! NO! LEAVE HIM ALONE...!
GRRRRR
GRRR
GRRR
¡WOOF!
GRRRRR
¡WOOF!
IK!
GRANDMA! GRANDMA!
61

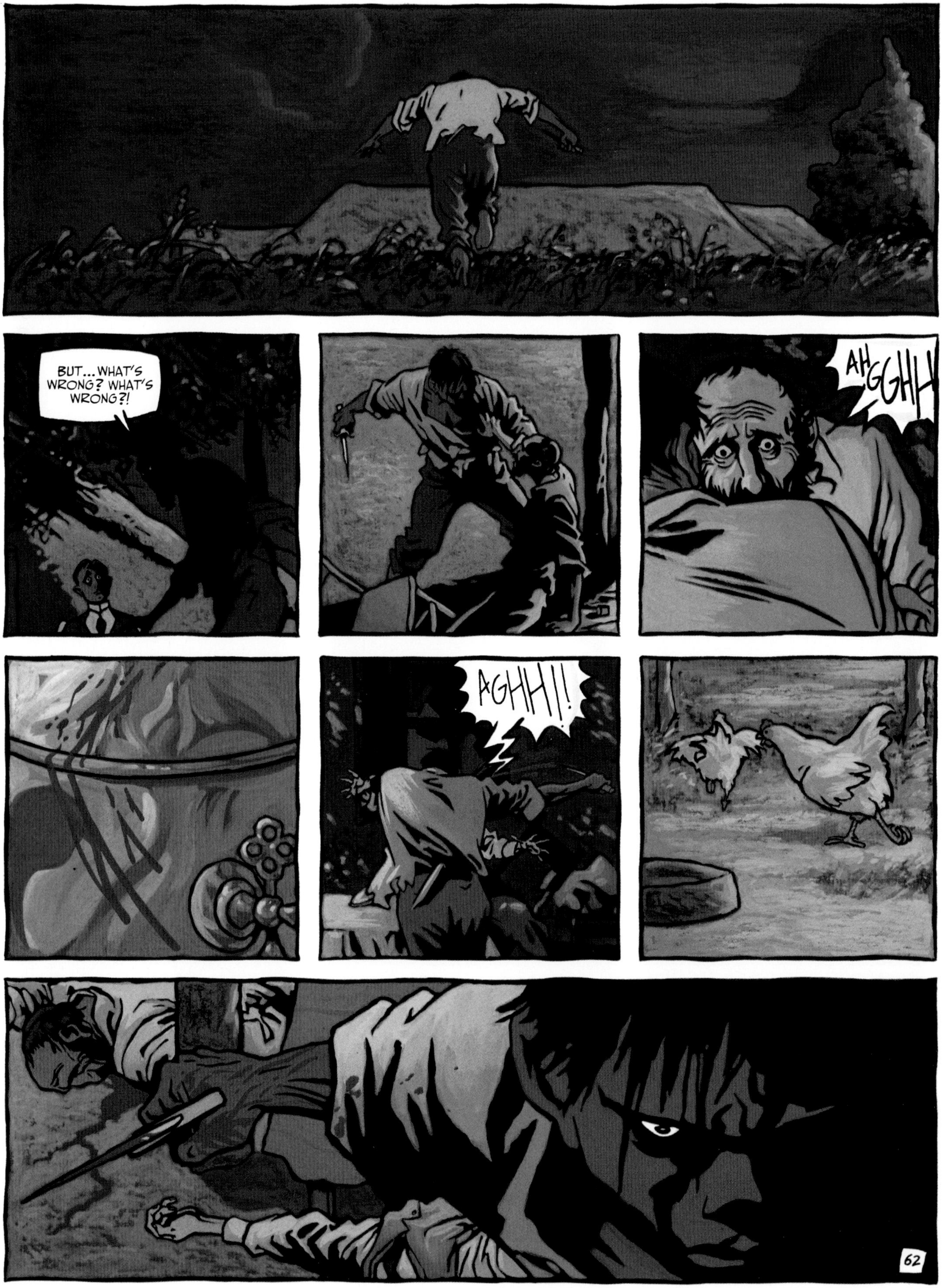
BUT...WHAT'S WRONG? WHAT'S WRONG?!
AHGGHH
AGHH!!
62

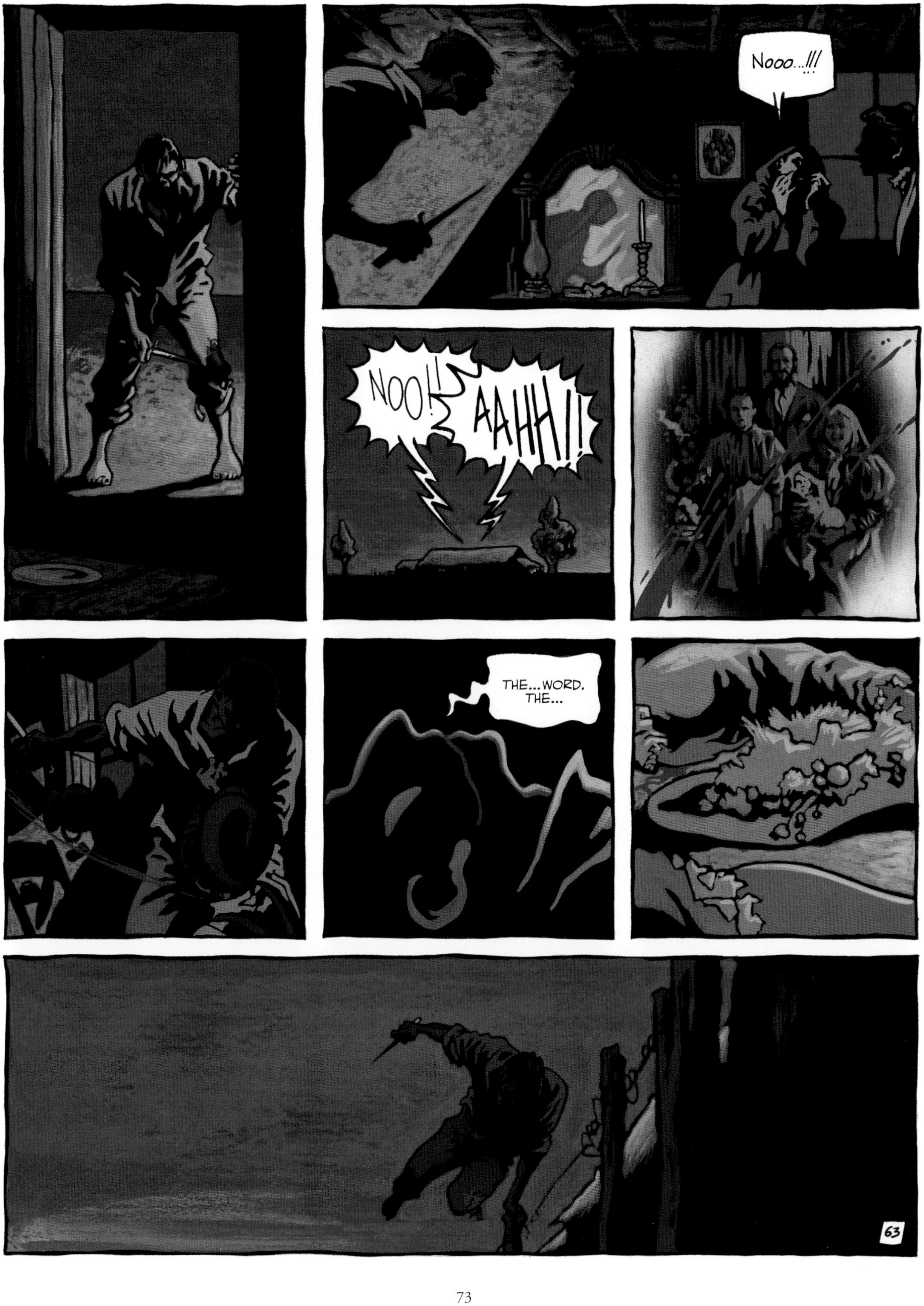
Nooo...!!!
NOO!!
AAHH!!
THE... WORD. THE...
63

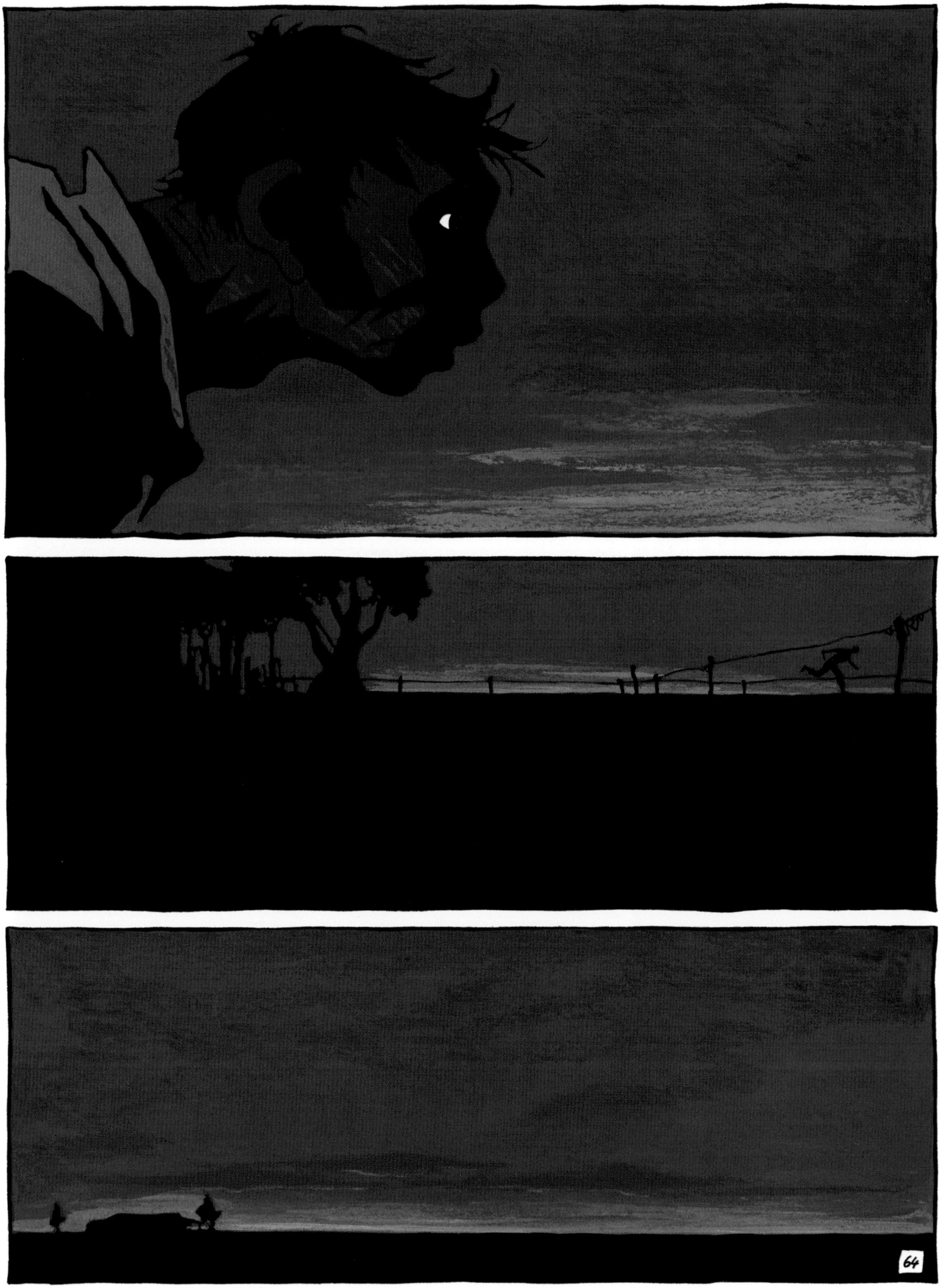
64

CHAPTER SIX

BUENOS AIRES

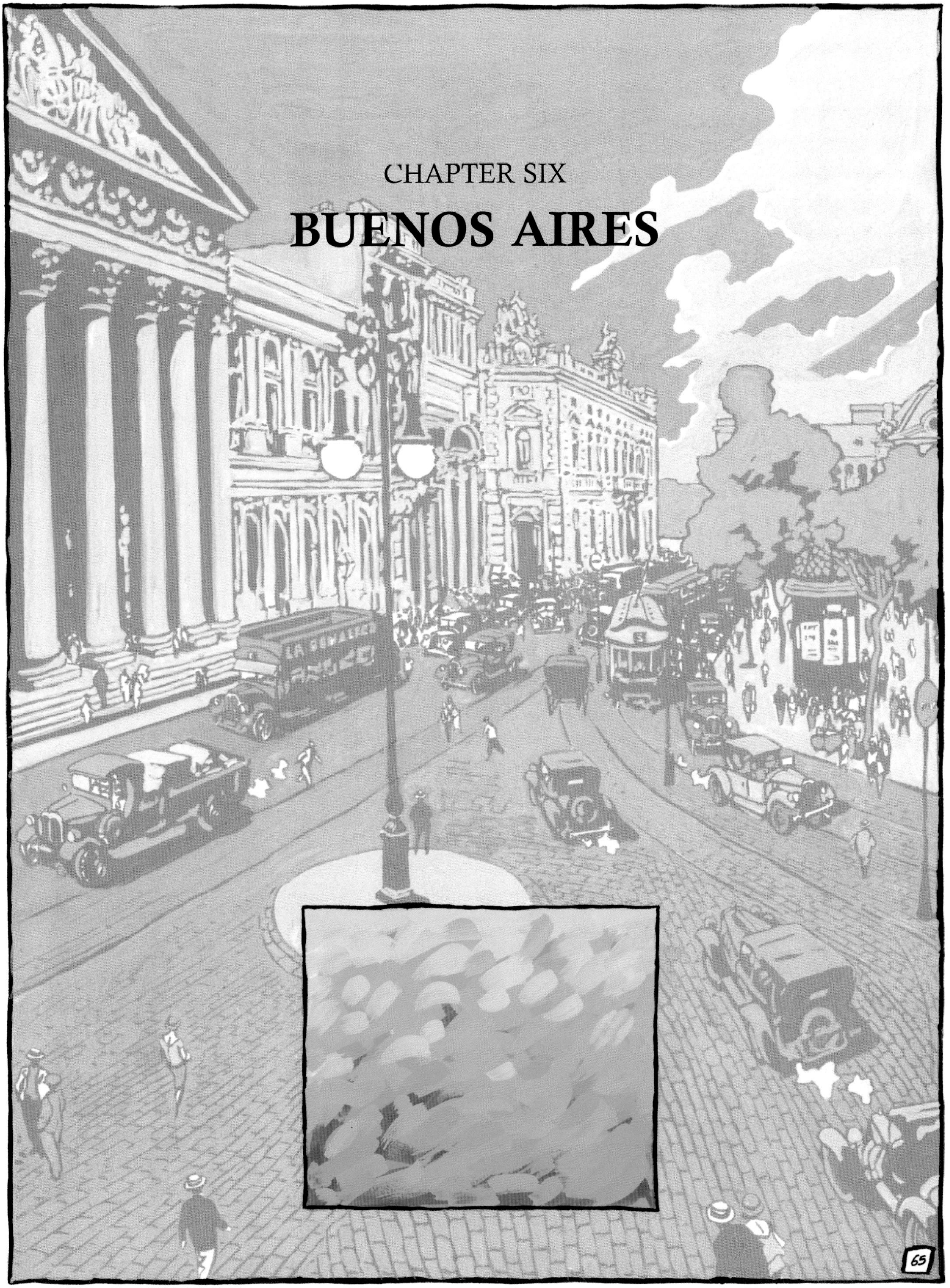
65

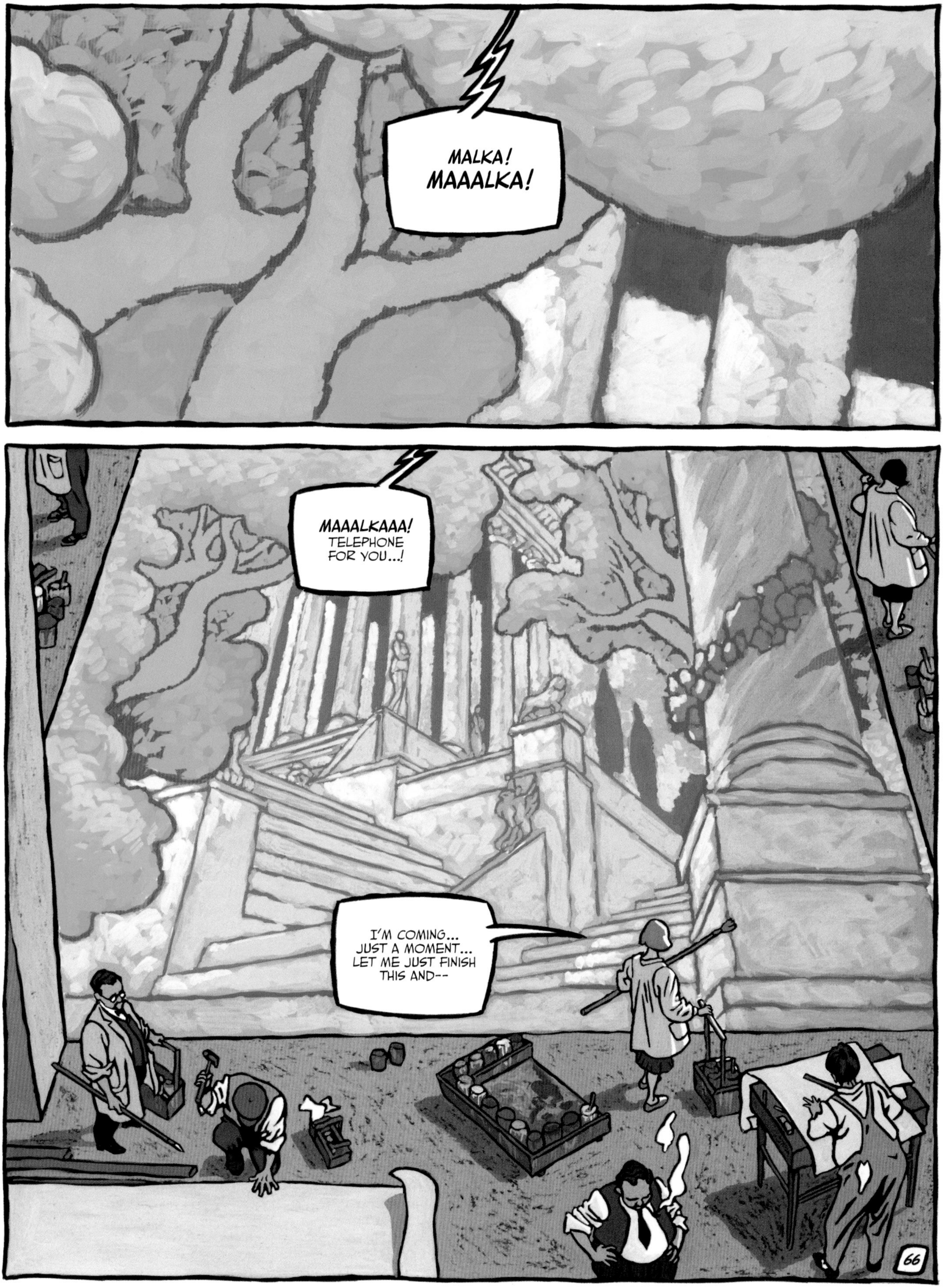
MALKA! MAAALKA!
MAAALKAAA! TELEPHONE FOR YOU...!
I'M COMING... JUST A MOMENT... LET ME JUST FINISH THIS AND--
66

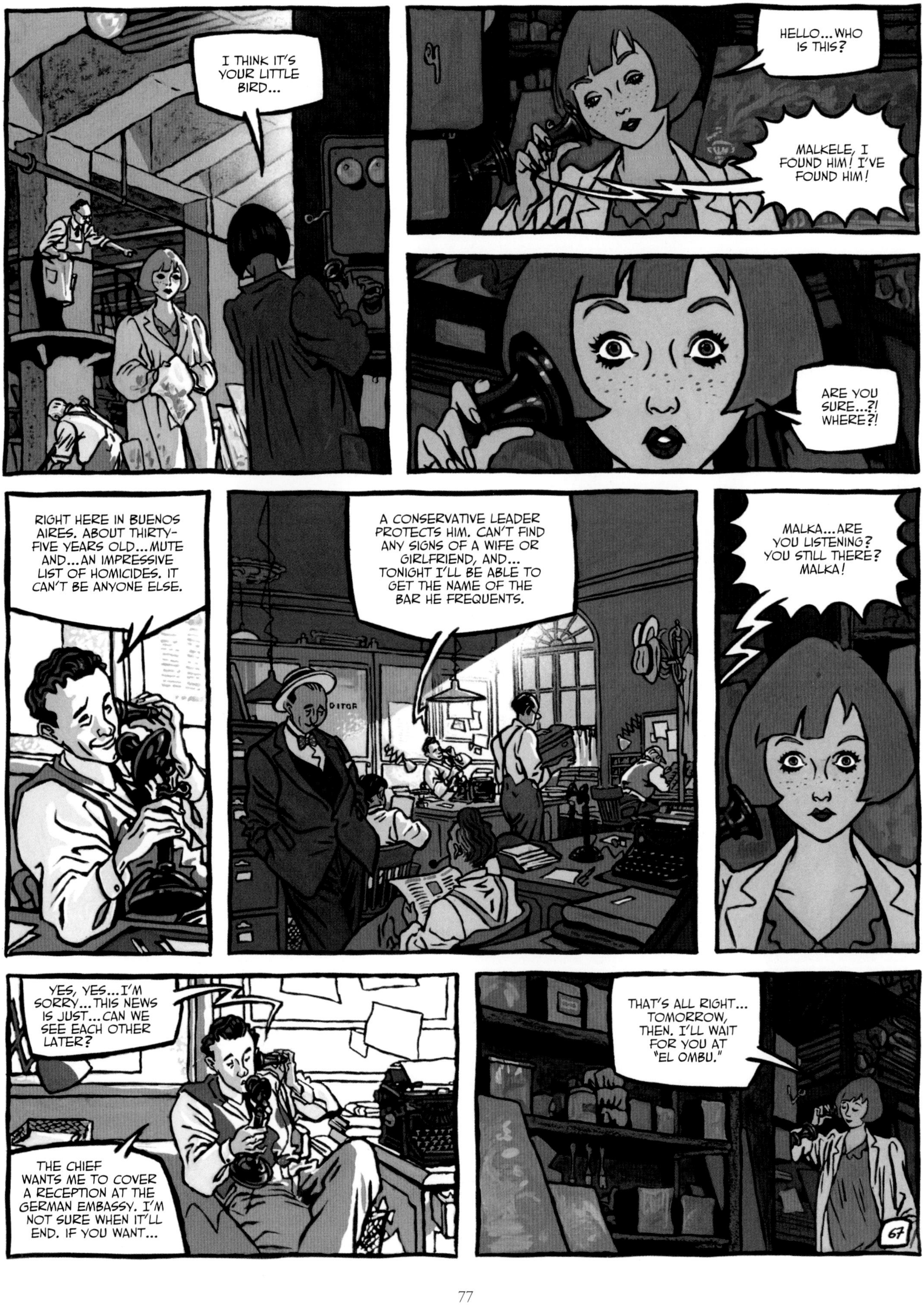
I THINK IT'S YOUR LITTLE BIRD...
HELLO...WHO IS THIS?
MALKELE, I FOUND HIM! I'VE FOUND HIM!
ARE YOU SURE...?! WHERE?!
RIGHT HERE IN BUENOS AIRES. ABOUT THIRTY-FIVE YEARS OLD...MUTE AND...AN IMPRESSIVE LIST OF HOMICIDES. IT CAN'T BE ANYONE ELSE.
A CONSERVATIVE LEADER PROTECTS HIM. CAN'T FIND ANY SIGNS OF A WIFE OR GIRLFRIEND, AND... TONIGHT I'LL BE ABLE TO GET THE NAME OF THE BAR HE FREQUENTS.
MALKA...ARE YOU LISTENING? YOU STILL THERE? MALKA!
YES, YES...I'M SORRY...THIS NEWS IS JUST...CAN WE SEE EACH OTHER LATER?
THE CHIEF WANTS ME TO COVER A RECEPTION AT THE GERMAN EMBASSY. I'M NOT SURE WHEN IT'LL END. IF YOU WANT...
THAT'S ALL RIGHT... TOMORROW, THEN. I'LL WAIT FOR YOU AT "EL OMBU."
67

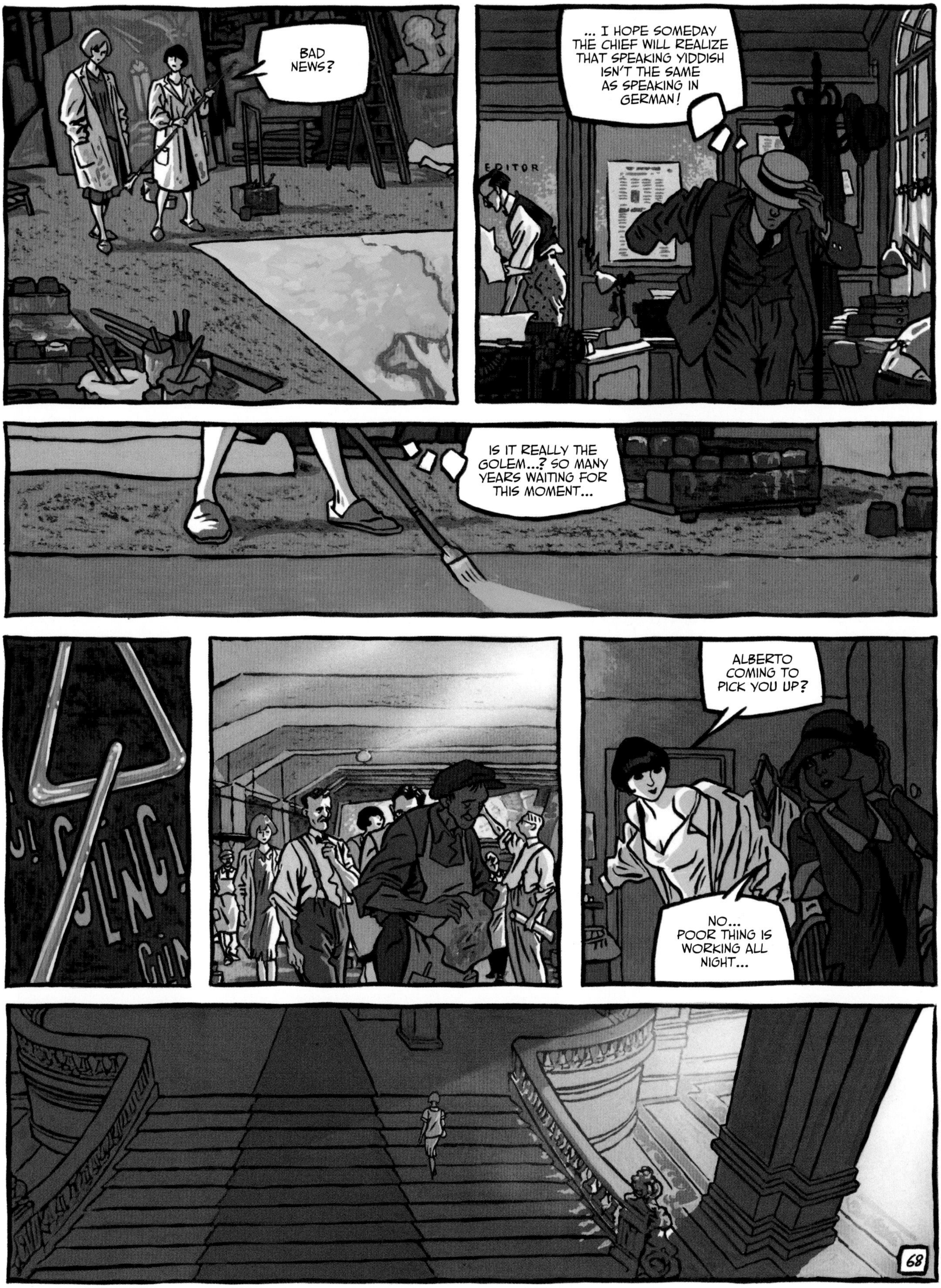
BAD NEWS?
... I HOPE SOMEDAY THE CHIEF WILL REALIZE THAT SPEAKING YIDDISH ISN'T THE SAME AS SPEAKING IN GERMAN!
EDITOR
IS IT REALLY THE GOLEM...? SO MANY YEARS WAITING FOR THIS MOMENT...
ALBERTO COMING TO PICK YOU UP?
NO... POOR THING IS WORKING ALL NIGHT...
68

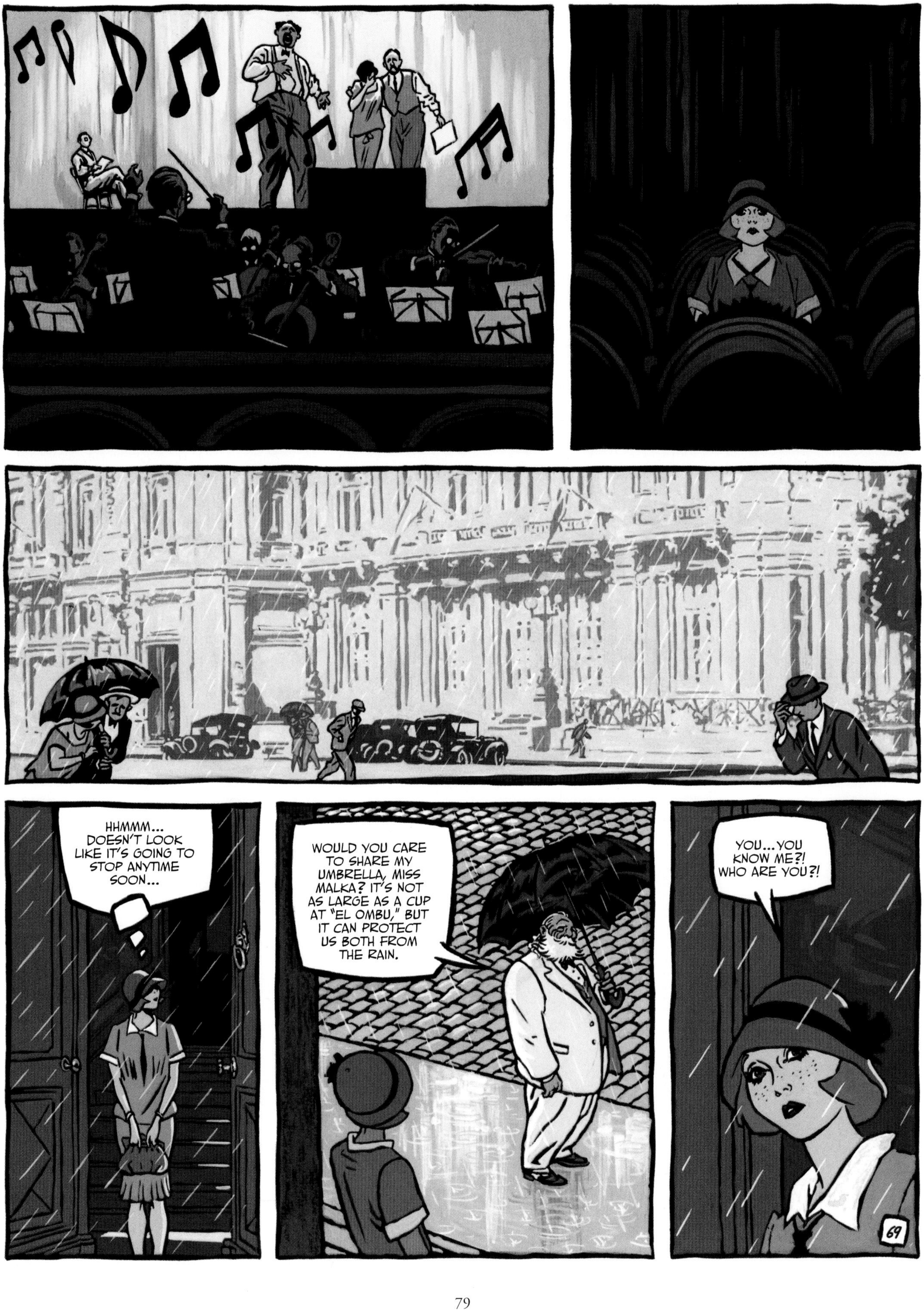
HHMMM... DOESN'T LOOK LIKE IT'S GOING TO STOP ANYTIME SOON...
WOULD YOU CARE TO SHARE MY UMBRELLA, MISS MALKA? IT'S NOT AS LARGE AS A CUP AT "EL OMBU," BUT IT CAN PROTECT US BOTH FROM THE RAIN.
YOU...YOU KNOW ME?! WHO ARE YOU?!
69

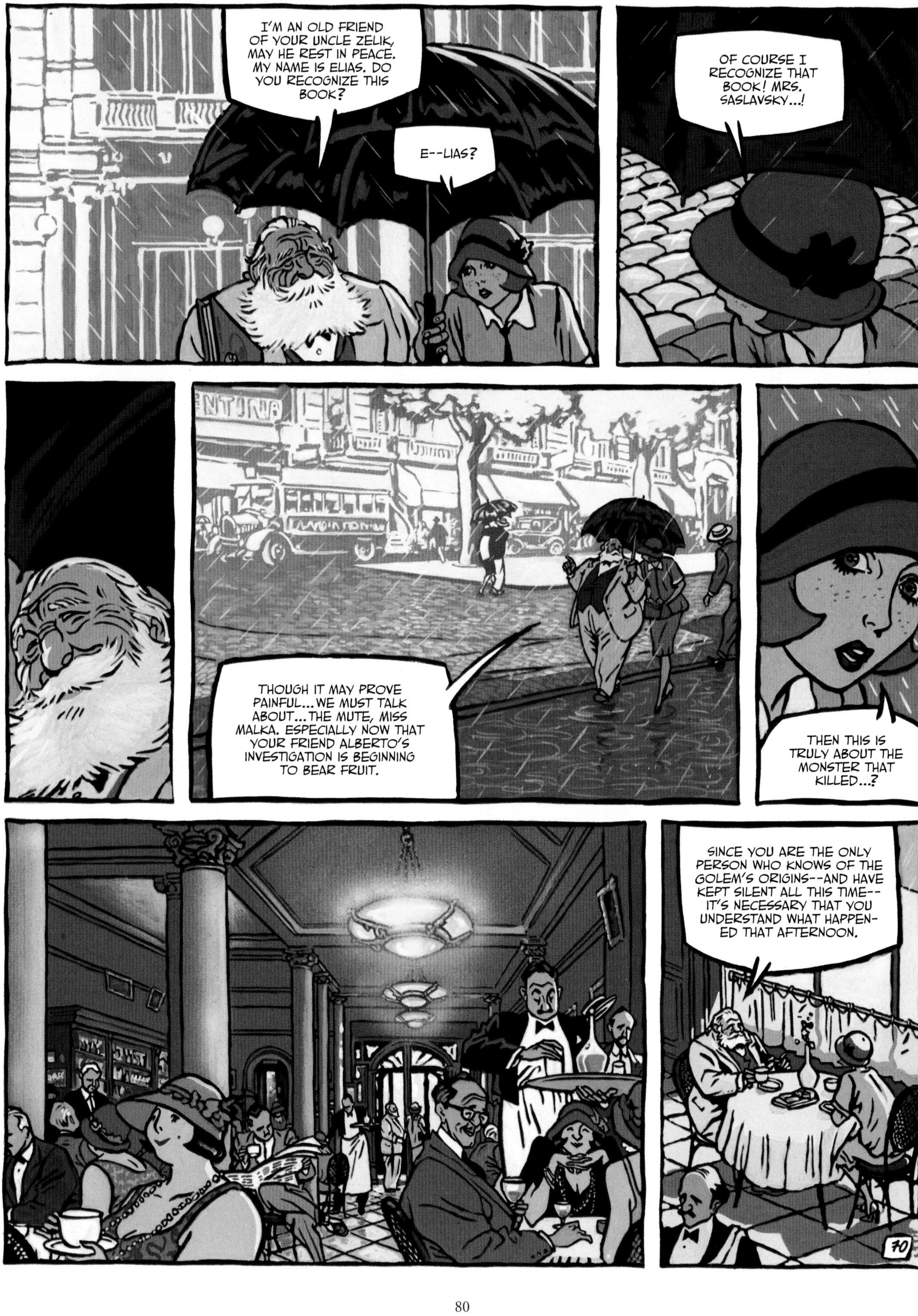
I'M AN OLD FRIEND OF YOUR UNCLE ZELIK, MAY HE REST IN PEACE. MY NAME IS ELIAS. DO YOU RECOGNIZE THIS BOOK?
E--LIAS?
OF COURSE I RECOGNIZE THAT BOOK! MRS. SASLAVSKY...!
THOUGH IT MAY PROVE PAINFUL...WE MUST TALK ABOUT...THE MUTE, MISS MALKA. ESPECIALLY NOW THAT YOUR FRIEND ALBERTO'S INVESTIGATION IS BEGINNING TO BEAR FRUIT.
THEN THIS IS TRULY ABOUT THE MONSTER THAT KILLED...?
SINCE YOU ARE THE ONLY PERSON WHO KNOWS OF THE GOLEM'S ORIGINS--AND HAVE KEPT SILENT ALL THIS TIME--IT'S NECESSARY THAT YOU UNDERSTAND WHAT HAPPENED THAT AFTERNOON.
70

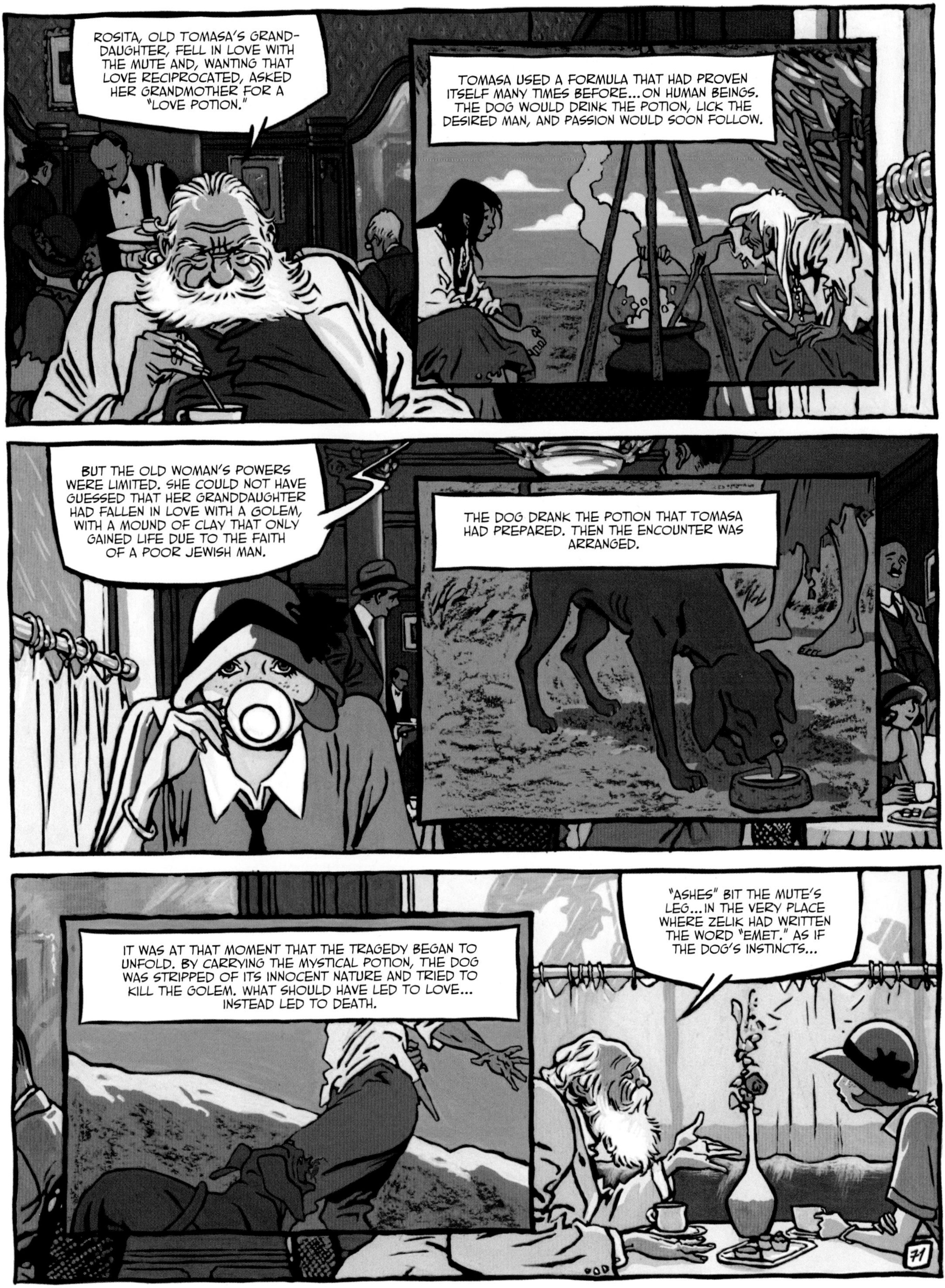
ROSITA, OLD TOMASA'S GRAND-DAUGHTER, FELL IN LOVE WITH THE MUTE AND, WANTING THAT LOVE RECIPROCATED, ASKED HER GRANDMOTHER FOR A "LOVE POTION."
TOMASA USED A FORMULA THAT HAD PROVEN ITSELF MANY TIMES BEFORE...ON HUMAN BEINGS. THE DOG WOULD DRINK THE POTION, LICK THE DESIRED MAN, AND PASSION WOULD SOON FOLLOW.
BUT THE OLD WOMAN'S POWERS WERE LIMITED. SHE COULD NOT HAVE GUESSED THAT HER GRANDDAUGHTER HAD FALLEN IN LOVE WITH A GOLEM, WITH A MOUND OF CLAY THAT ONLY GAINED LIFE DUE TO THE FAITH OF A POOR JEWISH MAN.
THE DOG DRANK THE POTION THAT TOMASA HAD PREPARED. THEN THE ENCOUNTER WAS ARRANGED.
IT WAS AT THAT MOMENT THAT THE TRAGEDY BEGAN TO UNFOLD. BY CARRYING THE MYSTICAL POTION, THE DOG WAS STRIPPED OF ITS INNOCENT NATURE AND TRIED TO KILL THE GOLEM. WHAT SHOULD HAVE LED TO LOVE... INSTEAD LED TO DEATH.
"ASHES" BIT THE MUTE'S LEG...IN THE VERY PLACE WHERE ZELIK HAD WRITTEN THE WORD "EMET." AS IF THE DOG'S INSTINCTS...
71

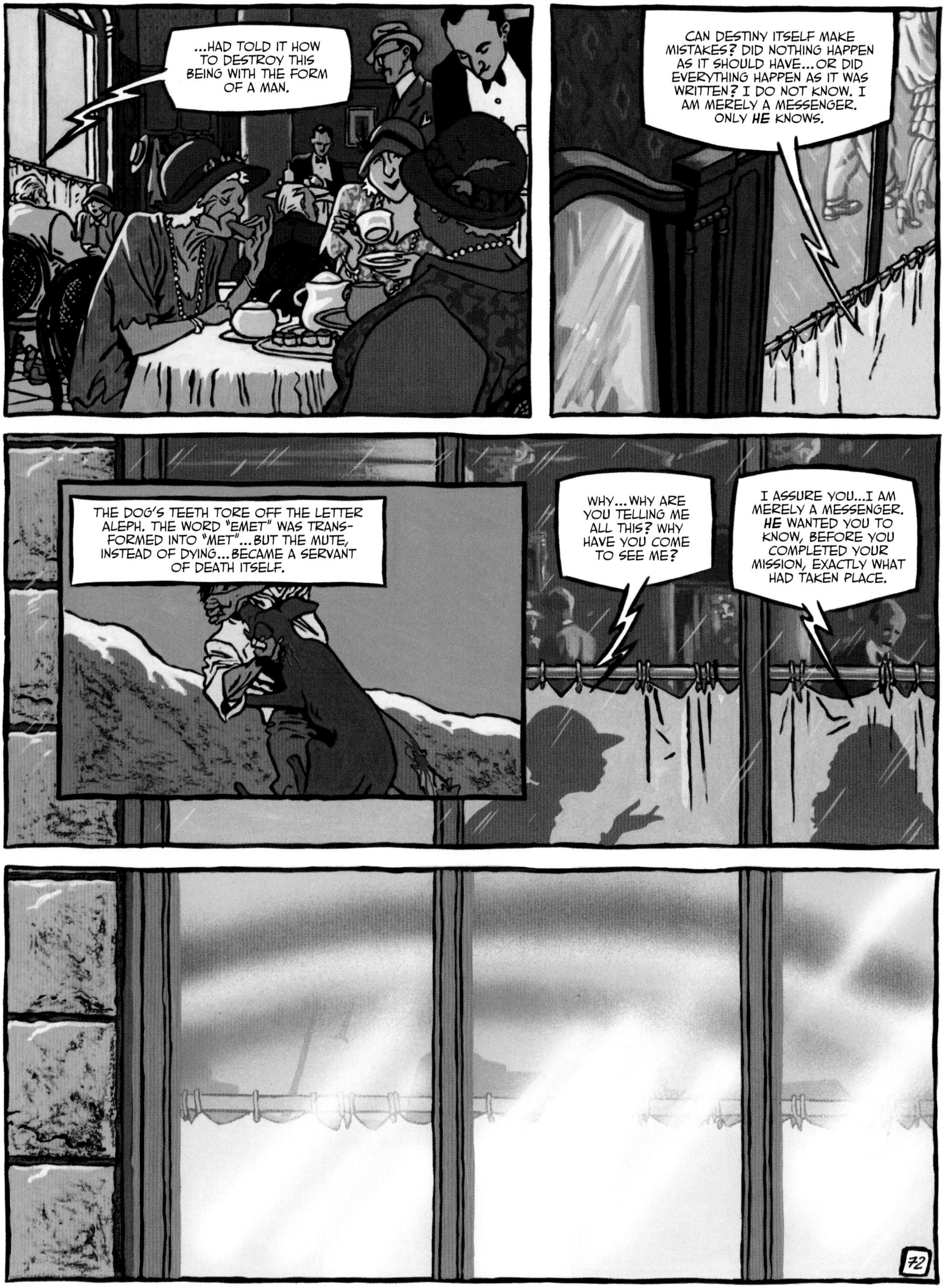
...HAD TOLD IT HOW TO DESTROY THIS BEING WITH THE FORM OF A MAN.
CAN DESTINY ITSELF MAKE MISTAKES? DID NOTHING HAPPEN AS IT SHOULD HAVE...OR DID EVERYTHING HAPPEN AS IT WAS WRITTEN? I DO NOT KNOW. I AM MERELY A MESSENGER. ONLY HE KNOWS.
THE DOG'S TEETH TORE OFF THE LETTER ALEPH. THE WORD "EMET" WAS TRANSFORMED INTO "MET"...BUT THE MUTE, INSTEAD OF DYING...BECAME A SERVANT OF DEATH ITSELF.
WHY...WHY ARE YOU TELLING ME ALL THIS? WHY HAVE YOU COME TO SEE ME?
I ASSURE YOU...I AM MERELY A MESSENGER. HE WANTED YOU TO KNOW, BEFORE YOU COMPLETED YOUR MISSION, EXACTLY WHAT HAD TAKEN PLACE.
72

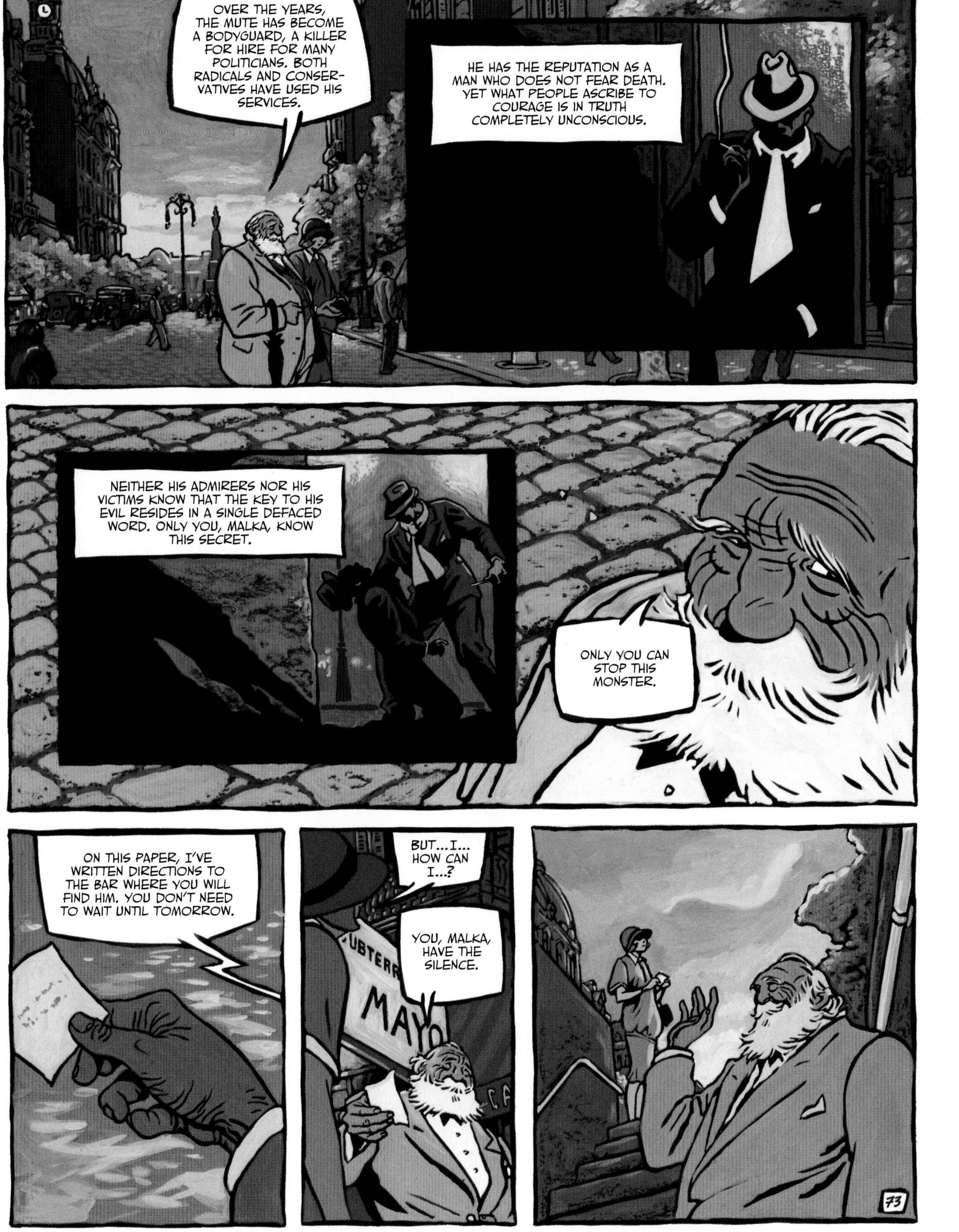
OVER THE YEARS, THE MUTE HAS BECOME A BODYGUARD, A KILLER FOR HIRE FOR MANY POLITICIANS. BOTH RADICALS AND CONSERVATIVES HAVE USED HIS SERVICES.
HE HAS THE REPUTATION AS A MAN WHO DOES NOT FEAR DEATH. YET WHAT PEOPLE ASCRIBE TO COURAGE IS IN TRUTH COMPLETELY UNCONSCIOUS.
NEITHER HIS ADMIRERS NOR HIS VICTIMS KNOW THAT THE KEY TO HIS EVIL RESIDES IN A SINGLE DEFACED WORD. ONLY YOU, MALKA, KNOW THIS SECRET.
ONLY YOU CAN STOP THIS MONSTER.
ON THIS PAPER, I'VE WRITTEN DIRECTIONS TO THE BAR WHERE YOU WILL FIND HIM. YOU DON'T NEED TO WAIT UNTIL TOMORROW.
BUT...I... HOW CAN I...?
YOU, MALKA, HAVE THE SILENCE.
UBTERR
MAYO
73

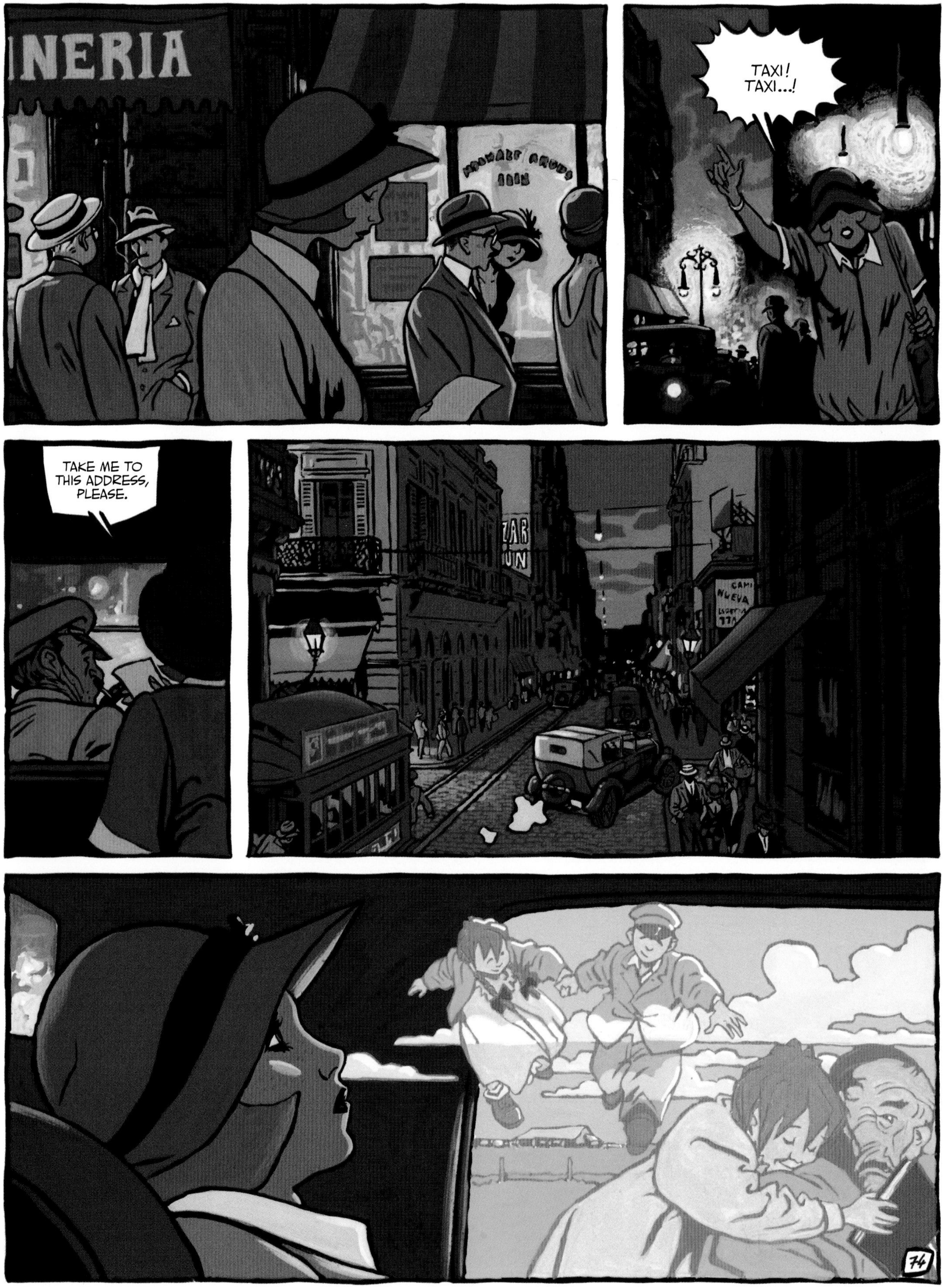

NERIA
TAXI! TAXI...!
TAKE ME TO THIS ADDRESS, PLEASE.
74

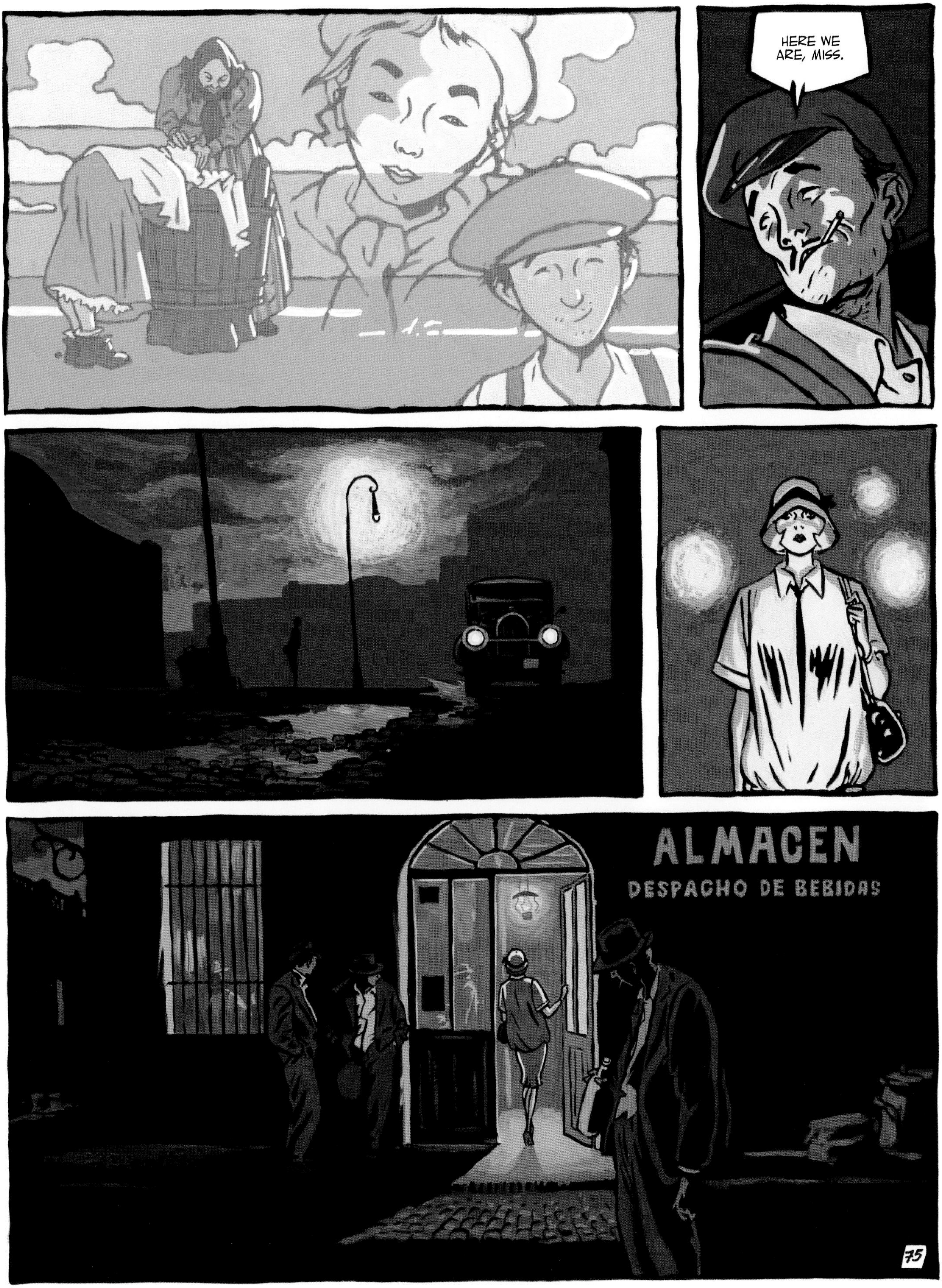
HERE WE ARE, MISS.
ALMACEN
DESPACHO DE BEBIDAS
75

TRY THE
TABLE IN THE
BACK.

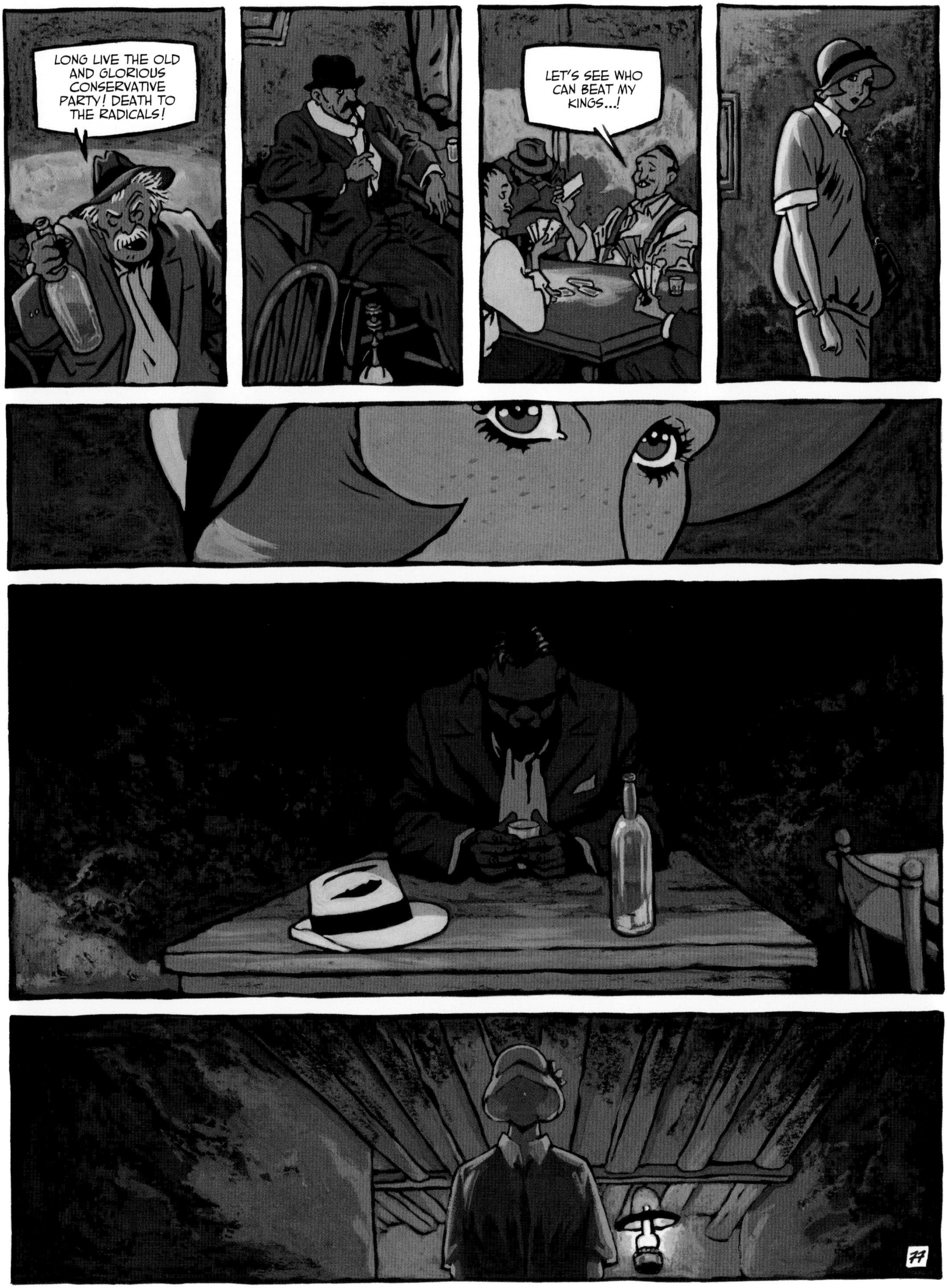
LONG LIVE THE OLD AND GLORIOUS CONSERVATIVE PARTY! DEATH TO THE RADICALS!
LET'S SEE WHO CAN BEAT MY KINGS...!
77

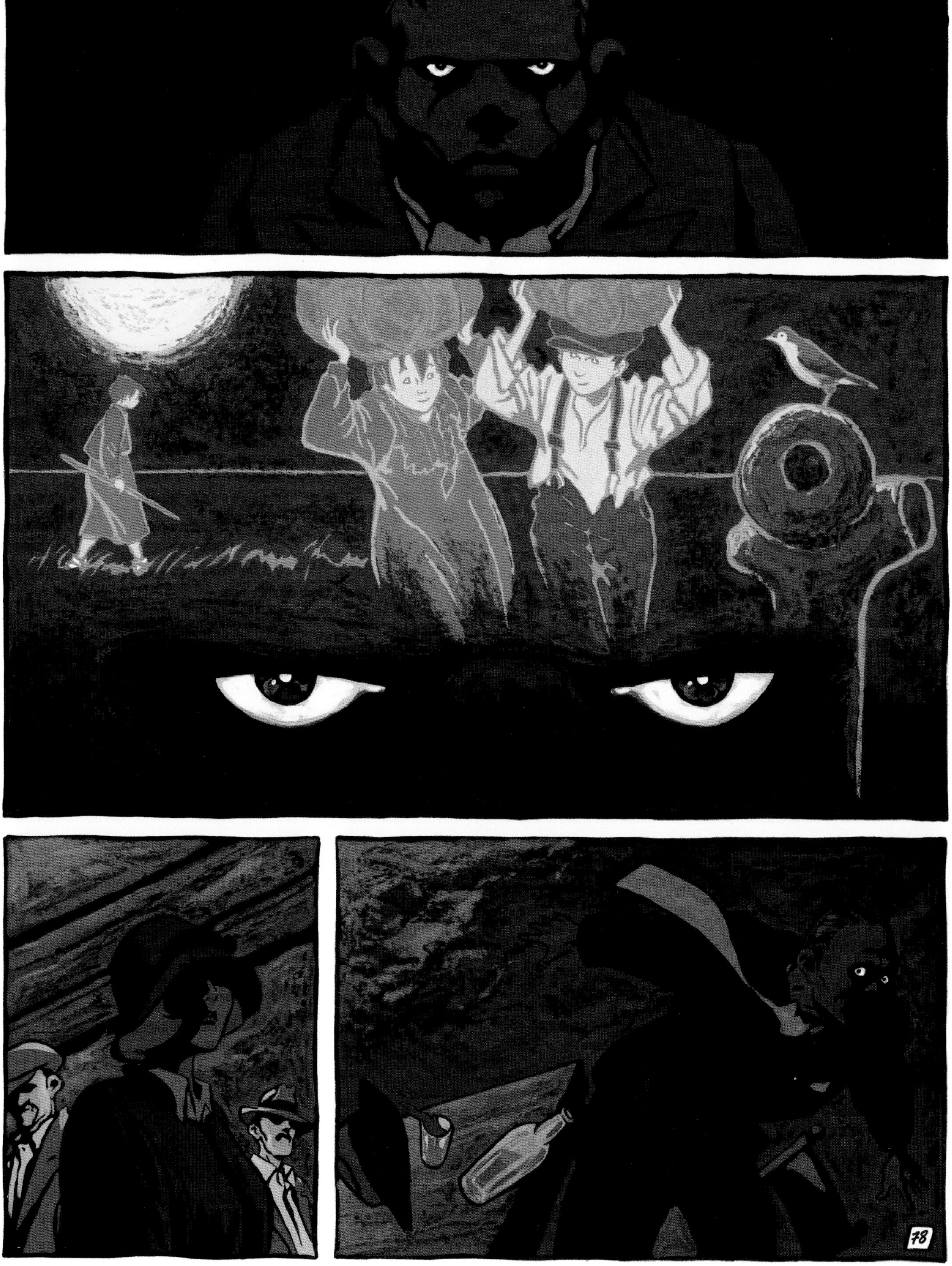
78

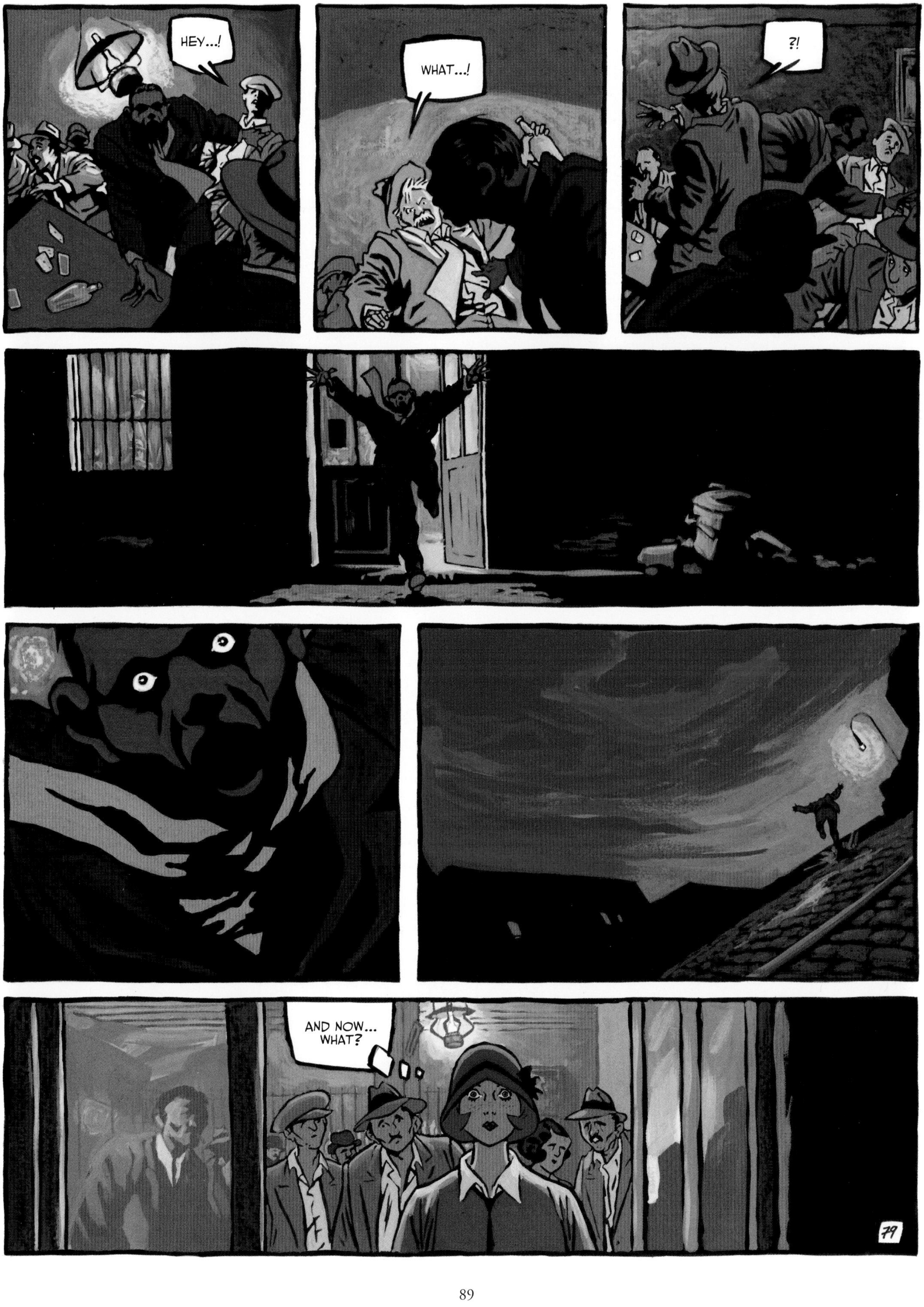
HEY...!
WHAT...!
?!
AND NOW... WHAT?
79

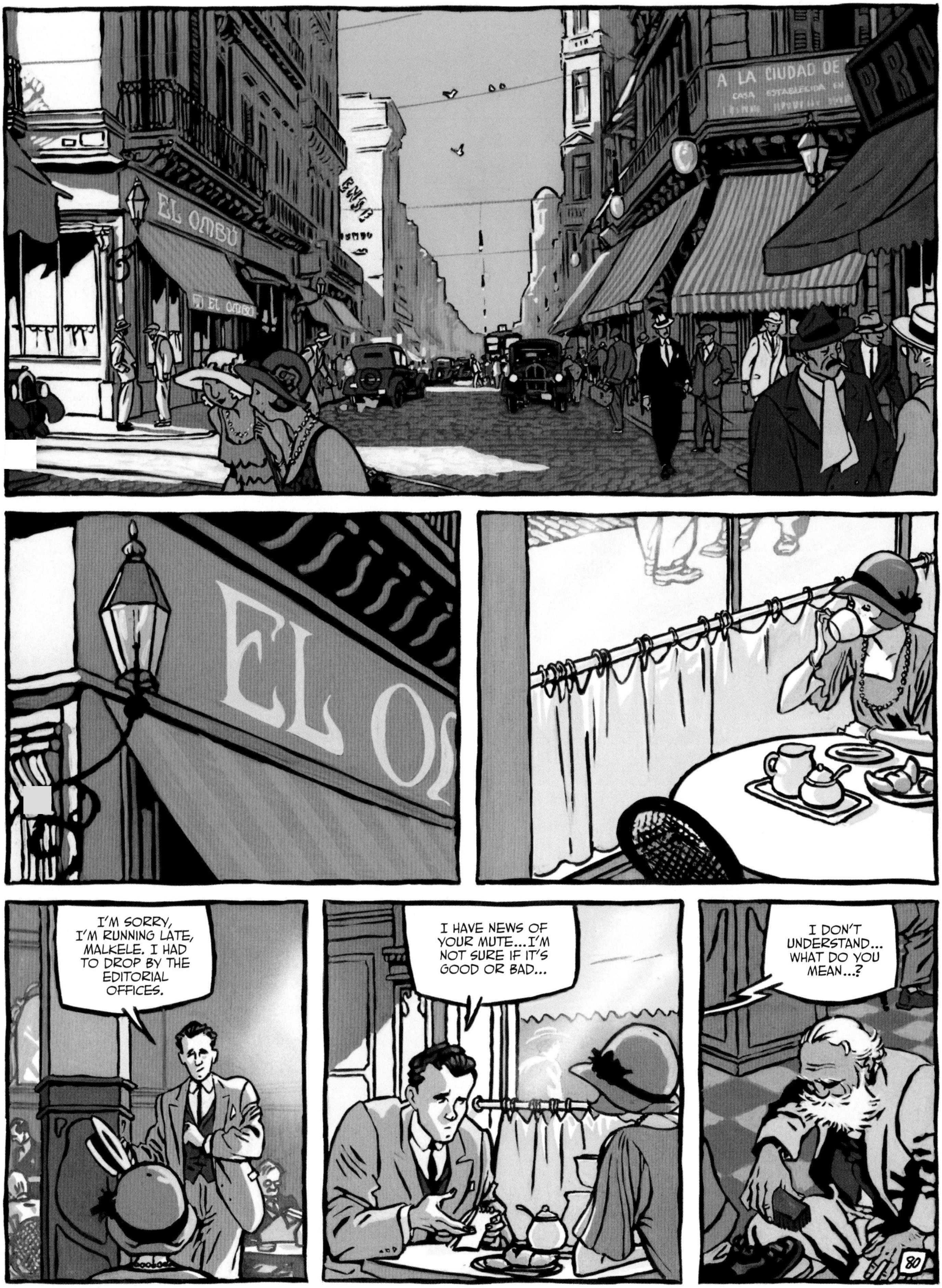
EL OMBÚ
EL OMBÚ
A LA CIUDAD DE
CASA ESTABLECIDA EN
EL O
I'M SORRY, I'M RUNNING LATE, MALKELE. I HAD TO DROP BY THE EDITORIAL OFFICES.
I HAVE NEWS OF YOUR MUTE...I'M NOT SURE IF IT'S GOOD OR BAD...
I DON'T UNDERSTAND... WHAT DO YOU MEAN...?
80

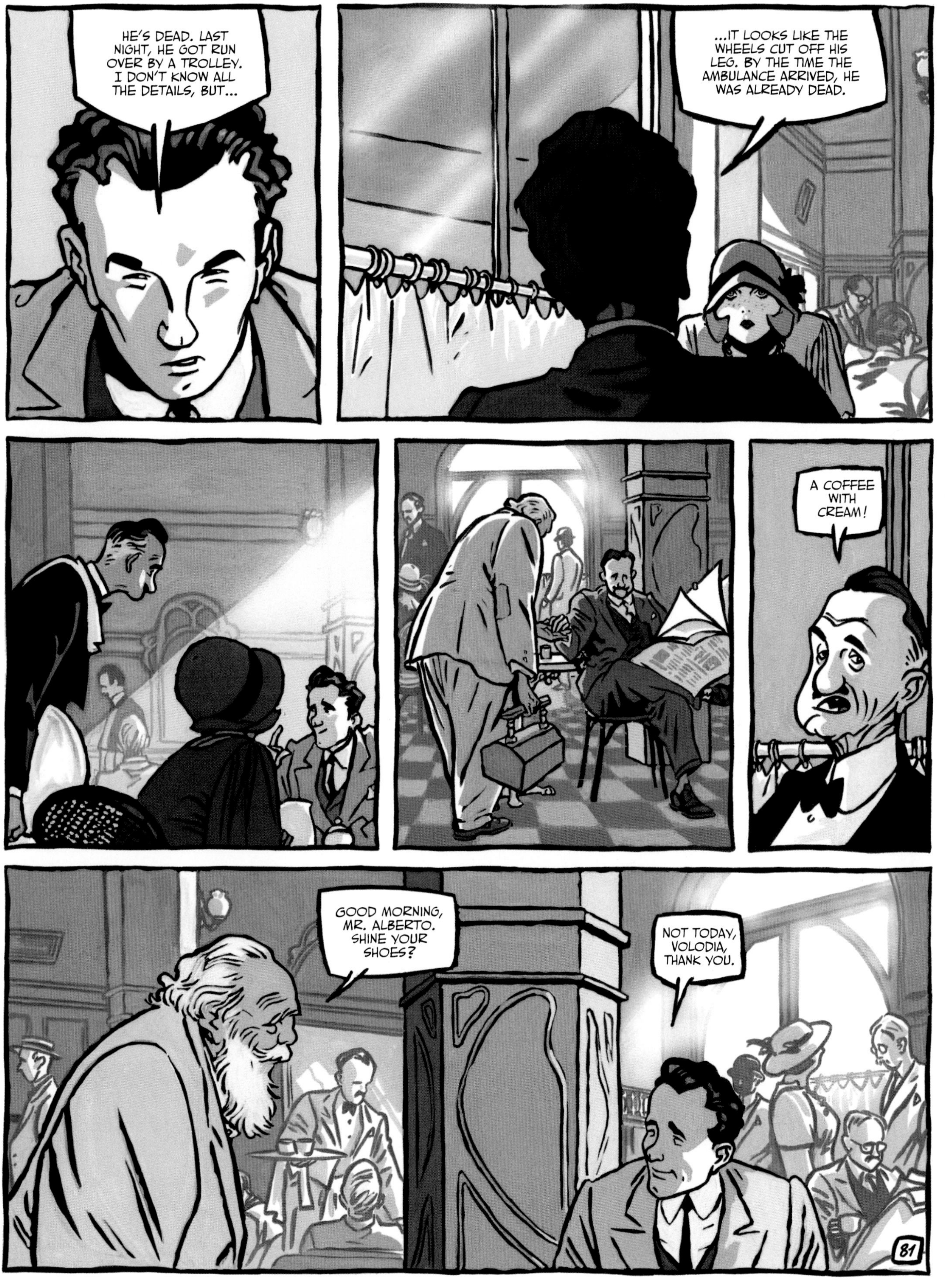
HE'S DEAD. LAST NIGHT, HE GOT RUN OVER BY A TROLLEY. I DON'T KNOW ALL THE DETAILS, BUT...
...IT LOOKS LIKE THE WHEELS CUT OFF HIS LEG. BY THE TIME THE AMBULANCE ARRIVED, HE WAS ALREADY DEAD.
A COFFEE WITH CREAM!
GOOD MORNING, MR. ALBERTO. SHINE YOUR SHOES?
NOT TODAY, VOLODIA, THANK YOU.
81

...VOLODIA? I DON'T KNOW. HE SOMETIMES SETS UP HERE. HE SAYS HE WAS A COUNT IN RUSSIA, BUT...YOU KNOW HOW IT WAS AFTER THE REVOLUTION...ALL THE EXILES CLAIM THEY'RE NOBILITY.

TO TELL THE TRUTH, I DON'T MUCH CARE IF HE'S LYING OR NOT. GENERALLY, WHEN HE SHINES MY SHOES, WE TALK ABOUT LITERATURE. ACCORDING TO HIM, HE WAS GOOD FRIENDS WITH TOLSTOY.

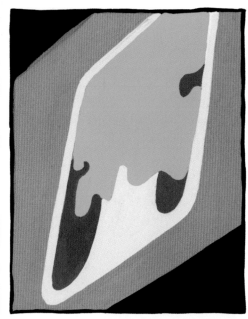

The Silence of Malka was serialized in issues 209 to 214 of the magazine *À suivre* between June and November 1995.

Two years later, Jorge Zentner and Rubén Pellejero reprised the characters in a three-page story to commemorate the final issue of the magazine, in December 1997.

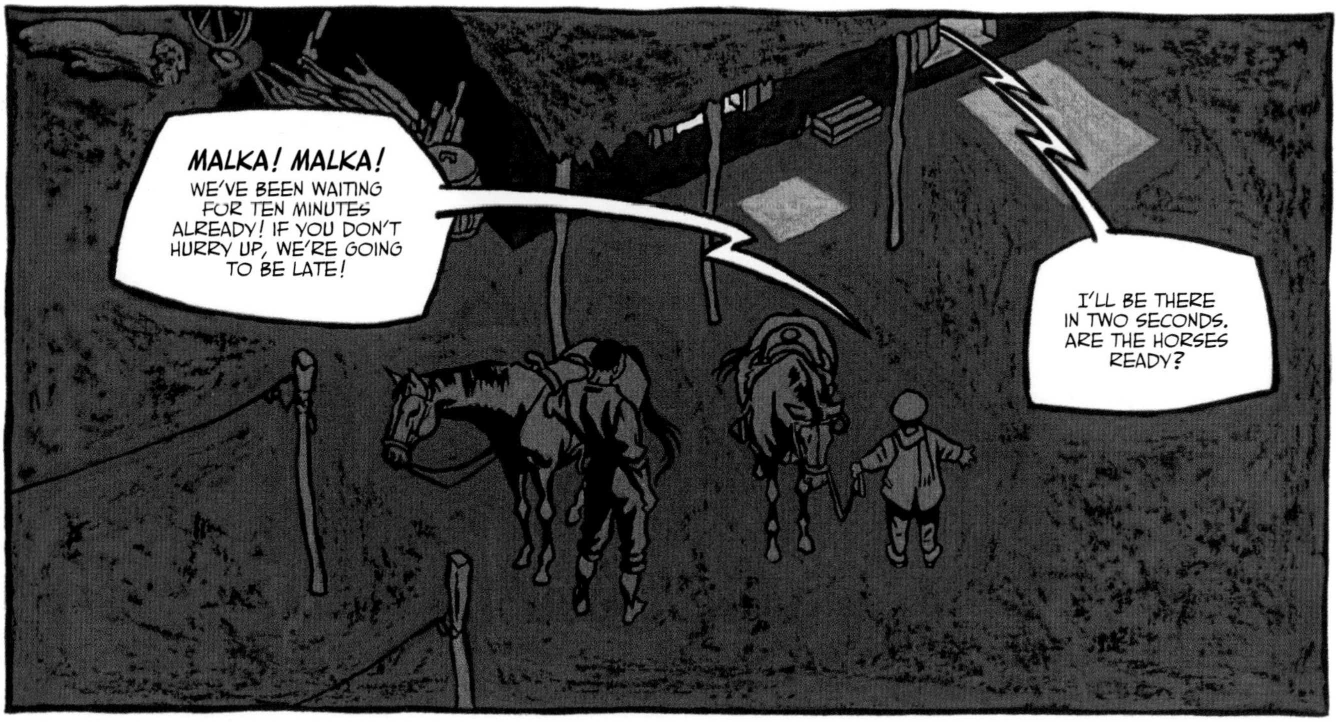
MALKA! MALKA!
WE'VE BEEN WAITING FOR TEN MINUTES ALREADY! IF YOU DON'T HURRY UP, WE'RE GOING TO BE LATE!
I'LL BE THERE IN TWO SECONDS. ARE THE HORSES READY?

"AT SCHOOL ONE DAY, AFTER THE TEACHER, MISTER EFRON, FINISHED ONE OF HIS LESSONS, I HAD AN IDEA. AT FIRST NO ONE BUT DAVID WAS VERY ENTHUSIASTIC ABOUT IT--NOT MY PARENTS OR UNCLE ZELIK. WE WERE ONLY ABLE TO GATHER THE MONEY WE NEEDED AFTER MANY WEEKS OF PLEADING AND PROMISING. FINALLY, THE BIG DAY WAS HERE."

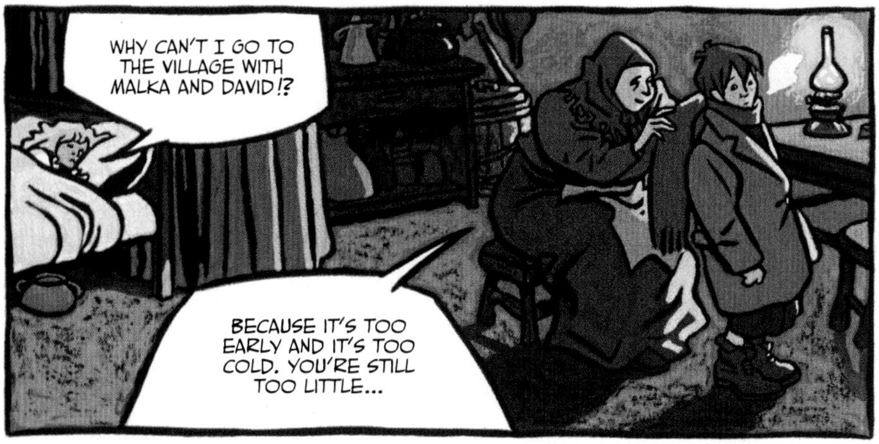
WHY CAN'T I GO TO THE VILLAGE WITH MALKA AND DAVID!?
BECAUSE IT'S TOO EARLY AND IT'S TOO COLD. YOU'RE STILL TOO LITTLE...

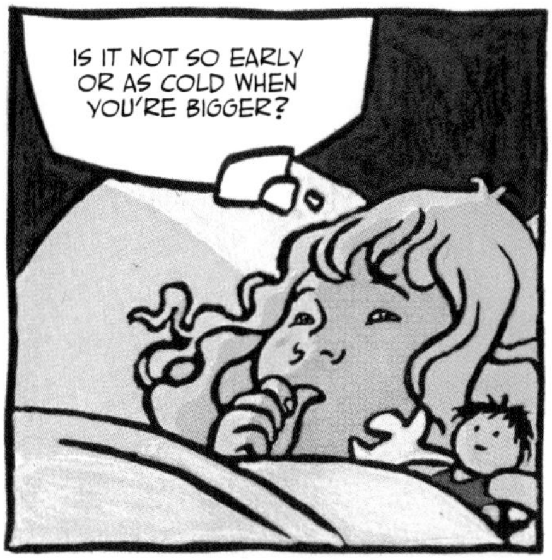
IS IT NOT SO EARLY OR AS COLD WHEN YOU'RE BIGGER?

"I HAD WAITED SO LONG FOR THIS MOMENT THAT I WASN'T EVEN BOTHERED BY MY LACK OF SLEEP OR THE FRIGID COLD. THE THREE HOURS ON HORSEBACK THAT SEPARATED US FROM THE VILLAGE PASSED QUICKLY. THE SUN WAS ONLY JUST RISING AND WE ONLY HAD A LITTLE MORE THAN A HALF AN HOUR TO GO. DESPITE THAT, WE HEADED STRAIGHT FOR THE STATION...TO MISS THE TRAIN'S ARRIVAL WOULD BE UNFORGIVABLE ."

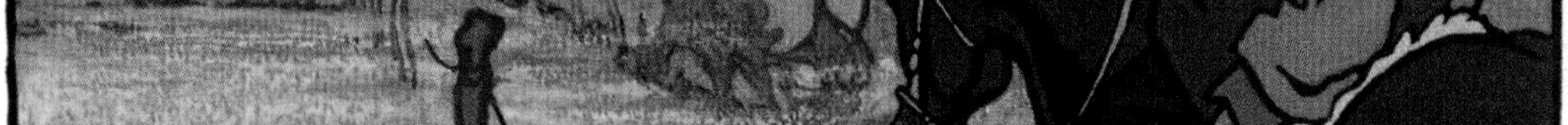

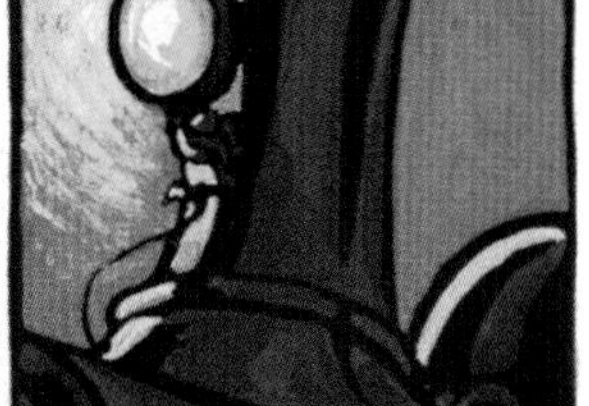

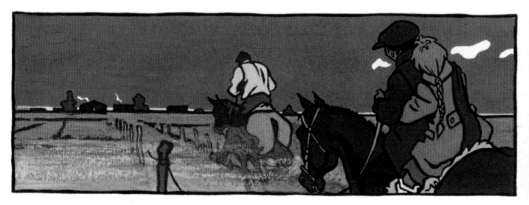

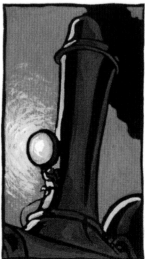

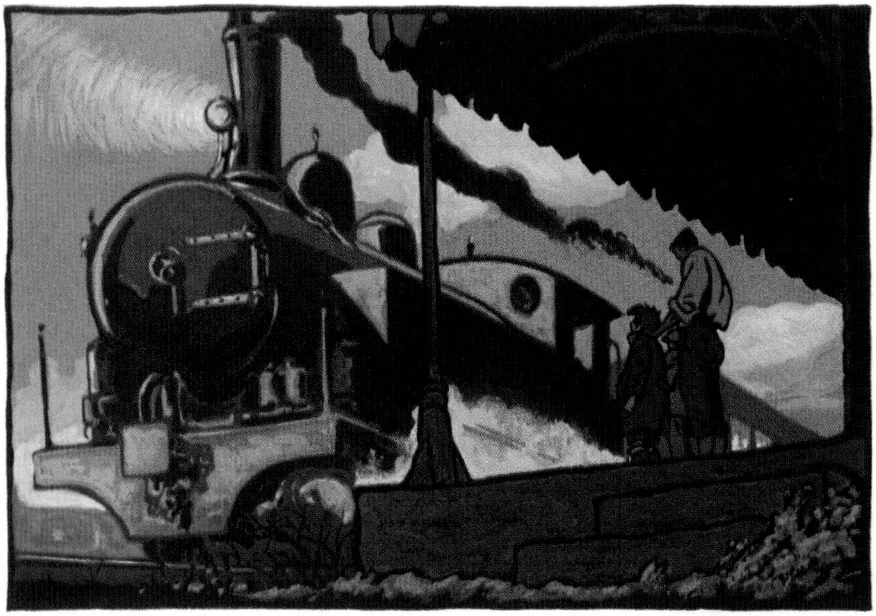

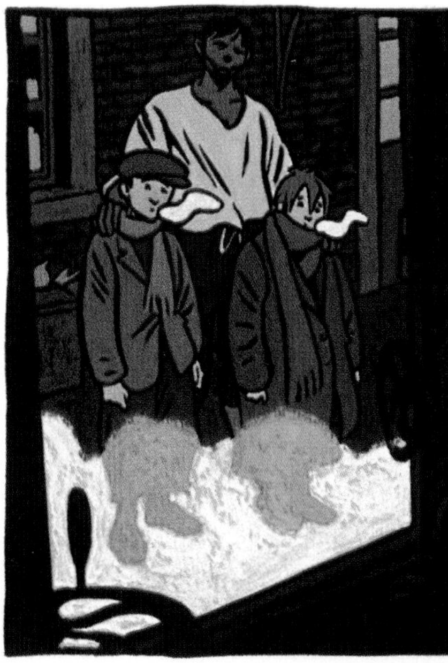

"THE TRAIN WAS INCREDIBLE, BUT MISTER EFRON WARNED ME THAT IT WOULD ONLY STAY AT THE STATION FOR A FEW MINUTES BEFORE IT CONTINUED ON ITS WAY TOWARD BUENOS AIRES. IF I WANTED TO ACCOMPLISH MY GOAL I WOULD NEED TO ACT FAST AND RUSH TO THE LAST CAR."

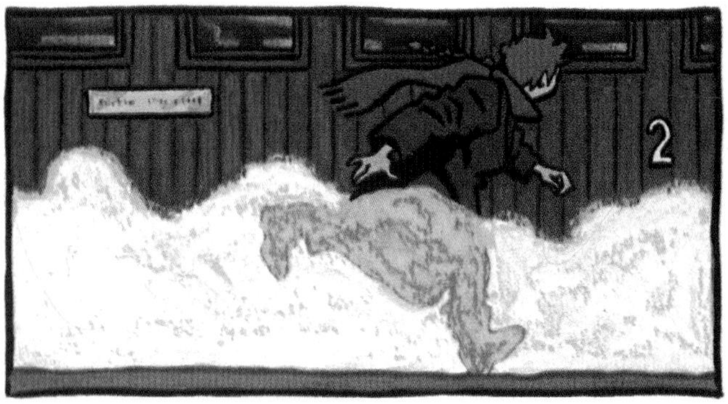
2

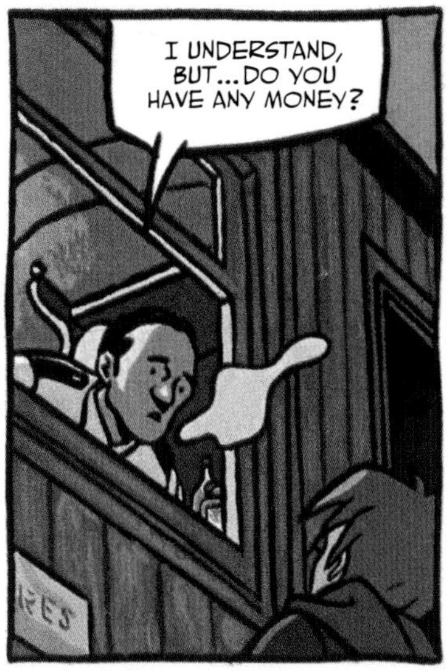
I UNDERSTAND, BUT... DO YOU HAVE ANY MONEY?

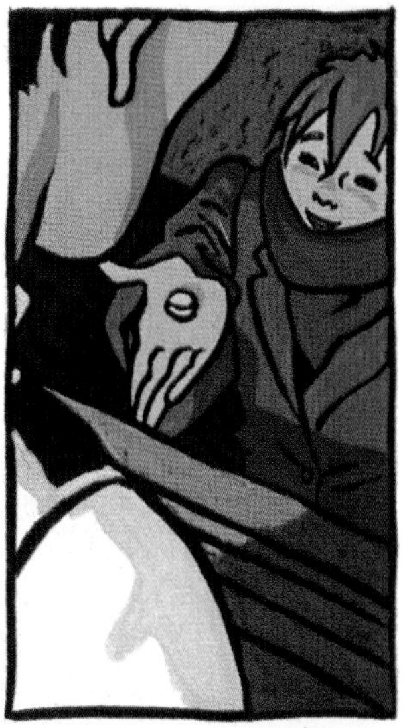

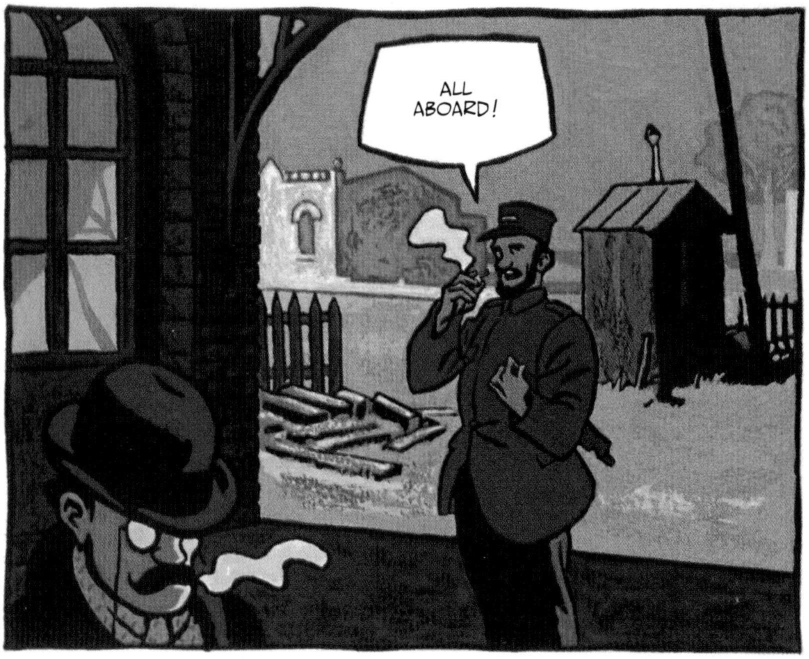
ALL ABOARD!

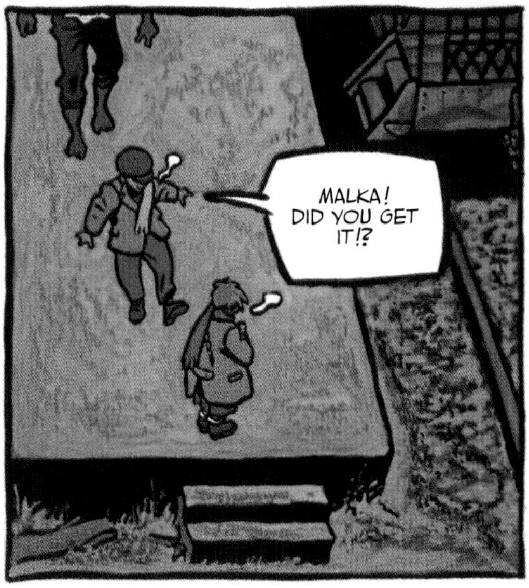
MALKA! DID YOU GET IT!?

"I WAS SO EXCITED, THAT I WAS JUST STUNNED SPEECHLESS."

"THAT NIGHT, DAVID AND THE GOLEM LIT A LARGE FIRE IN THE YARD. AFTER DINNER, THE WHOLE FAMILY GATHERED AROUND. IT WASN'T ANYONE'S BIRTHDAY, BUT THERE WAS A FESTIVE FEELING TO THE NIGHT."

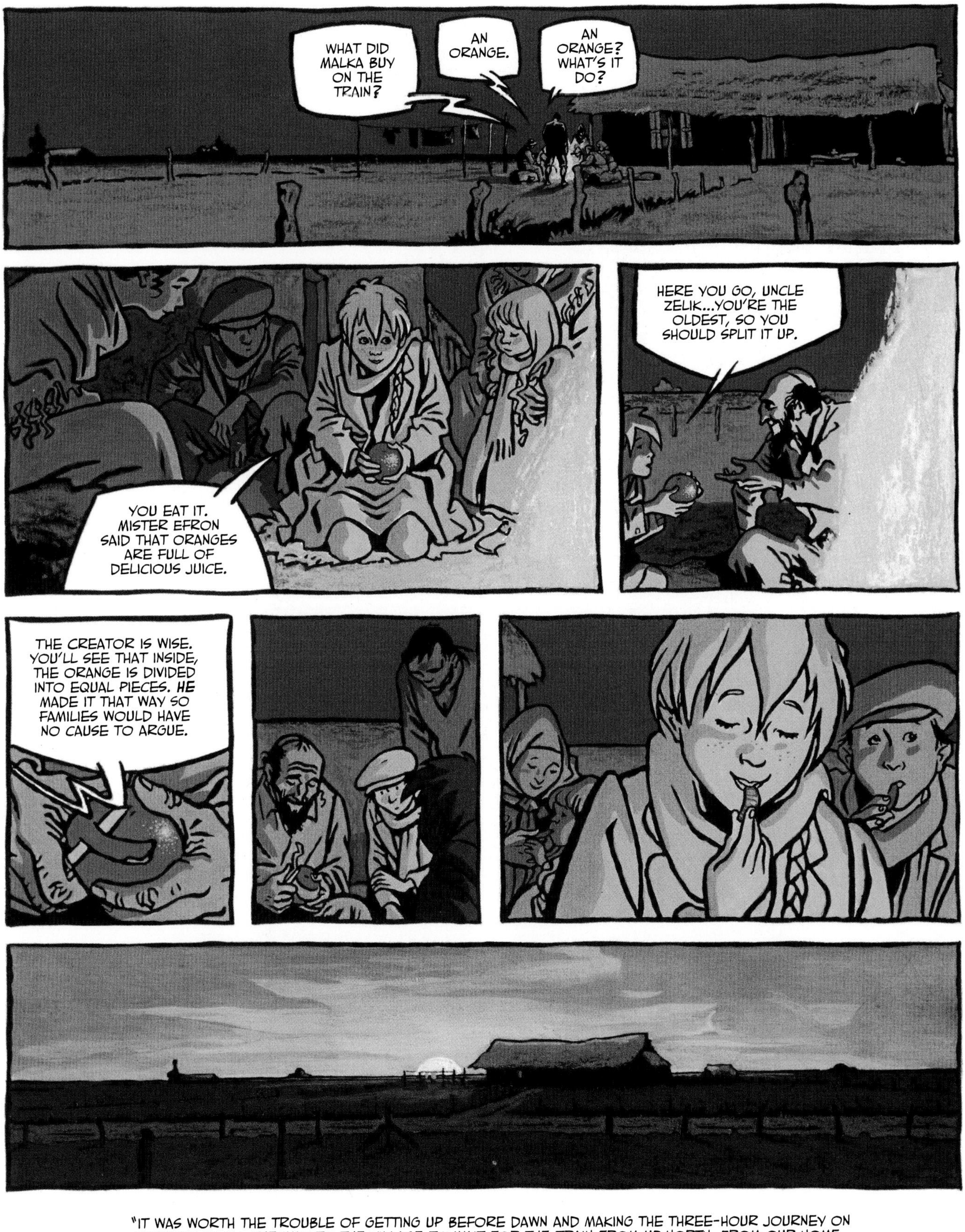

WHAT DID MALKA BUY ON THE TRAIN?
AN ORANGE.
AN ORANGE? WHAT'S IT DO?
YOU EAT IT. MISTER EFRON SAID THAT ORANGES ARE FULL OF DELICIOUS JUICE.
HERE YOU GO, UNCLE ZELIK...YOU'RE THE OLDEST, SO YOU SHOULD SPLIT IT UP.
THE CREATOR IS WISE. YOU'LL SEE THAT INSIDE, THE ORANGE IS DIVIDED INTO EQUAL PIECES. **HE** MADE IT THAT WAY SO FAMILIES WOULD HAVE NO CAUSE TO ARGUE.

"IT WAS WORTH THE TROUBLE OF GETTING UP BEFORE DAWN AND MAKING THE THREE-HOUR JOURNEY ON HORSEBACK ALL THE WAY TO THE VILLAGE TO WAIT FOR THE TRAIN FROM UP NORTH. FROM OUR HOME, OUR YARD, WE SAW THE SUN EVERY DAY. BUT WE HAD NEVER TASTED ANYTHING QUITE LIKE THAT ORANGE."

One thing Pellejero and Zentner have in common is that both creators plied other trades in their respective fields—illustration and writing—before bursting into comics at the forefront of the scene. Born in Argentina in 1953, Jorge Zentner made a living from writing, as a journalist, until the mid-1970s, when he was forced to flee his country's military dictatorship. A decisive encounter with Carlos Sampayo (co-creator of the series *Alack Sinner* with José Muñoz) prompted him to turn toward comics in 1979. Born in Barcelona in 1952, Rubén Pellejero had been an illustrator since the early 1970s. But not until 1983 did he publish his first comics—in *Cimoc*, a comics monthly from Spanish publisher Norma Editorial. At the same time, the artist met Zentner, with whom he went on to produce some fifteen graphic novels, among which *The Silence of Malka* holds a particular pride of place.

Though set in a believable, well-researched, and real (if colorful) world, the stories of Pellejero and Zentner always manage to surprise readers by taking the most unexpected detours into realms of the imagination. Their most famous creation, the *Dieter Lumpen* series, inspired by noir and hard-boiled detective stories, gave rise to astonishing developments rooted in fantastical genres. This blending of influences, along with a gift for storytelling as effective as it was original, made the duo stand out, securing a place for them among the most exciting talents in the Spanish-language comics scene.

Published in installments starting in 1995, *The Silence of Malka* is (along with Vittorio Giardino's *The Childhood of Jonas Fink*) one of the last great novelistic sagas from Casterman's landmark comics monthly *À suivre* ("To Be Continued"). Jorge Zentner found the seed for the story in an anecdote from his grandmother's childhood, when she was saved from drowning by her braids. Building on this endearing episode, Zentner found an opportunity to compassionately revisit the story of his own family, which had fled to Argentina in the early 20th Century to escape anti-Semitic persecution in Eastern Europe.

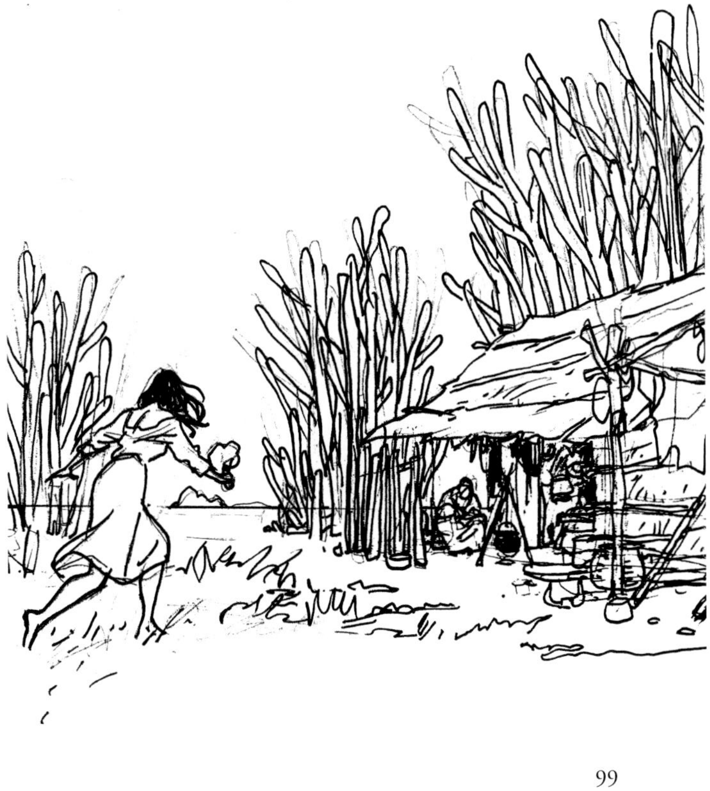

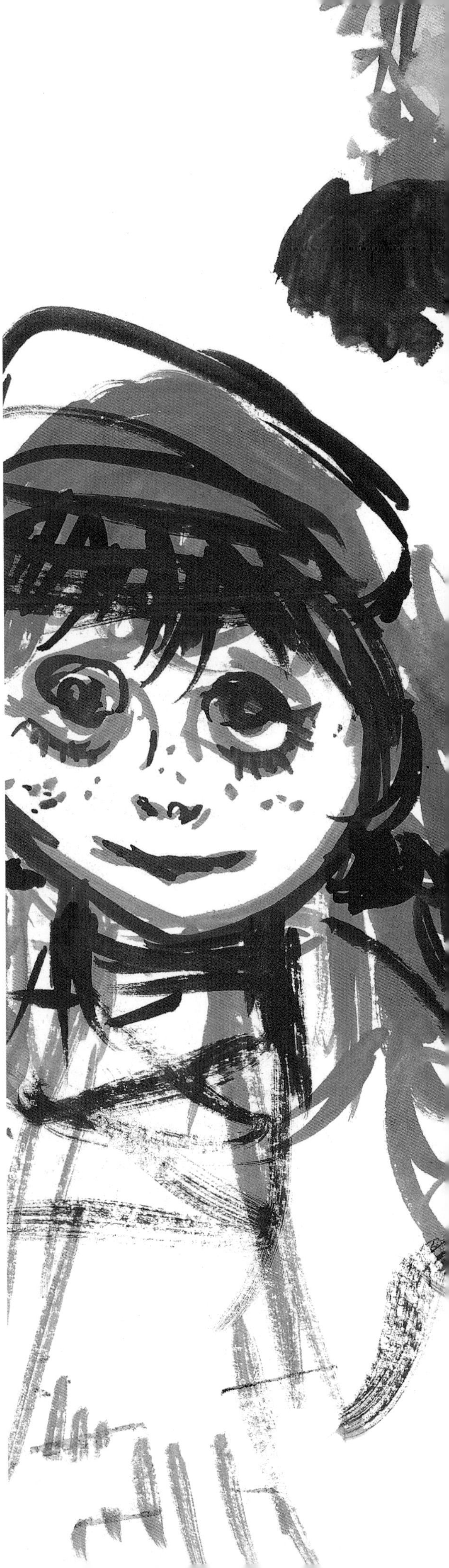

So it is that the book opens with the horrific depiction of a pogrom. Among the great strengths of this cruel fable is its use of the Golem, a mythological figure, in an almost naturalistic context. By reinterpreting this fertile legend, Zentner delivers a parable on the vagaries of Providence that can also be read as a veiled account of a clash between cultures: it is because young Rosita calls upon her grandmother's Native American magic that the Golem becomes an instrument of death.

Favoring the suggestive poetry of images, the story makes great use of silent panels to sensitively convey a range of ineffable emotions. Pellejero knows how to subtly vary panel size to suit the intensity of the action, like a musician modulating his rendition in concert. He also breaks with his penchant for very fine linework, akin to the nervous energy in the inks of his fellow countryman Jordi Bernet, not to mention the expressiveness of Hugo Pratt (whose landmark series *Corto Maltese* Pellejero would take over in 2015). The full-bodied brushwork here on display favors pronounced contours and warm colors painted in gouache right on the page.

Without resorting to easy melodrama or irrationality, Pellejero and Zentner serve up, in *The Silence of Malka*, one of the high points of their collaboration and moreover, one of the most remarkable works in Casterman's catalogue from the 1990s. The jury at the 1997 Angoulême International Comics Festival, with artist André Juillard presiding, rightly recognized the book with the prize for Best Foreign Work. This new edition, augmented with previously unpublished material, is a testament to how the evocative power of this masterpiece has lost none of its intensity in the last twenty years.

—Benoît Mouchart

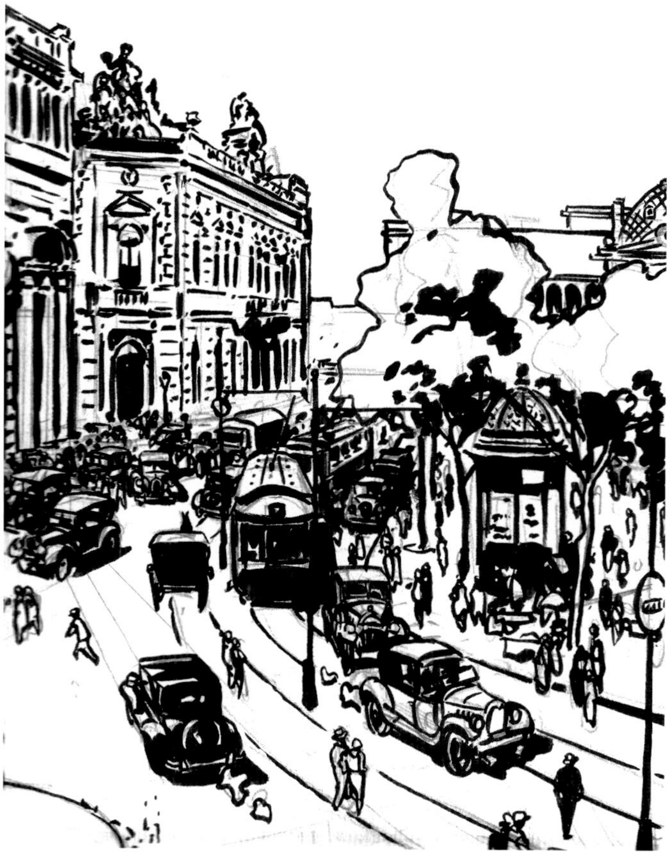

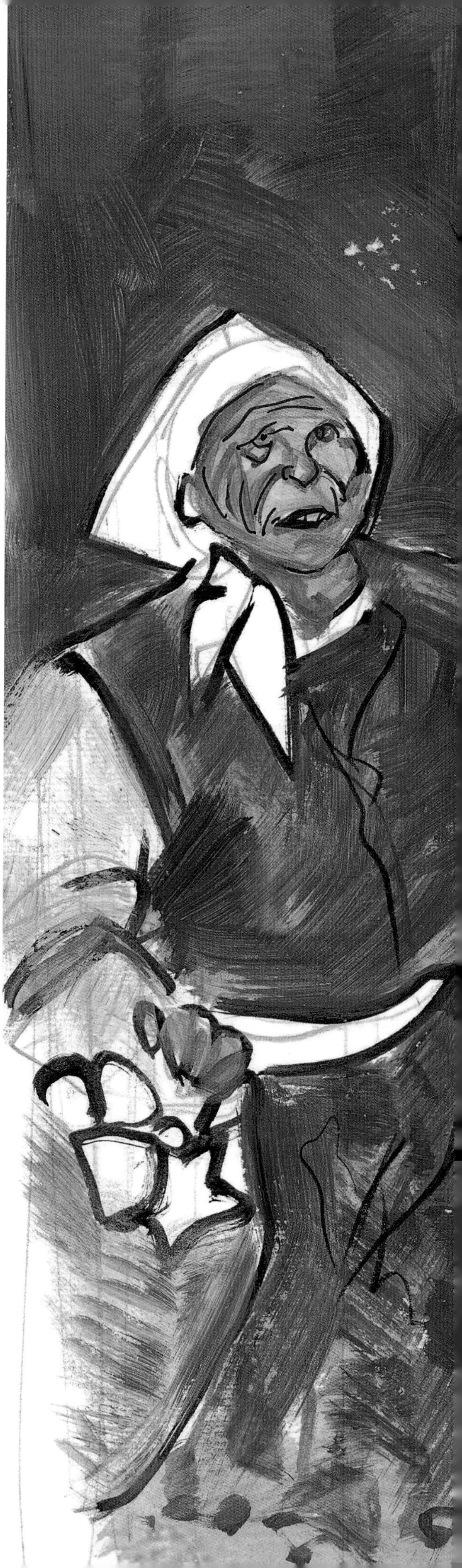

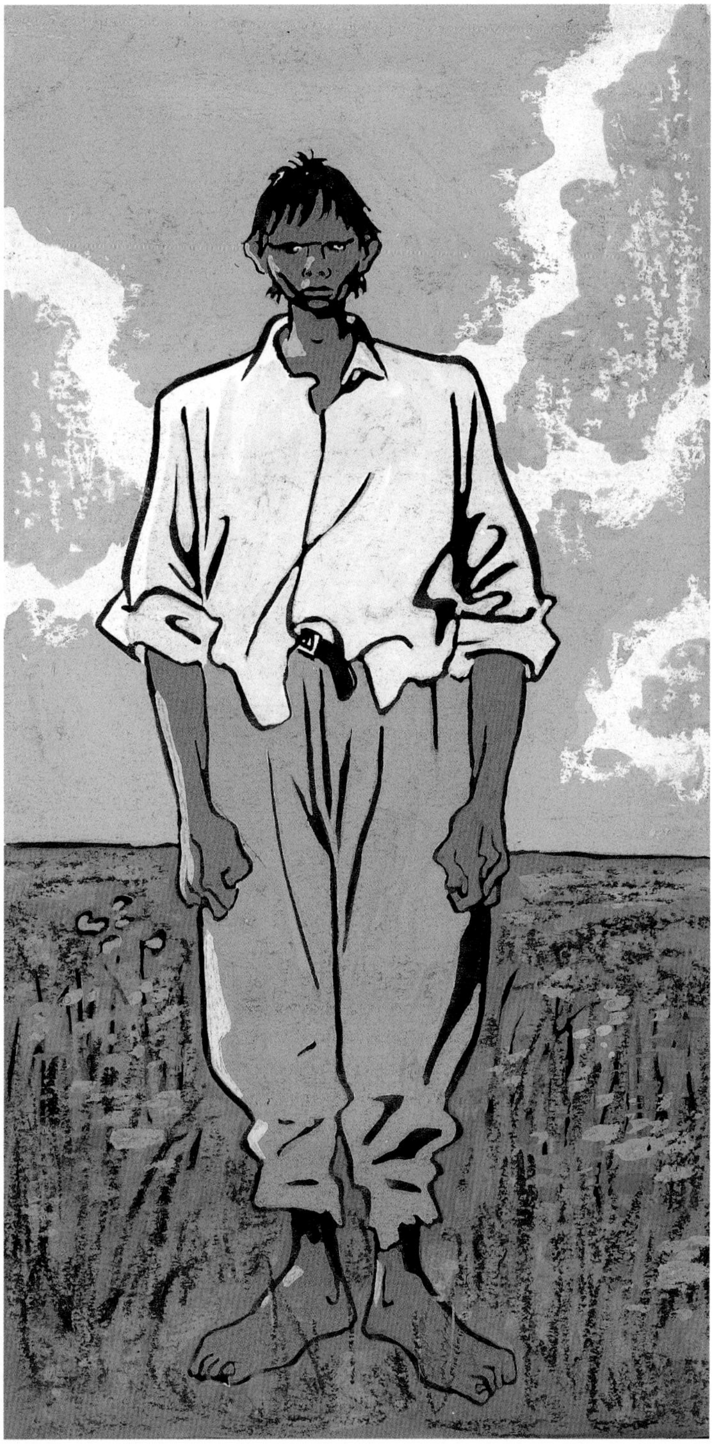

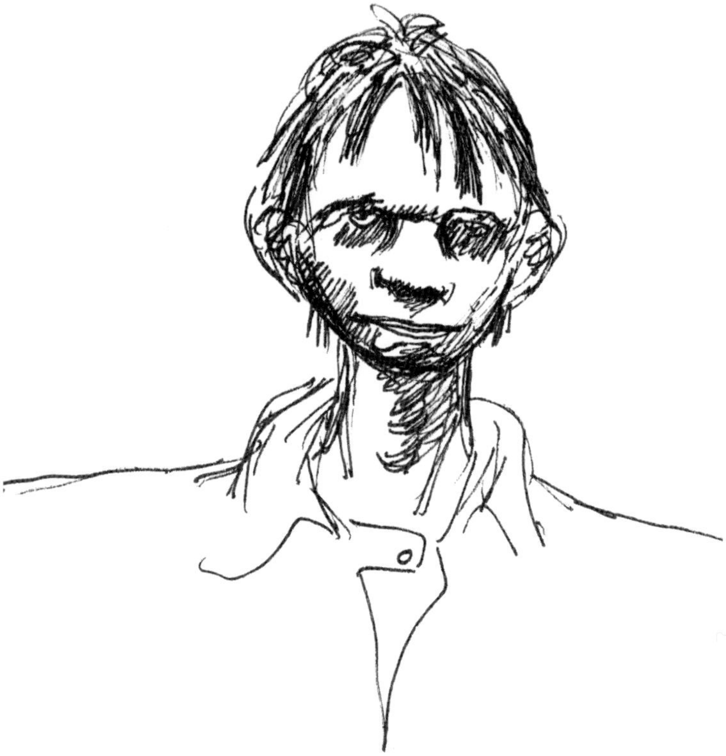

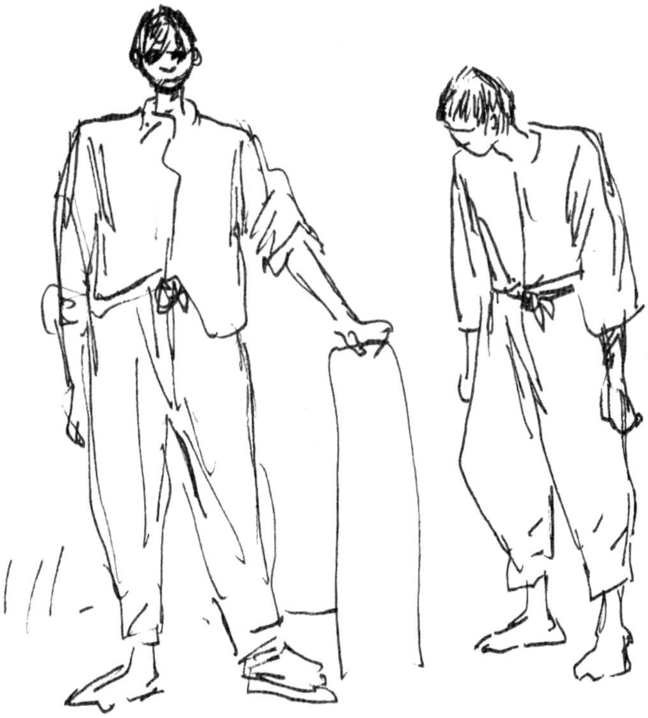

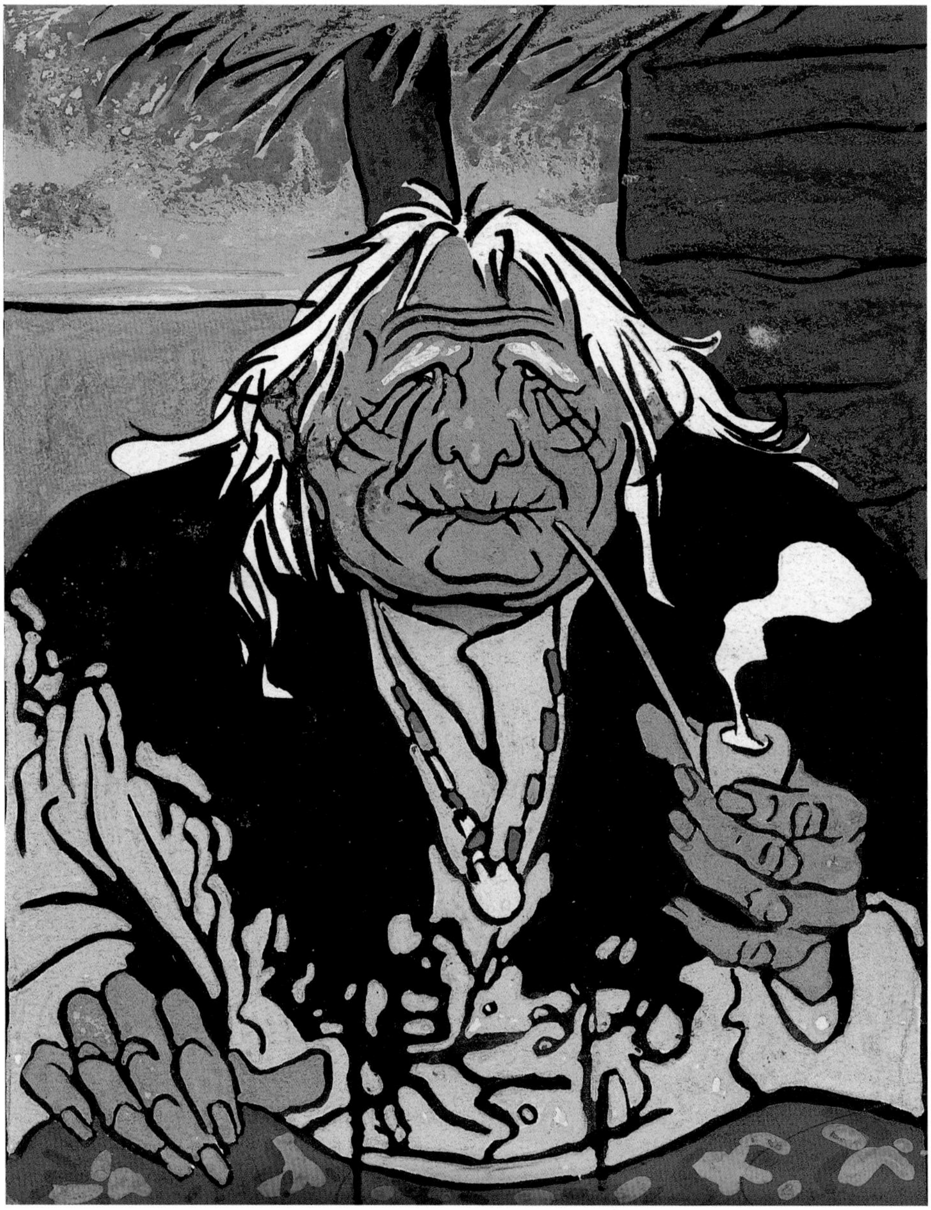

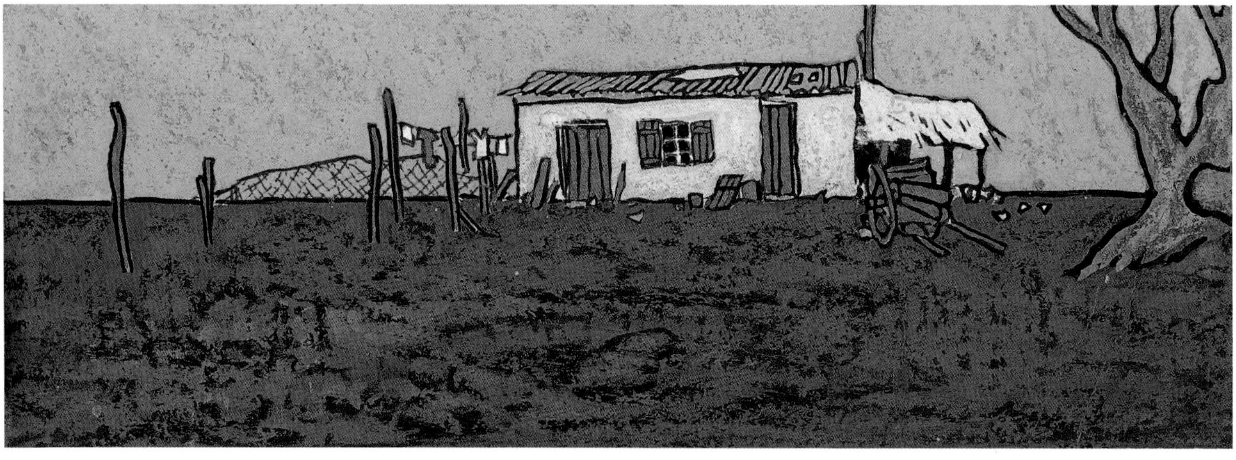

PROFETA ELIAS

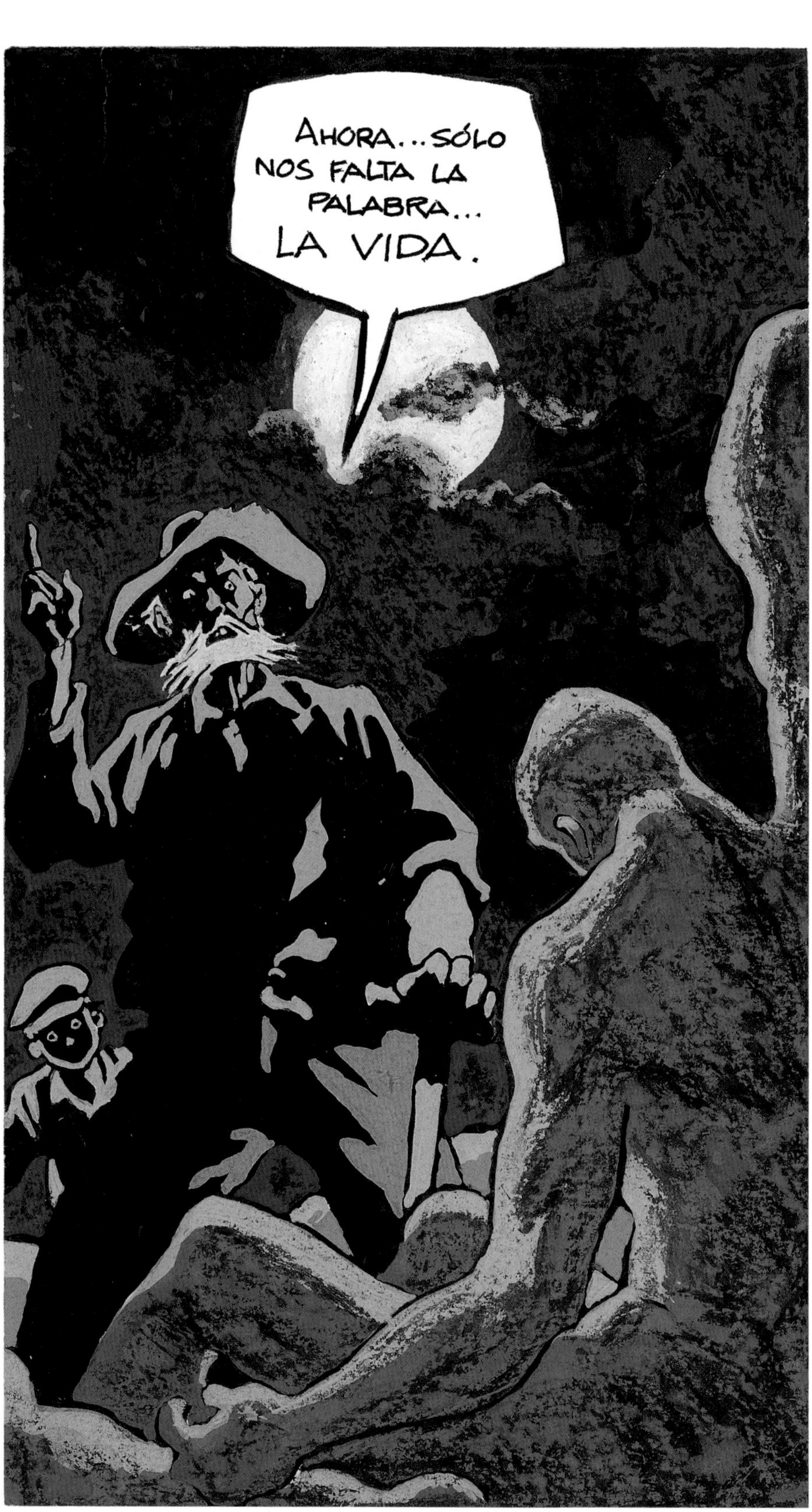
AHORA... SÓLO NOS FALTA LA PALABRA... LA VIDA.

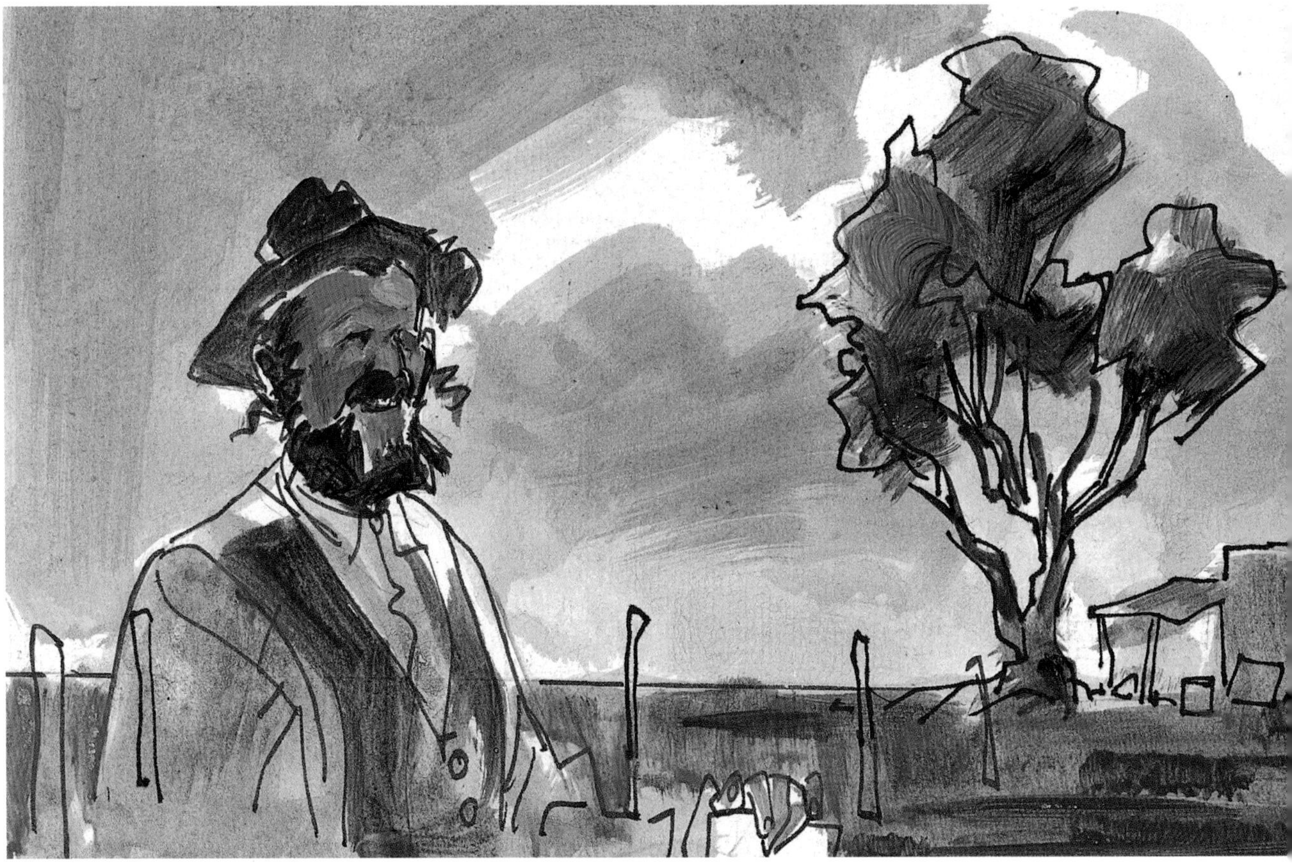

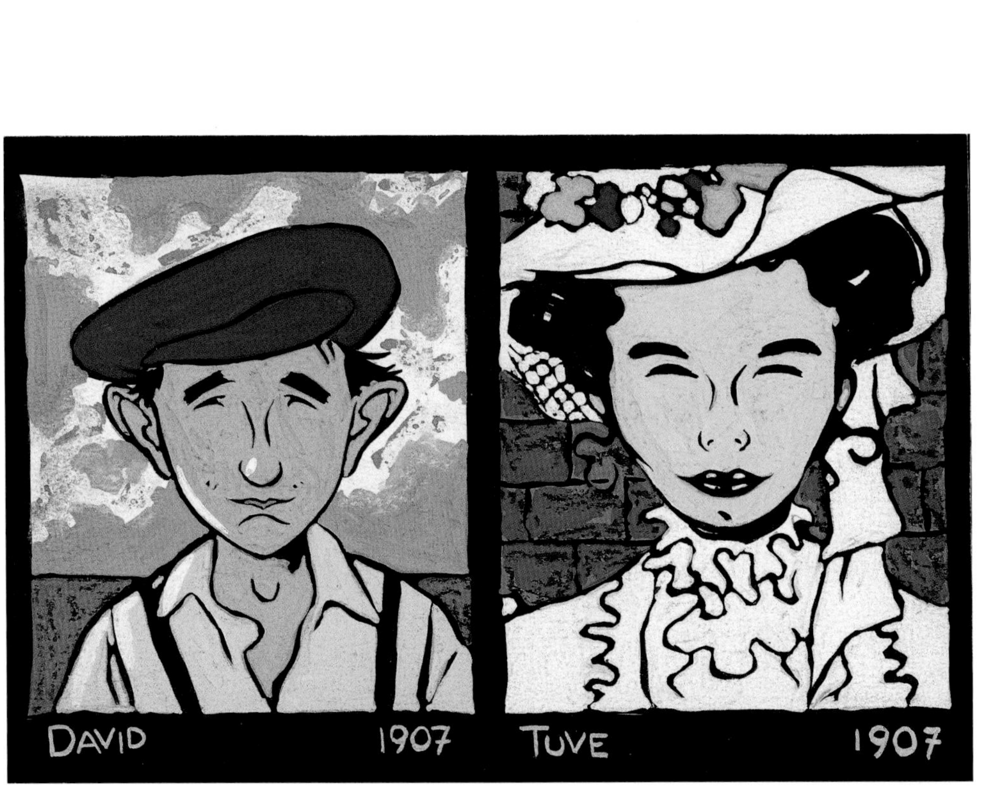
DAVID
1907
TUVE
1907

MADRE   1907

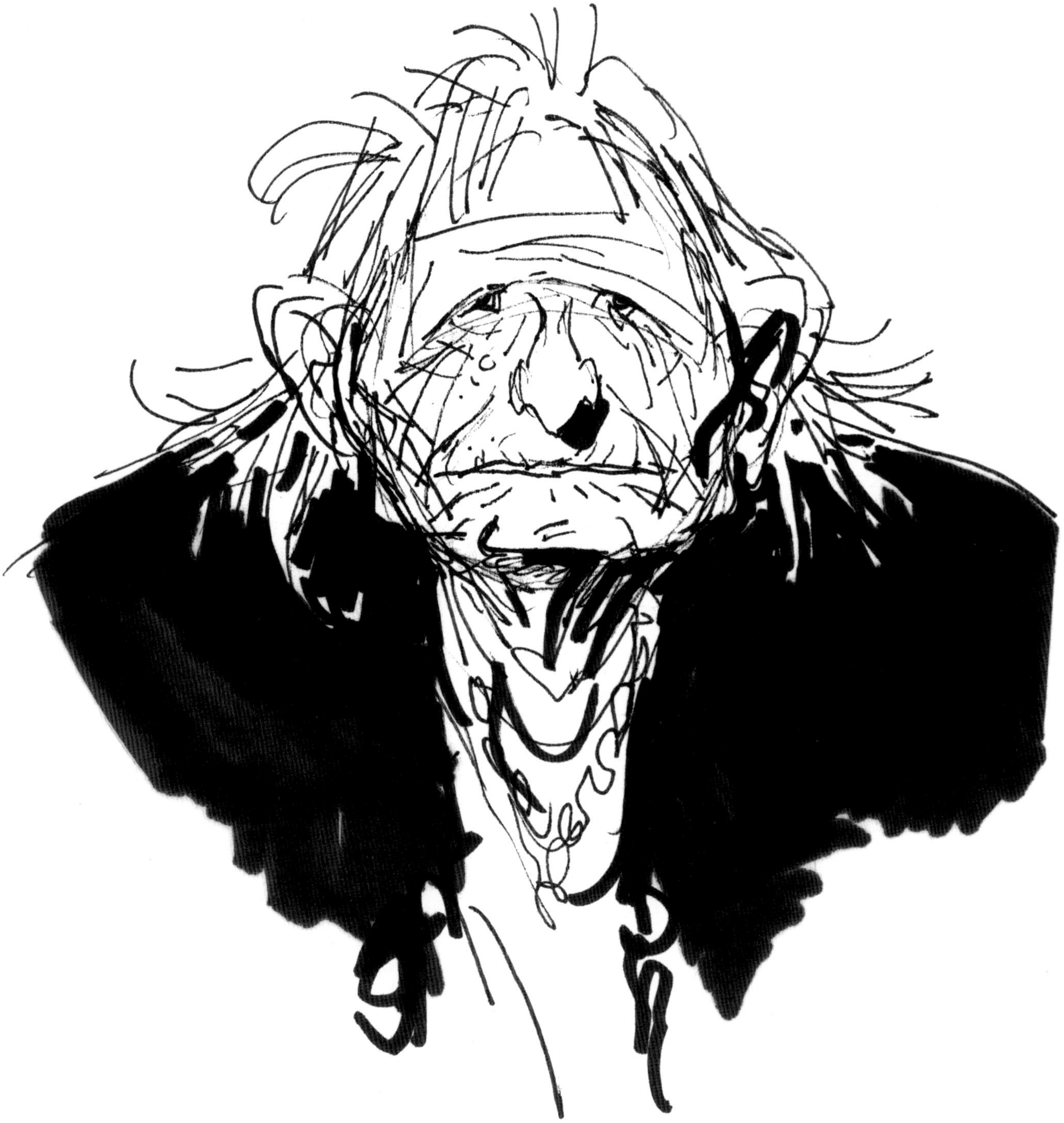

ALSO BY JORGE ZENTNER AND RUBÉN PELLEJERO

DIETER LUMPEN

OTHER BOOKS FROM EuroComics/IDW

EuroComics.us

CORTO MALTESE BY HUGO PRATT

ONE MAN, ONE ADVENTURE BY HUGO PRATT

PARACUELLOS BY CARLOS GIMÉNEZ

ALACK SINNER BY JOSÉ MUÑOZ AND CARLOS SAMPAYO

THE REPRIEVE BY JEAN-PIERRE GIBRAT

FLIGHT OF THE RAVEN BY JEAN-PIERRE GIBRAT

LIGHTS OF THE AMALOU BY CHRISTOPHE GIBELIN AND CLAIRE WENDLING

JEROME K. JEROME BLOCHE BY ALAIN DODIER

TALES FROM THE AGE OF THE COBRA BY ENRIQUE FERNÁNDEZ

VIOLETTE BY TERESA RADICE AND STEFANO TURCONI

FOUR SISTERS BY CATI BAUR AND MALIKA FERDJOUKH